SPIRIT ROAD

An Ensley Markus Mystery, Book 3

PEGGY STAGGS

Spinone Press, LLC

Spinone Press, LLC

Eagle, ID 83616

Visit our website at www.peggystaggs.com

Copyright © 2016 Peggy Staggs
Spinone Press, LLC
All rights reserved.

ISBN- 978-0-9968951-3-2

In memory of my dad, Col. William R. Cook. A man always ready with a story or a joke. I miss his smile.

Acknowledgments

A special thank you to Brad Devroude and Rexford Wilkosz of the Eagle Fire Department.

Chapter One

I'd told myself a hundred times a day in the past two weeks I wouldn't return to Spirit Springs. Yet I'd driven straight here from the Boise Airport. Now I sat parked across the street from Jack Trace's perfect home. Two weeks to the day I'd left him lying horribly beaten on the floor in his library. Yes, I'd called for help before I walked out. Only after he'd confessed to being a thief and a murderer.

It didn't match the man I'd come to know. The one who'd risked his life to help me find my father's murderers. Yet his confession stood between us. A barrier between me and the man I was afraid I'd fallen in love with.

Christmas Eve had been roiled in a hundred-year blizzard, Jack's kidnapping, and the unexpected arrival of my ex-fiancé, Don March. It ended with the heartbreak of Jack's admission to being a murderer and a thief. Christmas Day found me on a plane back to D.C..

Worse, Jack's confession had implicated my dad and Uncle Stan. Were the two men I'd trusted my whole life thieves, too?

For the second time in three months, I found my lifeline ripped from my hands. Had I succumbed to Jack's good looks, easy manor, and alpha presence? This time, the pain was different. The loss of my job was nothing compared to my dad's death. But this, this, my heart gave a spasmodic double beat.

I leaned against the steering wheel as I took in the long driveway leading to Jack's. If I were smart, I'd turn around, sell the bed and breakfast and leave this quaint western town in my rearview mirror.

The problem was, my heart refused to listen to common sense.

I'd devised a plan: I'd sell the bed and breakfast my dad left me. If dad's money came from a theft, I trembled at the thought. I didn't want it.

Moreover, if I sold the B&B what would become of Jane? We were the innocents in all of this, yet we'd pay the highest price.

Jack said he didn't want me any longer, that he was breaking things off. The thought crushed my heart. I'd tried to convince myself a relationship based on one traumatic experience after another couldn't last. And I knew nothing lasted forever.

Still, I sat here craving the truth. Was my father a thief too. Worse had he played a part in the deaths of those men in Africa? I had to know. That meant facing Jack. It would require every ounce of strength, mental and emotional I had. I needed closure and answers even if that brought with it unbearable agony. I had to hear the whole story.

I knew only one thing for certain; today's hurt was going to be with me forever. I tried to pull in a calming breath, but found I couldn't draw in the icy air.

Jack's brick two-story home rose strong and powerful out of the drifting snow covering the valley. After I sorted the lies from the truth, I knew only one thing; I wouldn't go back to Washington, D.C. That was my past.

I parked at the bottom of the sweeping sandstone steps leading to his front door. The wreath we'd picked out before Christmas was gone, but it should be in January.

I left the warmth of the car for the bitter cold air of Idaho's high desert. My breath formed frozen gasps of fog that floated away on the wind.

Beneath my feet the snow crunched as I made my way up the

expansive sandstone steps. Maybe he wouldn't be home. Of course, he'd be at work.

The turmoil ripped at my heart. I didn't know who or what to believe. My dad's last words were for me to trust Jack. But—oh, God could this get any worse?

Don's comment still haunted me, "Ensley, I realize how attractive he is to women. I've used his appeal on missions in the past. He doesn't hesitate to use his looks to seize what or who he wants. He's not the boy scout he pretends to be for you."

I shuddered as I walked to the entry.

On the other side of the glass paneled front door Lois, his Spinone, hurried toward me, a toy in her mouth. She sat down and wagged her stubby tail as she gazed up at me with warm golden eyes. She looked so happy. With the sight of her, the memories of Christmas Eve engulfed me. Her fuzzy face and gentle way had helped me through the horror of that night. She wouldn't be able to help me today.

I glanced up as I rang the doorbell. Jack stood at the foot of the stairs dressed in slacks and a blazer. When he saw me, he didn't hesitate, his deliberate steps matched his determined expression.

I swallowed hard as he opened the door. "Ensley. Come in." He stepped aside.

The expanse of the hardwood floors gleamed in the afternoon sun. On Christmas Eve, his home had been wrecked in a horrible fight that left two men dead. Now, all the furniture was set right. The broken things removed, but not replaced.

Every time I closed my eyes the images from Christmas Eve returned. A body lying in the upstairs hall, with the words scrawled above it, "We have him." Or the crazy woman holding a shotgun on us, or – I took a halting breath – the memories of that night populated my nightmares still.

So much destruction, so much pain, and so much heartache. A hurt so deep I couldn't sleep. I couldn't eat. In the last two weeks, I'd lost the five pounds I'd been struggling with and a few more.

"I heard Don's side of the story, but I promised myself I'd hear your side." Technically, I had. He'd told me Don's version was right. Don lies. "I... " Damn it.

"In here." He motioned to the living room.

I had to keep this clinical. I do clinical, very well. "How are you healing?"

"The bruises are almost gone." He indicated the sofa. "The broken ribs will take a while."

As I sat on the couch, my heart began pounding so hard I could hear it in my ears.

He settled on the matching sofa across from me. I'd rehearsed this as many times as I'd said I wouldn't come back. I raised my chin against the inevitable. "I have Don's version of the events in Africa. I came to hear yours." Keep it direct. Businesslike. I'd get his side, sell the B&B and move on. All business. As if I was buying a car.

"You know the purpose of the mission." His tone was firm and confident.

His self-assurance took me by surprise. Maybe because I felt so vulnerable. No, terrified this would end and knowing it already had.

Jack leaned forward, rested his elbows on his knees and clasped his hands. When he began, he glanced at me. "When we got there," He shook his head as his eyes darkened with the memory. "Boko Haram refused the diamonds they'd agreed to. They'd raped the diplomat's daughter so many times—" The knuckles on his hands grew white with the pressure of his grip. "She died three months later. Her mother drowned herself in liquor, and her father shot himself. A family destroyed for what? A handful of rocks." His torment stole the life from the room, leaving behind breathless despair. "The rest of the girls are mending."

"And the drug lord's daughter?" I needed him to tell me it wasn't true, he *had* to tell me he hadn't murdered her.

Jack's shoulders slumped.

I felt my stomach cinch into a knot so tight the pain screamed through me.

"I tried to persuade her to ask her father for more time. I even bribed her with a new life anywhere in the world. In the end, she told her father everything." His hands hung lifeless, and his eyes held a profound sorrow. "When we found out the helicopters weren't coming, some of my men volunteered to hold off our attackers to give us time to escape. I lost them all. Five good men, friends." His silence held all the agony of that day years ago.

I felt his pain from across the room. "And the drug lord's daughter?" All I could manage was a whisper.

He gave a weak smile. "I'm not good with women. She'd been offended by my offer. At least, that's what she said before she put a bullet in me. I had all those lives to protect. When she turned her weapon on one of the girls, I killed her."

"And the diamonds? Are they the reason you can afford all this?" I would have waved my hand to indicate his magnificent home, but it was all I could do to breathe. "Did my dad and Uncle Stan share in it?"

"What?" I think it was at that moment that he realized what he'd admitted to all those anguished filled nights ago. He shook his head. "Your father and Stan are two of the most honest and honorable men I've ever known." He looked me right in the eye. "All we brought out were the hostages and the bodies of our friends."

He glanced down at his hands as if trying to hide the pain I could see in his eyes.

"I told you I'd never lie to you." I could see the soul-wrenching sadness he felt etched on his face. "I did on Christmas Eve. It's haunted me every minute of every day since."

Deception, lies, and hate had filled that bitter night two weeks ago. That's when Jack told me he didn't want me any longer. I was still paying the price for his words. That left only one question. My fingers dug into the arm of the couch. The first and last one on my list. "And me? Was I a way to get back at Don?" I held my breath waiting for the answer I wasn't sure I could survive.

He stood, walked over, and sat beside me. "God. No. March has nothing to do with us."

I thought I was ready, but like always with this man, I found the turmoil in my heart unbearable. I struggled to my feet. "I said I'd hear your side. I... I believe you." I swallowed hard as I fought against my gathering tears. "I know what you want. I won't stay. I can't... " What? Be so close to you? See you every day and not want to be with you? "I'm selling."

He rose. "You have to understand, I wanted—"

"No, I don't."

"I wanted—"

I had to get everything Don had told me out, or I'd explode. "I know you and Lacey were lovers. I've seen the way you look at her now. I couldn't bear it if you looked at me that way. I can't stay."

"Who the hell told you that?" He squeezed his eyes shut. "March. Son-of-a-bitch." He reached for my hand. I pulled back. "Ensley, forget him. He's the past."

"Lacey told—"

"There never will be, anything between Lacey and me. Ensley, please," His words rushed out in a stream of frustration.

"What's left to say? You came to break things off that night didn't you?" I held my breath waiting for the answer.

He reached for me again.

I stepped away. I couldn't let him touch me or I'd never leave.

"I thought the only way you'd be safe was if you weren't here. Weren't with me."

"You get your wish, I'm leaving."

"I hate that you've been shot at, that you had to rescue me from that basement hell. Ensley. Listen to me."

"No." I turned my head.

"Ensley," His voice became stern.

"What? I have to *understand*? Well, I don't. How could you do the things you did, say what you said, and have them be lies?" I walked to the door and grabbed the latch. No. I was going to make him appreciate how deeply he'd hurt me. I whipped around. "All you had to do was say a few kind words, and I fell for you. Not much of a challenge."

I couldn't look at him.

He pulled my hand from the door. "Ensley, I meant those things I said to you." His voice was soft in my ear. He turned me to face him.

"You don't... " I pressed my back against the cold panes of the door. The smell of his warm citrusy aftershave surrounded me. I could feel his strong hands as they gently held mine. I had to center my thoughts.

I tried and failed.

6

"Tell me." His words were tortured with remorse.

"Oh, what the hell." I steeled my resolve. "Maybe it'll make a good story for your next poker game with the boys."

He closed his eyes. "God, what have I done?"

"I'll tell you exactly what you've done. I spent two weeks in D.C. not sleeping, or eating. All I did was run with Sophie, and cry." I pulled my hands free and reached for the door handle. "You broke my heart. No one has ever done that before. You want to know why?" On the plane, I'd come to the conclusion my heart was broken. By the time I landed in D.C., I knew it was permanent. "Because I've never cared this much about anyone. Ever. Get it?"

He looked down at me, his hazel eyes soft and moist. "I'd die if you got hurt."

"Oh. Oh, right." I put my hand in the middle of his chest to hold him back as I exchanged my pain for anger. Good, if I got mad I could leave. I can do all kinds of stupid things when I'm mad. "If I were hurt? Well, too late. I may not have been wounded or beaten, but I pulled the bullet out of you up on that mountain." I pointed to the resort area south of town. "You don't have the memory of seeing you hanging from the ceiling in that basement. Do you have any idea how many times *that* car battery and *that* basement brought me screaming out of a nightmare? I won't live long enough for *that* particular hell to fade." I squeezed my eyes shut. Seared into my memory was the sight of him nearly naked, hanging by his wrists, bloody and beaten. The car battery sitting by his feet. I pulled free again. "So, yeah! I was hurt." I leaned hard against the door as I fumbled for the handle. All my mad had drained away, and raw emotion stepped forward. Damn it. "If I was so important, why didn't you call me in D.C.?"

"Because what I needed to say couldn't be said in a phone call. I needed to see you, to touch you."

We stood there for an eternity.

Me trying to leave and knowing I couldn't.

Him watching me with his extraordinary hazel eyes, the brown centers melting into glistening gold that flows into a lush, earthy green.

Was I going to leave? Being this close to him, hearing his voice, feeling his touch, I knew that possibility was slipping away.

"Ensley, I—"

"Stop it. You only call me Ensley when you're annoyed with me."

"You told me never to call you Ens."

"Of course I did." I let go of the door handle and stopped pushing against him. This was not supposed to be happening. I had a plan.

"Don was on one side, telling me you were a mercenary who lived hard and threw away women. You were on the other side telling me he was right. And I, I was in the middle wanting so desperately for it not to be true. No, needing it to be a lie." I took a trembling breath. "Which is it? The man who kept track of all those girls to be sure they were safe. Or the mercenary?"

He wiped a tear from my cheek. "You know the answer. If you didn't, you wouldn't be here fighting so hard." He brushed the hair from my neck. "You can't leave any more than I can let you go. You've got to give me another chance." He gently pulled me into his arms. His warm kiss filled me with the desire I never thought I'd feel again.

On the nights, I wasn't having screaming nightmares—and waking up Sophie's whole family—I was dreaming of his tender kisses. Of how he made me feel, and the warmth of his embrace.

As a military brat, I learned early to imagine the worst-case scenario. Then figure out a way to survive it. No matter what I'd tried, I hadn't been able to devise a way to continue without Jack in my life.

I'd pictured every outcome for today. I'd even half-expected to find Lacey here. I'd fully anticipated driving out of Spirit Springs with no hope for happiness. Ever.

Me wrapped in Jack's arms, with his kiss warm on my lips, was not one of the outcomes.

When he started to pull back, I stopped him. "Oh, no."

"Ens, I still can't breathe very well." He led me back to the couch.

That's when I saw the suitcase by the stairs. "Were you going some-where?" I sat beside him.

"I was coming after you."

"How did you know where I was?"

He smiled. "I have contacts."

Of course he did.

Chapter Two

I pushed open the back door of the House at Road's End, and called, "Jane?" On one hand, I couldn't wait to see her. On the other, I had a lot to think about. It had been so easy for Jack to lie to me. I knew he said it was so I'd leave and be safe … but.

I'd phoned Jane from Boise to let her know I'd be home today. I smiled as the word ran through my head. "Home."

When I'd called her from D.C. she'd wanted to tell me Jack's version of what happened in Africa. I wouldn't let her. I didn't want one more secondhand story, I needed to hear it from Jack.

"Boss, you're here." She hurried into the kitchen and gave me a hug.

She stepped back. "You look," she tilted her head and peeked at me over her new lavender glasses, "what's wrong. I know you've been to see him. It doesn't take five hours to drive up here from Boise." She pushed her glasses up into her blonde hair. "You look as if something is weighing on you. But you do look happier than the woman I talked to a few days ago, the one who couldn't go three words without crying." She busied herself with something on the counter. "Talk to me."

"I have so much to consider."

"Don't make me pull the words out of you."

I'd spent two hours in Jack's arms as the afternoon had faded into evening. "We have things straightened out. Jane, I almost didn't come back." I slumped against the counter as the gravity of my words sunk in. "It took everything I had to face him."

She snapped her towel at the countertop. "I knew you'd be back. You belong here, this is your home." She gave me a sideward glance. " You understand that now, don't you? Besides you left those cats here."

I nodded. "It took me a while, but yes, I do." It was until things changed. They always do. Nothing lasts forever.

"Tell me what he said."

"He told me Don's version was correct so I'd leave and be safe. Can you believe it? I might be run over by a bus, or struck by lightning, or taken by aliens. Anything could happen." Okay, maybe not the aliens, but who knows?

"He said the same to me. It didn't sound any better then," Jane said. "Men are crazy creatures."

I settled against the counter as my thoughts battled. I wanted to be with Jack, but the devastating pain of our separation … I shuddered. If this happened again I'd have to walk away no matter what the cost. Maybe I should have this time.

"Boss, you with me?"

"Sorry, so much has happened in such a short time." That sounded rational. "Something's been bothering me about the kidnappers. There was another man there, he stayed in the shadows, so he was nothing but a dark form. I got the idea he was calling the shots. I asked Jack, but he wouldn't tell me who he was." Why? Was there something he'd left out of his story? Or was it a lie of omission?

"I couldn't get much out of him. Except what I could see. I don't think I've ever seen a man so torn up." She tilted her head. "You know, he's only been to work three or four times since you left."

"What? Broken ribs hurt, and the bruises had to be painful, but he only missed one day with a bullet hole in his shoulder and a painful leg wound." I know one thing for sure about men—probably the only thing—they get their self-worth from their jobs. For Jack to stay away from the one he loved was serious.

"His hurt was a lot deeper than a few broken ribs and some bruised shins. And I'll say no more about it."

Jane is an open book. Until she decides to keep something to herself, that's when she closes the book. Permanently. "Do we have any guests?"

"We do, and I don't mind telling you, I'm glad you're back. It's no fun doing this alone."

I smiled. "Who do we have?"

"Mr. Tyson." She grinned. "He's going to get the resort started again. The whole town is excited. Still, it's like they're holding their breath. They don't want to end up worse off than they are. They learned the hard way not to go all in on a promise."

A year and a half ago, the town had put its hopes and money behind a new ski resort. Instead of becoming prosperous, they ended up with a hand full of sand and a lot of debt. "I bet the mayor is delirious."

"He is. We've got a couple other guests."

"No one we know, right?" I'd shut off my phone while I was in D.C. If I wanted to talk to someone, I called them.

She frowned. "He won't be staying here ever. When he left, I pointed out the fact that he wasn't welcome back."

We were referring to Don March, the man who'd nearly ruined my life twice now. "I don't think we have to worry about him again." I knew better. He'd show up at the worst possible moment. He is a determined man when he wants something. "Who are our guests?"

"A pleasant couple from Utah. Three women passing through on some kind of journey of self-discovery. Then there's a professor from back east somewhere."

"Knock, knock. Good afternoon, ladies." Mr. Tyson stood in the doorway, his curly blond hair in perfect order. "Jane told me you were back. I'm glad. I was hoping you'd be here before the party. I brought this for you." He handed me an envelope. The sort an invitation comes in.

"Thanks, I'm excited you're moving forward with the resort."

"We are." He indicated the envelope he'd given me. "We've invited some investors to a get-together at the new Broadmoor Hotel in Boise. I'm headed there now to get things ready for Saturday." He glanced at Jane. "I've invited several people from town. I hope you can make it."

"Of course."

"Good. We can count on you ladies then?" Ross glanced at his watch, "Right now, I've got to get on the road. I'll see you both this weekend." He left by the back door.

"Sounds like fun." Jane smiled. "If you don't mind, I'll stay here. Besides, someone has to fix breakfast and feed the cats."

"I'll tell Mr. Tyson I can't go. I've left you to do all the work for two weeks. It isn't fair."

"I won't hear of it. Go. Have some fun. I haven't spent the last two weeks of my life being miserable." A twinkle lit her blue eyes. "Stan left yesterday." She grinned. "I've had a great time."

My Uncle Stan and Jane have an understanding. "Want to help me pick out something to wear?"

"I've got some leftovers I can bring out. We'll have dinner and pick out a dress."

Someone had scraped a path in the snow between Brique House, my two-story home, and the B&B.

On the porch, I slipped out of my boots and let the front door swing open. The night before Christmas Eve, Don March stood here. He'd said he wanted Jack to exchange money for information, and to tell me he'd gotten my old job back for me. He really thought I'd go back to work for the woman he'd slept with while we were engaged. His honesty comes in many shades. It ranges from filthy black lies to... well, they never quite make it all the way to the white truth.

I'd refused to see him in D.C. He'd sent flowers, Mama Bianchi— my best friend Sophie's mother—had enjoyed them. She said it wasn't the flowers fault Don was a culo. I'd asked what it meant. Papa said she shouldn't talk like that in front of us kids. Franco is their youngest, he's thirty. Yes, they'd taken me in as one of their own.

My favorite path to the kitchen is through the library. The dark oak bookcases line three of the walls. I ran my hand along the spines of the leather-bound volumes. A red brick fireplace sits opposite the door.

My dad had lived here until he moved into the B&B. That move had set off a series of events, events that brought me to this place at this time.

I set my purse on the kitchen counter. I figured I'd have a refrigerator full of veggie slime and green mold. Instead, the bottle of wine Jack had brought over the night everything went to hell sat alone on the shelf. I'd forgotten the wine. I held it. You don't take someone's favorite wine and whisper seductively that you'll be back if you're ending things. Leaning against the counter I held the cold bottle, staring at the label. Why hadn't I realized it? I felt like an idiot.

A knock on the front door stopped me. The last time I'd answered the door, it had been Don. I set the wine down.

In the entry, I saw Jane standing on the other side of the glass-topped door. Her hands full.

"I've got salad and Swiss steak," she said as I pulled the door open.

"Sounds great." Jane is amazing in the kitchen. She bakes bread for the town's two restaurants, cinnamon rolls for the truck stop, as well as making breakfast for our guests. I help, but I'm not certain how much assistance I am.

Back in the kitchen, I turned on the oven while she put the salad in the refrigerator.

"I didn't know if I should throw this out or keep it." She held the bottle of La Crema, Chardonnay. "I know Jack brought this over before," she let her voice trail off.

"No. If I'd remembered this bottle," it was all I could say after so much turmoil.

"You knew without the wine." She peeked over her lavender glasses. They suited her perfectly. The unexpected color was every bit Jane. She looks like a farm girl, but she keeps company with my Uncle Stan, a retired Major General, and a very smart man. Her brand of uncanny common sense and her ability to read people astounds me. Jane is an unexpected treat. Like the second piece of your favorite chocolate in a Whitman's Sampler. It shouldn't be there, but you're happy it is.

"I wish I could see life the way you do. It takes me so long to figure things out."

"You're a ponderer. Most brainy types are. Take Stan. He thinks things through for a good long while before he acts." She paused as she watched me. "And when you have two scared people in love, it takes longer."

"What?" Did everyone know? "Jane, I've only known him for a couple of months. I can't be in love." I'd spent my time in D.C. denying how I felt. I'd almost convinced myself it wasn't real love, until I realized I even knew the moment it had happened. The instant I'd fallen in love with a total stranger. Still, I knew one day I'd have to walk away and learn to live without him.

I had to change the subject. This was all too fresh. Too raw. "What did Uncle Stan get you for Christmas?"

"A diamond necklace." She grinned. "Biggest diamond I've ever gotten. I told him he shouldn't have spent all that money. He told me I was worth every penny." Her smile lit her face.

He was right.

I put the wine back in the refrigerator. "Let's go pick out a dress for the party while dinner warms up." When I came out here, I'd jammed most of my things in the back of my SUV. The movers brought out the rest later. So everything had either been *crammed* in an SUV or stuffed in boxes.

When I'd arrived, I'd hung things with no thought as to their well-being, or order. I should arrange them by style and color.

As we climbed the stairs, my phone rang. Howard Harris' name appeared on the screen. "Hello, Mayor." Unlike his daughter, Lacey, he's very friendly

"Ensley, it's so good to have you back," the mayor said. "You've heard the great news, haven't you? Did you get an invitation from Ross?"

Jane and I walked into my room as I marveled at the town's grapevine. After only a few hours my return had gotten around. "I have. It's great news. This will benefit everyone."

"You are going to the party in Boise, aren't you? You have to. We're counting on you as one of the town's leading business owners."

I'd gone from a researcher secluded in a lab to, it would appear, a prominent businesswoman in a small town. I liked the change. I watched Jane as she began sorting through my evening gowns. With all the parties Don had taken me to, I had a lot. I should have donated most of them before But I left D.C. I'd been in a hurry and they hadn't been a priority.

"I am. It's important for everyone to be there."

His silence had me wondering if we'd been disconnected. Finally, he said, "Do you think you can get the sheriff to go?"

"I don't know why he wouldn't."

"I'm sure you're right." He didn't sound convinced. "If you'd invite him." More silence. "Since he's the sheriff, I think it's important to have him there. He is the most powerful man in town, next to me, of course."

"I'll ask him."

Jane held up a blue silk cocktail dress. I like silk. Seriously, who doesn't? I shook my head. I'd gotten that one for a reception the night Don had received a commendation. I needed to get rid of all the bought-for-Don stuff. I'd go through them when I got back. I'm sure the girls around here could use them for Prom.

"Thank you." I heard the relief in his voice. "Well, I'll see you there if not before."

We said goodbye. "That was odd."

"What did he want?" Jane asked.

"He wants me to make sure Jack is going to the event in Boise."

"He'll be there if you wear this." She held up a black cocktail dress.

It's one of those dresses you buy because you can't resist it, and your best friend won't let you leave the store without it. You have to have it for no other reason than it's the most elegantly beautiful dress you've ever seen. When you get home, you can't find the nerve to wear it. The layers of chiffon flow over the strapless silk sheath beneath. The straight neckline is interrupted by a 'V' in the center. Each row of black chiffon twists and curl at the hem. It's cut short in the front and drapes gracefully down to my ankles in the back. "I don't know."

"It's stunning. I keep telling you, you've got to let Jack see what he's missing." She grinned. "This is perfect."

I held up the dress as I glanced in the mirror. "I've never worn anything like it." All the other evening dresses I'd gotten to wear to events with Don. This one I'd bought for me. "Maybe." I twirled around. "Jane, I'm going to wear it. I have some silver shoes that will be perfect with it."

"I've only got one thing to say." Her grin held a full measure of mischief. "You better be sure you're ready for the reaction you'll get."

Chapter Three

Saturday afternoon the snow glittered in the sun, only the way it can in the high mountain air. Millions of tiny sparkles carpeted the valley like a flurry of white sequins. Our drive to Boise would only take three hours, and our stay overnight would be short. Still, we'd be together. I smiled. Together.

"Are we staying longer than one night?" Jack asked as he reached for my suitcase.

I pushed his hand away. "I'll do that." I learned a long time ago to never pack for less than three days. I've been caught in an airline strike, a storm delay lasting two days, and a computer glitch grounding flights around the world.

"I'm fine," he protested.

"It isn't heavy, and my ribs don't need to heal." I tossed my bag in the backseat and hung my dress on the garment hanger over Jack's suit. "And don't tell me you're fine. I know how badly broken ribs hurt."

He raised one eyebrow. "When was the last time you broke your ribs?"

"Never, but I know. Medical school, remember?" I turned and slipped my arms around his shoulders and brushed my lips against his. "This is a great day."

"Hmm, and getting better." He drew me closer and didn't let go.

»§«

I never leave home without checking my destination out thoroughly. Boise is an oasis in the brown sea of southwestern Idaho's winter. The city has lots of trees, a crystal clear river running through the middle of it, and lots of restaurants downtown. If we had time, and Jack felt up to it, they have a greenbelt stretching from Lucky Peak Dam through the city for twenty-five miles along that sparkling river. I wasn't planning on doing the whole distance. However, a walk in the cold air would be great.

The best-laid plans...

Above the city, snow smothered the mountain tops. As the hills sloped down toward the valley, they rounded and became gentler until they resembled folds of crumpled velvet. As the terrain leveled out, the buildings of downtown rose up in an assembly of new and old. A gray-brown froth of leafless trees surrounded the crisp gathering of buildings.

With no snow in town, I can wear my Manolo Blahniks without the worry of breaking an ankle. Now that I'm a B&B owner, I was going to have to find less expensive shoes. Thousand dollar heels weren't a problem when I was working for JPL Corp. in D.C. With my inheritance I can afford them, the problem came more with the Idaho terrain. The four-inch heels of my Christian Louboutins aren't practical in Spirit Springs. Still, they look great. I glanced over at Jack and smiled. He reached out, took my hand and kissed it.

In case I lost my nerve, I'd brought along a simple black dress. I'd been to lots of parties with diplomats and world leaders. People you only see in the newspaper, on TV, or the cover of magazines. No, it wasn't the situation, it was the man beside me. Since my return, he'd been different. When he held me it was as if I was the most important thing in the world to him.

Christmas had changed us both. I was determined to make the most of our time together. For Jack the difference was subtle, but it was there. Right now, I was happy to let things be.

»§«

The hotel had a fresh feel that only comes with brand new. The lobby had an ultra-modern appearance. Either that or not all the furniture had arrived. Whichever, they should leave it as it is.

We were on our own for a while. The investors were being treated to a dinner presentation before the party at seven.

Jack promised me a late supper. I'd missed our meals together. I couldn't wait to be alone with him.

He said he had some calls to make. I went to soak in the tub until my skin turned pink. The tension came when my makeup refused to cooperate. I'd taken it off twice. Nothing would coordinate. It was either the way the eye shadow looked with my gray eyes or the fact that my stubborn hair refused to obey the curling iron. I looked at the black dress hanging on the back of the door. Did brown hair go with black chiffon?

I squeezed my eyes shut. I was driving myself straight into crazy town. It wasn't the dress or the party for the investors, I could handle that. It wasn't even Jack. It was the soul-wrenching events that had been thrown at me lately. What I needed most right now were calm days and peaceful nights. I wouldn't be greedy and wish for a month of ease. No. I figured a few days or maybe a whole week would do the trick. Just a little time to breathe.

Finally, satisfied with my makeup, I put on dress number two. The sheath looked ordinary, but *nice*. That wasn't going to work. I didn't want plain-but-nice. "This is dumb. Jane will kill me if I don't wear the one she picked out." I changed into the strapless dress and fluffed the layers of black chiffon. "If he doesn't like it, I'll change. Plan made. Problem solved."

I slipped into my sparkly silver Christian Louboutin's as I heard a knock. I pulled open the hotel door. "Hi."

"Wow." Jack turned me around. "Wow."

"It's okay?"

"The only problem I can see is I'm not armed."

I knew better. Jack doesn't go anywhere unarmed. I smiled. "Thanks." I stretched up and kissed him. "You look amazing," I whispered. More precisely, unreasonably hot. His black suit fit his broad shoulders perfectly. His soft brown hair is stylishly short, setting off his even features and high cheekbones. He can alter his appearance in an instant by changing his expression. One minute he appears warm and welcoming, the next as hard as steel and scary as hell.

"Shall we go?"

I handed him my room key.

He raised his eyebrows. "Oh?"

"I don't have any pockets." I held my hands out to the side. "I'm not taking a bag. It's a pain to keep track of."

I was still struggling. I felt like I was on an unstable roller coaster. I'd gone from the worst depression ever to being blissful. With the inevitable lurking just out of sight, I'd decided to make enough memories to sustain me when we parted. With all the many severed relationships in my life, I know nothing is everlasting. I'm not a fatalist, just a realist. I've learned nothing stays the same. We change, and people and events around us shift. With every adjustment comes new challenges.

Jack pushed the button for the elevator. He leaned over and whispered, "I can't wait for dinner, and we're alone."

A shiver of anticipation bubbled through me and stole the words from my brain as the doors whooshed open. There stood the mayor and his daughter.

Of course. Lacey.

She hates the sight of me, because in her eyes if it weren't for me, she'd be with Jack.

I smiled. "Good evening Howard, Lacey."

"Mayor." Jack nodded. "Lacey."

We stepped inside.

Elevator rides are at best interesting, at worst intolerably uncomfortable. Either you're with strangers, and everyone faces the door, eager for it to open. Or you're stuck in a confined space with someone who wants to scratch your eyes out. Lacey would have liked nothing more than to open a trap door in the floor and let me fall to the bottom of the shaft.

I hoped no one on a lower floor had pushed the call button. My luck didn't hold. We stopped twice.

I heard the rustle of Lacey's beaded dress as she hugged up behind Jack to make room for the newcomers. *It wasn't that crowded.* Yes, I'm tired of outside forces inserting themselves where they didn't belong. I had enough doubts of my own to keep me off balance, I didn't need help.

Music from a small band flowed out into the lobby. Inside, the ballroom we found a flurry of energy, of people laughing and dancing. Investors and towns people were gathered around the tables scattered throughout the room. The lights were at the perfect level for conversation and dancing. Ross and his partner, Cullen Riley at Blazer Development, were pros. If anyone could, they'd make the resort a success.

Ross greeted us. "Good evening. What a lovely dress, Ensley." He smiled at me.

"Thank you," I said.

He shook Jack's hand. "Sheriff, I'm glad you were able to make it. You'll all make a great impression on the investors."

"I wouldn't miss it," Jack said.

Ross turned to the mayor and Lacey. "You look charming, Lacey."

"Thanks." She sounded like a bored teenager.

"Mayor, I think you're going to be very pleased with the results tonight. I have a few investors interested not only in the resort but, the town, too."

A wide grin lit Howard's face. "That's great news. I want them to know the town is behind the resort one-hundred percent."

"Let's go meet some people." Ross guided the four of us around introducing us to the investors.

This was easy, small talk with strangers. At least here, I knew what everyone was after. In D.C., this week's ally maybe the one trying to destroy you the next. Here, everyone wanted money. The town needed it, and the investors wanted to make it. Perfect fit.

Someone brought me a glass of wine. I don't drink at these functions. I've seen too many unforced errors due to one cocktail too many. With few exceptions, I never drink anything I haven't seen poured.

I carried the glass around. It kept anyone from bringing me another unwanted beverage. I danced with Ross and chatted with his partner Jeffery. He was as stiff as Ross was relaxed. Interesting how partnerships form.

Across the room, Jack chatted with a woman draped in diamonds. I bet the sparkle from her gems could be seen from space. Jack has a comfortable, refined manner. I watched him and wondered about his past. He'd fit in at any Washington gala or embassy ball as well as the battlefield. He's a puzzle. I do like a good riddle. But right now that was the problem.

Howard walked up and held out his hand. "Would you like to dance?"

"Yes, thank you."

He put his arm around my waist. "I'm sorry about Lacey. She... well she's had a hard time since her mother died." He glanced over at Jack and Lady Diamonds.

"I wish—"

"Please, don't take it personally. She'd hate anyone who," he pressed his lips together. "She thinks a lot of the sheriff." He changed the subject, and we made small talk for the rest of the dance. I thanked him as someone took my hand. I turned.

"I believe this is our dance." Jack smiled at me as he folded me into his arms. "This is so much better than being shot."

"Really?" I pulled back and grinned up at him. "That's your pick-up line?"

He brushed his face against mine until his mouth touched my ear. That only made it impossible to breathe. "I figure with our history, it should work," he whispered.

Someone tapped me hard on the shoulder.

"If you don't mind." It was Lacey.

"Not now, Lacey," Jack didn't let go of me.

"It's okay," I moved aside. She'd been drinking. Either that or she was wearing whiskey-scented perfume. The last thing anyone needed tonight was a scene. I stepped to the side of the dance floor.

"Care to dance?" Cullen asked.

"Yes." Over his shoulder, I watched Jack and Lacey.

"Ross tells me you own the bed and breakfast," Cullen said.

"Yes."

"It's going to be a great area when they get the road fixed."

Road? "We drove down today, and it was in excellent shape."

He smiled. "No, dear, the one up to the resort."

Woops. I needed to pay attention. "You're right, it needs a lot of work."

"From what I've been told, your bed and breakfast is the best in the state."

"Thank you. You've been talking to Howard, haven't you?"

"He's very proud of your little town."

I glanced up as Jack stopped dancing. He seized Lacey by the wrist and led her over to her father.

After a short exchange, Howard focused a glare at his daughter. Jack shook his head. He watched as a shocked Howard grabbed his daughter's arm and dragged her out of the room.

That couldn't be good.

Jack skirted a table as he walked over to us. He nodded to my companion. "Cullen, please excuse me. Ensley, my ribs ache if you don't mind I'd like to go back to the room."

"I heard about your, ah situation."

"Thank you. I overdid it a little today." Jack took my arm.

"I'm sorry to hear that." Cullen stepped back. "I hope you feel better soon, good evening." I half expected my dance partner to bow.

I thanked him for the dance. "What happened?" I whispered as we walked away.

"She's drunk."

We left the ballroom. Instead of heading for the elevators we went out into the lobby. "What did she say?"

He shook his head. "We're changing your room. I want yours next to mine."

I stopped. "What's going on?" My room was on the floor above his.

"Not here."

There are a few two-word statements that always prove to be toxic. This was one of them. Inevitably, what followed wasn't good for either of us.

At the front desk, Jack said, "We need a room change."

The young man behind the counter said, "Yes, Sir. Is there a problem?" His brow wrinkled as his gaze darted from Jack to me.

"We need adjoining rooms."

"Oh, I see."

I was pretty sure he didn't, because I had no idea why.

The clerk typed on this computer. "I'm sorry, sir, we don't have any adjoining rooms left. We do have one with two bedrooms, the Presidential Suite."

"Fine. Book it."

"It's four hundred—"

"Book it." Jack reached into his pocket. "Have our things taken from these rooms up to the new one." He wrote down our room numbers, took out a hundred dollar bill. He slid the room numbers, the cash and our key cards across the counter. "Now." He didn't release the items. "No one is to know about the room change. No one." He dropped the tenor of his voice for emphasis.

"Yes, Sir." The clerk handed us new key cards.

Jack put his hand in the middle of my back. "We're going for a walk."

Chapter Four

I thought about telling him it was midnight, it was freezing outside, and I wasn't wearing anything that could possibly keep me warm. I figured he knew.

He slipped out of his jacket and draped it around my bare shoulders.

"What's going on?" I asked. "What did Lacey say?"

"Bitch."

Okay. So, nothing good.

"In here." He opened the door to a small metro-style bar.

"Jack, tell me what happened?"

"Did you drink or eat anything tonight?" he asked.

"No. I never do at these things." Which reminded me, I was starving.

"Good." We found a table off to one side and ordered our drinks. Chardonnay for me, Scotch for him.

"What's going on?"

The worry lines between Jack's eyes were deep. "Lacey threatened to kill you."

I gasped as I raised my fingers to cover my open mouth. Finally, I said, "Tell me what happened between you two and I don't mean tonight. She's hated me from the minute she saw us together."

The waitress set our drinks on the table.

When we were alone, he said, "Last summer on the Fourth of July, Oliver and I were making rounds after the fireworks." He clinked the ice in his glass and took a drink. "I was checking the parking lot when I heard someone scream. Lacey's boyfriend was beating the crap out of her. I arrested him." He sipped more golden liquid. "Oliver hauled the boyfriend to jail, and I took Lacey to the hospital. I stayed with her until Howard arrived." He signaled the waitress.

"That was the right thing to do," I said.

When she came over, he said, "Water, please." Alone again, he went on, "The next day, I went back to the hospital to get her statement. It was cut and dried. At the same time, an ATF friend of mine was investigating the illegal sale of explosives. Lacey's boyfriend was in it up to his face tattoo."

"Was she involved?"

"No. I told her to find a nice guy and stay away from the dangerous punks. I felt sorry for her."

Jack leaned back as the waitress set the water on the table. "I ended up being her idea of a nice guy."

I understood, he is a great guy. "It happens more than you think."

He shook his head. "Once she was out of the hospital, she started coming to my house. It got to the point." He stopped. The ice in his glass made a clinking sound as he tilted it from side to side. He drank the rest of his Scotch and said, "I had to tell Howard. No matter how I try to avoid her, she always turns up."

"So, why the room change?" I asked. "She's drunk, there's no way she's going to do anything."

He rubbed the back of his neck. "Doc, we can't catch a break. First your dad's death, and being nearly killed up on the mountain, then Christmas Eve and now this."

It didn't appear so. "It'll be okay." Especially, when I found out what *it* was. "And the room change?"

"It's to keep you safe."

And again I didn't know what *it* was.

"She's gone too far. I can't let this go. I've got to arrest her." He picked up the glass of water.

Why couldn't the fates find something better to do than screw with us?

"God, this can't be happening," He put his hand to his ribs. They had to hurt. "She hired a hitman. She said it was so she and I could be together. I told her if she didn't get ahold of the guy and call it off she'd spend her youth in prison." His eyes narrowed. "I can't believe she's that stupid." He downed the rest of his drink.

"Jack," I said his name softly.

"She told me she couldn't call it off because she didn't even know his name."

Now that I knew what *it* was I began to shake. My quaking lips made it hard to talk. "What?" My voice came out squeaky and too loud. With a trembling hand, I reached for my glass. "I've never had anyone hate me this much." I stared at the last third of my wine, then gulped it down. I needed the rest of the bottle to dull the fear churning through me. "What are we going to do? And no. Leaving again isn't an option."

"I wanted you to know what was going on first. I'm calling Andy at ATF. He's local." He pulled out his cell phone. "Andy, I have a situation. You know where I am. When can you get here? Good." He hung up. We finished our water, and he said, "Let's go."

Outside I faced him, "Jack." This was the first time I'd been afraid for me. Until now, it had always been Jack in danger. It was *easier* for it to be me, sort of. My breathing became rapid. *Easier* didn't mean I wasn't terrified. At least this way, I wouldn't have to remove any bullets from Jack or see him tortured. "Is Andy as good at his job as Brad is at his?" Brad is the FBI agent who'd been there to wrap things up after my dad's death. I'd turned to him when Jack was kidnapped. It had been two and a half weeks since that day. The day I'd left Spirit Springs.

"Andy is—" Jack stopped. "Are you okay?"

"No."

"I won't let anything happen to you." We stood on the sidewalk in the cold. His warm jacket around my shoulders and the delicious

PEGGY STAGGS

citrusy scent of his aftershave filled me with a sense of his masculinity and pure power.

"I'm..." I couldn't process the situation. I pulled the jacket tighter around me and leaned against him.

"Do you have your .38?" he asked.

"What?" I was lost in the idea that Lacey wanted me dead.

He lifted my chin. "Your .38? Do you have it?"

"No. Besides, I don't have a concealed permit."

"We'll take care of that when we get home." We began walking.

"Home," I whispered as I slipped my hand in his.

"What?" He watched me.

"I remembered something Brad said when you... I was looking for you."

He frowned as he glanced down at me. "What did Brad tell you?"

We stopped. The stone of the old buildings absorbed the light glinting off the glass of the new structures around us. A horn honked signaling a driver's irritation. A muscle car roared past us, its pipes singing the praises of its engine's power. "He said these things don't happen to normal people. We aren't normal, are we?"

"With my past and you being you? No, Doc, we're not normal." He brushed a wisp of hair from my face. "Does that bother you?" Again the little worry lines appeared between his eyes.

"No. I just thought I'd check." I shivered more with the realization of the death threat than the cold.

"Let's get inside before you freeze."

The lobby lay empty at this late hour. The only sign of life was the desk clerk and the mellow sounds of the gathering we'd left earlier.

"Is our room ready?" Jack asked the attendant.

"Yes, sir. I think you'll find everything satisfactory."

"Is the kitchen still open?" I asked.

"I'm sorry, we're only doing catering right now until the restaurant is finished. It isn't much, but the continental breakfast room has fruit, cold cereal, and some juice drinks. There are snacks in the refrigerator in your room."

"Thank you," I said and looked at Jack. "I'd love an apple." I handed him his jacket.

28

"I don't want anyone to know we've changed rooms," Jack reiterated.

"No, Sir. Only two of us know. Me and the night maid."

To drive home his point, Jack pulled out his sheriff's badge and laid it on the counter. "Keep it that way."

I smiled as we walked toward the breakfast room. "Do you always carry your badge?"

"Always. You never know when it'll come in handy." He paused. "I'm sorry about dinner. When we get this straightened out, I promise we'll go out."

I found an apple, and we went back out to the lobby to wait for Andy.

The last strains of the music and fading laughter from the party filtered out around us. A couple left the festivities. I watched them as they walked across the lobby. It was Lady Diamonds and presumably her husband. We exchanged goodbyes as they passed.

"Dr. Markus." The clerk came out from behind the counter. "This came for you." He handed me a single red rose wrapped in cellophane and green florist paper. "There's a card with it."

I thanked him. The note read: *I'm sorry about what happened with Lacey. Howard.* "Poor Howard. That's kind." I handed the note to Jack.

I stripped the cellophane protection from the rose. The flower was so fresh it had tiny droplets of water on it. I inhaled its perfume. The ambrosial scent made my nose tingle. The droplets covered my nose and mouth. I didn't wipe away the delightful rose scented water.

The lobby doors swooshed open, and a man, Jack's age, walked in. He was two or three inches shorter than Jack and built like a linebacker.

"Jack," he called. As I got to my feet, he hesitated then shot Jack a surprised look.

"Ensley Marcus, this is Andy Buckingham."

"Nice to meet you." Did I know him? No. He wasn't someone you'd forget with that shock of bright red hair.

He shook my hand. "It's good to meet you, too. I'm sorry about your dad. He was a good man.

"Were you at his memorial service?" I asked Andy.

"No, I'm sorry. I was away on assignment."

I sat down as a pin, the kind you get with a corsage, stuck my finger. A tiny dot of blood blossomed on my fingertip. I raised it to my lips. More of the dew drops had rubbed off on my fingers.

They talked for a few minutes, then Jack said, "Let's go."

We went to the bank of elevators. The rose was so profoundly red. I took in the sweet, pleasant fragrance.

Andy stopped Jack outside the elevator. "Isn't that—?"

"Yeah. Later."

In the mirrored panel of the elevator, I saw Andy give Jack a what-the-hell glance.

Jack shook his head.

Hmm, I'd ask later.

As the elevator approached the top floor, I watched Jack pull up his pant leg and retrieve the gun he keeps in an ankle holster. The doors slid open, and both men moved into the hall.

"Have you seen anyone in the hall?" Jack asked a woman walking past.

She gasped and clutched an ice bucket to her.

"ATF." Andy took out his wallet.

"Sheriff." Jack showed her his badge.

"I haven't seen anyone." She hurried away.

"Thank you," Andy called.

They'd scared her half to death. "Poor woman." I know they would have frightened me if I didn't know they were the good guys. I smiled. Jack is a good guy.

At the end of the hall, Jack opened the double doors of the Presidential Suite. Jack and Andy cleared the rooms before they let me enter. I was supposed to stay in the doorway.

I walked into a spacious living room. A white sofa cozied in around a chrome and glass coffee table. The top sparkled as if it were made of a million tiny multicolored gems. The designer had set off the brilliant white couch with vivid lime green accents. I like the bright green.

"Pretty." I ran my hand over the back of the silky couch as I walked to the window. Below, downtown was a mosaic of light and dark. On the street, a string of white and red lights from the passing cars wound up the road and out of sight. Beyond the glow of the city center, the dark line of the river was dotted with delicate lights. They mingled with the bare tree branches in the chilled night. I reached out and touched the glass with my fingertips. Rainbow colored halos surrounded the dim bulbs of the lights that flowed along the dark waterway.

The Boise River splits the business district from the University beyond. On the hill above the school, the train depot reigns over downtown. Bright lights are hidden in the shrubs collided with the white stucco exterior in a blaze of light. I looked at the bright red apple in my hand and laid it on the kitchenette counter.

I needed to figure this out. I took a hotel notepad from beside the phone. I'm a list maker. They help me focus. I lifted the flower to my nose. I didn't know what to put on my list. I laid the pen down as I glanced across the room at Jack and Andy.

Jack was shaking his head. I heard him say, "I don't," He lowered his voice, and I couldn't hear anymore. Jack's voice is deep and warm. I like it. A lot.

I fluffed the folds of my delicate black chiffon and silk dress. It made me feel special. I watched Jack talk to the other man. What was his name again?

"Wow," I whispered. That's what Jack had said when he'd picked me up. I felt a smile tickle my lips and reached up to touch it.

Everything had turned soft and easy as if I were floating. I lifted the top layer of chiffon on my dress. Through it, everything looked gray and blurry. I didn't want dark and unfocused. I wanted bright and happy. Jack made me happy. I let the fabric fall and walked over to him. I slipped between Jack and the other man.

Jack smiled down at me. "Doc?"

I stared into his eyes as I ran my fingers across his mouth.

"What's going on?"

I wanted my dance. "Jack, I need to feel—"

"Doc?"

Something was wrong, or was it? I kissed him.

He wasn't kissing back. "Jack."

"I better go," someone said.

"No." Jack's voice sounded troubled. He put his hands on both sides of my face and tilted my head back. "She's stoned."

I looked up at him as the edges of my vision grew dark. I watched the darkness shrink to a pinpoint and go black.

"Ens, wakeup."

I opened my eyes.

"The ambulance is almost here," someone said.

"Jack." I tried to pull him down to me. I ran my hands up his arms. "You have great shoulders."

"She okay?"

Jack shook his head. "No."

"Lacey stole my dance."

"Lie still."

Why was Jack frowning? I'd ask later. Right now, the pillow was so soft, the blanket so warm, and he was so close.

"I'm right here." He brushed my cheek with his thumb as he cradled my face in his palm.

I laid my hand on his arm and closed my eyes.

"Why didn't you warn me? It's Goddamn her. She's real. I nearly shit when I saw her downstairs."

Why didn't he think I was real? I held onto Jack.

"Andy, keep your voice down."

"Don't worry, she's out. You told us it was part of a cover story. Does she know?"

"No. She's not going to. If you say a word, I'll shoot your ass. Got it?"

"Yeah, not a word."

Chapter Five

The sunlight ripped through the window and collided with my face. Where was I? I squinted at the room around me. A hospital room? I started to sit up and almost vomited. I sank back against the pillow. What had happened? Where was Jack?

An IV ran from my arm to a bag above. I covered my eyes against the onslaught of sun. I felt horrible. What had I eaten that made me sick? Nothing. I remembered having one glass of wine and a glass of water.

My head pounded in time with my heartbeat. With my eyes closed, I felt around for the call button. I pressed it.

"How do you feel?" the nurse asked as she turned off the call light.

"Like I've been run over by a truck and a train. Where am I?"

"St. Luke's Hospital. Just relax. You're going to be fine."

"What happened?" A fuzzy memory of looking out the window at the train depot came back. I remembered walking over to Jack, and that was about it.

"You were drugged." She took something from the counter. "That handsome sheriff left this for you." She handed me an envelope. The note read:

. . .

Doc,

I'll be back as soon as I can. Don't leave the hospital. I have a police officer outside your door. You'll be okay.

Jack.

The last sentence was up for debate. Incoherent flashes began popping into my head. Vivid colors and snatches of a conversation.

"I have a horrible headache. It's about an eight on the pain scale. May I have some aspirin?" I kept my eyes closed against the invasion of light.

"I can get you some Tylenol."

"Aspirin is more affective for me." I paused. "I'd like to take a shower and get dressed." Maybe that would make me feel better.

"You can take a shower, but you're not going anywhere until the doctor discharges you, and the sheriff gets back." She filled a glass from a pitcher on the rolling table next to me. "Drink some water, you'll feel better." When I took it, she moved the table around so I could reach it.

I drank a glass of water, then another, and a third.

The shower didn't work. I crawled back into bed. Half of me was sure my head was going to fall off, while the other half wished it would. It couldn't hurt any worse. Bits of last night came and went. I don't like not knowing what happened. I hate not being in control. Oh, I know you're never really in control. However, I find the illusion comforting.

"Good morning, Ensley."

The doctor entering my room was an old med school classmate of mine. The last I'd heard he was practicing in Kansas City.

"Stanton, what brought you to Idaho?" We'd studied together.

"I was tired of the big city life. I wanted a change of scenery." He gave me a hug.

"How are you? And Bev and the kids?" I asked as he stood.

"We're all fine." He shifted from one foot to the other." You, on the other hand, are not." He set my chart on the rolling table. The metal cover tipped as if to fall. He caught it. "The good news is, we isolated the drugs and they should be out of your system in the next twenty-four to forty-eight hours."

"I didn't take anything."

"I know that." He glanced out the window. "Want me to close the curtains?"

"Please."

As he moved the louvers he said, "You always avoided taking any medication when we were in school."

"What was it?"

He opened the file and shuffled through the papers. Finally, he closed the chart and said, "I'm waiting on the rest of the results. We counteracted the nasty cocktail of potent opiates and street drugs. They were on the rose." He shoved the clipboard under his arm. "Who is that guy?"

"What guy?"

"The one who brought you in?"

"Jack."

"I don't mind telling you he scared the shit out of me. I got the feeling if you didn't survive, neither would I."

I smiled. "He can be intimidating. I'd tell you his bark is worse than his bite, but it isn't."

"Yeah, I got that. You have some interesting people around you." He glanced at the open door.

Between the CIA, the FBI, now the ATF, and Jack, life *had* gotten exciting. With the personal risk level going from school zone crossing to Indie Five-hundred at light speed.

"The last I heard you were an up-and-comer at JPL. What are you doing out here?"

"It's a long, story." Enter the CIA in the guise of Don March, my ex-fiancé. "I'm no longer in medicine. I moved to a small Idaho town." Enter Jack, the FBI, and an assortment of bad guys. "I have a Bed and Breakfast in Spirit Springs. You and Bev should come up." I took a sip of water. "They're beginning construction on a new ski resort. We came to Boise to meet the investors." Enter the ATF and my current problem: Lacey.

"A bed and breakfast weekend, sounds relaxing. I'll talk to Bev."

"When can I get out of here?"

"I'll check in later and see how you're doing then." He looked at the metal clipboard. "You absorbed the drug around your mouth and nose. There was DSMO on the flower. I want you to drink lots of water and have something to eat. I'll see you later."

"Horse liniment? It smelled like a rose."

"I checked. Believe it or not, you can get the stuff in a rose scent." He shrugged.

"That would certainly get the drugs into my system in a hurry." I rubbed my temples. "Stanton, would you order something for my headache." I laid back.

"It's on the way."

He passed Jack and Andy on his way out. Jack stopped him, and they spoke. When they were done, Jack came over to my bed.

"What happened?" I started to sit up. The effort had my stomach threatening to revolt. I hate to throw up. I know it isn't on anyone's favorites list, but I'll do just about anything to keep it from happening.

"What do you remember?" Jack asked.

"It's like a dream. The memories are there, but they don't make sense. I remember walking into the hotel room and looking out the window. Then I walked over to you." I held tight to his hand. "Everything's still fuzzy. I don't like this feeling."

"You're okay, I've got you." He brushed the hair from my face.

»§«

I was so hungry even the hospital food tasted good. I closed my eyes. I still felt shaky, probably low blood sugar. It would take a few minutes for the food and the medication to get into my system. I lay against the cool pillow and closed my eyes.

My headache eased as the sun warmed my face.

A gentle hand caressed my cheek. "Jack." I opened my eyes.

"How do you feel?"

"Better. What happened last night?"

He smiled. "You're something on drugs."

I squeezed my eyes shut as a flutter of anxiety filled my stomach. "What did I do?"

"Let's just say," he leaned down and whispered. "The next time you make a pass at me, I'm not saying no." He kissed me.

"I like hospital kisses." The first time he'd kissed me we'd been in a hospital. That time, he had a bullet wound in his shoulder, and mine was immobilized from a bad pull. Awkward, but great. Really great.

A nurse came in. "You're not supposed to sit on the side of the bed."

"When can she leave?"

"Doctor is on his way," she said as she shooed Jack from the side of my bed, then took my blood pressure.

Stanton paused in the doorway when he saw Jack.

"Hello, Dr. Hayden," Jack moved toward him.

"How are you?" Stanton's voice was as tight as his posture.

"Good. Thanks for listening to me last night." Jack shook his hand.

Stanton's smile faltered. "It was very helpful information. With her sensitivity to drugs, she was lucky you were there." He turned to me. "You're all set to leave. I want you to take it easy for at least the next twenty-four hours. It would be better if it were forty-eight, and don't forget to drink lots of water and eat something with calories." He pulled a card from his pocket and handed it to me. "Call me if you have any symptoms. Any. My cell is on the back."

I promised, and he left.

"I'll be outside, while you get dressed," Jack said and followed Stanton out the door.

All I had was my dress from last night. Hardly daywear.

Downstairs in the truck, Jack said, "I talked to Howard earlier. He didn't leave the note or the flower. We went out to the night clerk's house, and he said he didn't know where it came from, it was left on the counter for you."

"Was it Lacey?" I didn't want to think she'd follow through on her threat, but someone had.

"She was in her room fighting with her father from the time they left the party until the ambulance got there."

"If it wasn't Lacey? Then who?"

"The man she hired." He pulled into the parking garage at the hotel. "Either she won't tell me, or she doesn't know. We're banking on her not wanting to tell me. Maybe a couple of nights in jail will change her mind."

"She's in jail?"

We drove up the narrow concrete ramp. I hate parking garages. It isn't only because the parking spots are so small you can't get out of your car. No, it's the creep factor. All those empty cars for someone to hide behind. There's no one around, because who hangs out in a parking garage? It's probably due to all those movies where something bad happens in one. "People threaten people all the time. They don't arrest them."

"She hired a hitman. That's a Felony. It's out of my hands."

Chapter Six

When we entered the Presidential Suite, a uniformed officer stood to greet us.

I glanced around and discovered the couch was now everyday white, and the table didn't sparkle. Even the green accents had dulled.

"Good morning, Officer Royce," Jack said. "Was a package delivered for me?"

"Yes, sir, It's on the chair." He pointed to a folded black article. "An A3-level vest."

"Thanks."

"That's a bulletproof vest," I needlessly pointed out.

"And you're going to wear it at all times." Jack handed it to me.

In my bedroom, I hung my dress in the closet. The vest was easy to put on. The problem was it didn't fit under anything I'd brought, and it was uncomfortable. I tugged at the bottom of my sweater. With the vest on, it barely met the top of my jeans. At least my blazer covered everything.

When I came out, Officer Royce was gone, and Jack was talking on his cell phone. "When was she taken to the hospital? Yes, we're on our way."

"What happened?" Did I want to know?

"Lacey is in the hospital. She was beaten."

"Poor Lacey and poor Howard."

"Let's go."

"Do you think I should be there?" Even at the best of times, I was the last person she'd want to see.

"You're in protective custody. Mine. Where I go, you go."

"Is that why the vest?" I pulled the coarse fabric away from my skin.

"Yes. Let's get down there and see what the hell happened."

Jack is excellent at his job. I'd seen him focus when we were stranded on the mountain above Spirit Springs last fall. He'd zeroed in on the situation and hadn't let anything get in the way until we were safe. Right now, it looked like I was his mission.

He made a call. "Andy, we've got a problem. Lacey was beaten. We're on our way to the hospital. We'll meet you there."

I asked. "What's your code?" The only phone I'd had on Christmas Eve was his. It had been a problem, all the contacts were in an alphanumeric code.

"What code?"

"Your contacts are all alphanumeric."

He smiled as he pushed the button to call the elevator. "Yes, they are."

"It was a problem on Christmas Eve."

"I heard about it." We stepped into the elevator. "What no one's been able to figure out is how you got into it."

"What do you mean? I simply picked it up and used it." I'd held it tight as I'd searched for him.

"It's protected."

"No, it wasn't."

He pulled it from his pocket and handed it to me. "Make a call."

I slid the bar across the bottom, and an oval appeared in the center of the screen. "That wasn't there."

"You have to have my fingerprint to access it." He took his phone back. "Was March with you when you found it?"

"Yes." The elevator doors opened, and a man got on.

"We'll talk about it later."

40

I knew that tone. What had Don done?

Jack's new silver truck was wedged between a Cube and a Dart. "I'm glad you got your truck back." Men out here are very protective of their trucks. A bad guy had tried to get away in Jack's on Christmas Eve. It hadn't worked. Fortunately, for the bad guy, he didn't damage the vehicle.

"They caught him before he got out of town." Jack opened the truck door for me. When he got behind the wheel, he said, "About my phone."

"Don was there," I repeated.

"Did he ever take it from you?"

"A couple of times, when he talked to Brad. But it was never out of my sight." That night, it had been my tether to sanity. My only link to Jack. Until the connection was severed and I put it on the floor beside him and left. I held my breath against the memory and anguish of that night.

"Was his phone or anything like a phone near mine at any time?"

"You're asking me to remember a night I've been spending almost three weeks trying to forget."

"I'm sorry, it's vital."

I dragged my thoughts back to the heartbreaking memories. "No. He never had it. Wait, he pulled it out from under the bed. That's the only time."

He thought for a minute. "That fits with what we know. My phone wasn't breached. He had to have switched phones. Why go to all that trouble?"

I'd realized that night Jack knew some very influential people. You don't code your contacts if all you have on your phone are your best friend and the local pizza place. "Did I—" What? "I had no idea. I wanted to find you." I looked over at him. "I was so desperate I called Don."

"Doc, it wasn't your fault. You had no way of knowing. The first time you called Brad, they knew right away you weren't on my phone. Mine had gone dark. But my code showed up on Brad's phone." He started the truck. "There's no possible way for anyone besides me to access it."

"You don't think Don's coming back into our lives, do you?" Please. I kept thinking he was part of my past only to discover he'd inserted himself into my present.

"Men like March will do whatever it takes to get what they want. So, yes, he'll be back." He stopped and waited for a car to pass. "Where did you leave it when... ?"

"I left it on the floor beside you."

"March." He took my hand. "Don't worry. It made some people uncomfortable until we got it straightened out." He smiled. "It never hurts to give them a little heartburn once in a while."

Again, I wondered who Jack really was. At every turn I was learning he was a lot more than a small town sheriff. "Jack, what's your middle name?"

He stopped backing the truck out of the parking spot. "What?"

"I don't even know your middle name."

It had been a benign question, but the hurt in his eyes had me wishing I hadn't asked.

"I don't have one."

"Oh."

We left the garage in silence. Jack is like an intriguing, scary puzzle. An exciting one I want to put together, the problem is, I'm half afraid of what the whole picture will look like. Yet, I keep pressing on. Was I crazy? Should I be running in the opposite direction like Don had warned me? I'd taken that option off the table the day I returned to Spirit Springs.

We drove around the hospital's crowded parking lot looking for a space. We ended up at the far end of the row of cars. "Stay close to me," he said.

I was still pondering the middle name thing and his response. "I will." Everyone has a middle name. Okay, not Beyoncé. Some people even have two middle names, like George Herbert Walker Bush. It's not a big deal. Or it shouldn't be. Should it?

A policewoman stood by the door to Lacey's ER room. Jack showed the officer his ID, and we went inside. Lacey's eye was swollen, her cheek bruised and her lip split. I picked up a compress. The ice in it had melted.

"I'll be right back." I started for the door.

Jack stopped me. "Stay here."

Oh, right, the whole protective custody thing. I pressed the call button instead. "Lacey, what's your pain level?" I asked.

"I hurt everywhere." She groaned as she turned away from me.

I felt sorry for her. No one deserved this.

"Lacey," Jack's voice didn't hold the empathy mine had. "Are you ready to tell me?"

"Us." Andy entered the room.

"Tell us who you contacted?" Jack's voice remained firm.

"I told you, I did it for you and me," she angled so she could see Jack. "For us."

Jack's heavy sigh was one of frustration. "Why can't you understand, there is no *us*? There never was."

"There would be if she hadn't come along." She pointed at me.

I didn't want to listen to this. I'd been feeling sorry for her, now she was pushing it.

This time, it was Andy who said, "No. You don't realize—"

"Andy." Jack cautioned.

They exchanged glances, then Andy continued, "How much trouble you're in. Contract killers are ruthless. You're a lot better off dealing with us. The little scuffle you were in, was a warning. If he carries out your instructions, and you don't have his money, he won't come after you, he'll start with your father. Then he'll move onto anyone else in your family he can find. All for what?" He shot Jack a glance. "Something that never was and never could be."

I watched them and listened to all the words. There was a lot not being said. Something hidden below the surface. I remembered the way Andy had looked at me the first time we met. As if I was someone who shouldn't be there. Which didn't make any sense at all.

"I was mad." Lacey turned toward the wall. Andy walked around the exam table. Now no matter where she looked, she had to face one of them. "I wanted to be special like she is. I'm nothing but a bartender. I never went to college." She rose up and glared my way. "You're a doctor, why don't you go back where you came from?" Her effort took all her strength, and she slumped back to the bed. Her attention turned to Jack. "She's not even from here, and you've seen how people treat her. That great looking guy, Don, came to town, he wanted to take her with him. Oh, sure she left for a couple of weeks, now she's back."

The nurse came in, and I turned my attention to her. I didn't want to hear *Lacey's* humiliation. "She needs a couple more ice packs and a sedative. If you'll talk to the attending, maybe he'll prescribe something for her pain."

Her eyes narrowed as she glanced over at Lacey. I was sure Lacey had been Lacey to her. I figured her scuffle in jail had more to do with her attitude than the hitman.

Lacey began to cry.

"She's suffering. Please, see what you can do."

"I'll get the ice and talk to the doctor."

"Thank you." I pitied Lacey. She thought all she had to do was be with Jack, and everything would be different. I leaned against the doorjamb. She didn't understand. You can't get your self-worth from someone else. It isn't a gift or a prize you win. You have to work for it. I'd worked all my life to become a doctor, only to find I was happier as an innkeeper. A B&B owner in a small town with a sheriff who was more of a puzzle than any of my research projects.

"How did you get ahold of the hitman?" Andy asked.

Time and again she'd turn her head, or stare at the ceiling, but remain silent. She wanted Jack so badly she was willing to kill to get him. The thought was even more chilling when I stopped to think I was the target.

The nurse returned. "Here's the ice. I've paged the doctor." She left. Lacey's animosity was coming back on her.

"Thank you," I whispered after her. I stood there with three ice packs.

There was a lull in questioning, and I went to her bed. "Lacey, here are some ice packs for your face." I laid one of them on her swollen jaw and the other over her eye. I handed her the third one. She put it across her rib cage.

In an effort not to make things worse, I went back to the door.

I watched as the two men asked the same question in different ways. Their skill was impressive, their delivery smooth and seamless. I could tell they'd done this a hundred times.

Finally, they left her.

Out in the hall, Jack put his arm around me. "After what she's done, she doesn't deserve your kindness."

I smiled up at him.

"I was impressed after all she's put you through." This time, it was Andy.

I stood between them. "I didn't do anything. I just stayed out of the way."

A second later I felt the impact but never heard the shots.

Chapter Seven

The sound of running footsteps faded down the hall.

"Doc, breathe. You're okay, breathe."

"Did I get shot?" Pain raced from the center of my chest outwards.

"Yes. You're fine."

"It hurts."

"I know. Like getting hit with a baseball bat." He put his hand to my face. "It would have hurt a lot more if you hadn't had that vest on."

I'd take his word for it.

"Put her in here," a woman's voice instructed.

Jack started to lift me, and I pushed his hand away. "Your ribs." I struggled to my feet. The hall tilted, and Andy caught me before I fell. He picked me up and laid me on an examination table. Finished he said, "Jack. Outside."

The nurse helped me off with my sweater and the vest. I looked at the vest as she pulled the last Velcro strap loose. In the center, three slugs still stuck in the material. Underneath, the impact had torn my skin. Blood stained my bra and ran down my stomach as a massive bruise formed.

"Honey, that's going to hurt for a while." She held a compress against the wound and said, "You won't need stitches. A couple of butterflies wouldn't hurt, though." She smiled. "You doing okay?"

"It feels like someone hit me with a sledgehammer."

"Little thing like you, I can imagine. Lay still, I'll dim the lights. The doctor will be right in." She spread a blanket over me. "Relax. I'll be back with some ice."

I laid there staring at the artificial lights above me—my chest aching. Silently, a policeman stepped inside. He stood, with his back to me, watching the door.

The nurse brought the promised ice, and I pressed it to the bruise.

Jack walked in, his face stern as he spoke to the officer. Finished, he came to me. "How're you feeling?"

"What happened?"

"Some piece of shit, dressed in scrubs shot you." I wasn't the only one capable of stating the obvious. He glanced at the vest on the counter. "Nice grouping."

"Not on this side. If I hadn't had the vest on, I'd be dead. The bullets would have blown my heart apart." The realization sent a shiver through me. Lacey's hitman had almost succeeded. I reached for Jack's hand.

His jaw tightened. "I'm sorry. I should—"

"What? Know things before they happen? When you develop that talent, let me know. I'd like some stock tips."

"Andy and I have an idea."

Andy walked in. "Sarge, he got away. A car was waiting for him."

Jack nodded. The shooter doesn't know you had a vest on. According to the hospital, you're going to be in ICU."

"I can't take up a bed they may need."

"You won't be there. You're going to be with me at the hotel. Right now, we're taking you out of here as if you died."

"Dead?"

"It's temporary."

And why not? Temporarily dead beat the other option. Besides, I was running low on firsts. I figured there were a lot more in my future. "Okay."

"You're not going to object?"

48

"I know how good you are at your job," I told him. Not long ago I would have said, "I trust you." Maybe … just maybe I'd feel that way again. I hoped. Right now the lie from Christmas still hung between us. As much as I wished it away it remained.

Jack smiled. Like I said, he has a great smile.

I put my arms around his neck.

He wrapped the blanket between my bare back and his arms.

Andy cleared his throat. "Is she ready?"

"Yes," I said. "What's next?"

"We're going to take you out through the morgue." Andy came farther into the room. "You've got to lie still."

"Then what?" This seemed like an elaborate plan to be hatched so quickly. "You've done this before, haven't you?"

"A few times," Andy said.

"Don't worry," Jack said. "It'll work. Any casual observer in the hall will think the shooter succeeded."

It didn't take long for the doctor to tell me what I already knew. My chest was bruised, and the abrasion was going to hurt for a while. He did apply a couple of butterflies.

After I was dressed, Jack and Andy came in, and Jack handed me the vest. "I want you to put this back on. It's going to hurt, but it'll keep you alive in case they try again."

"It has bullets in it."

Andy laughed. "Don't worry, it'll still work."

I could tell Jack was trying hard not to laugh too.

I ignored them both. "Why the Presidential Suite? It's my first choice, but won't someone see me?"

"It's all worked out," Jack assured me.

"You weren't out in the hall long enough to do much of anything." I marveled at his abilities. How had he arrange something like this so quickly?

"We know a US Marshal," Andy said.

Of course they did.

"One of their jobs is to hide people," Jack said.

"Is this US Marshal another poker buddy?"

"Part of my team."

I didn't have to ask what team. I knew. I'd seen the pictures on the wall in Jack's office. It occurred to me that a lot of Jack's Army buddies and team members lived in the area. They all seemed to be in law enforcement. That couldn't be a coincidence. I was a little surprised they were still together. Not much, but a little. "Is he in the picture in your office?"

"Yes. You ask a lot of questions for a dead woman," Jack said.

"Are you going to put me in a body bag?" That wasn't a first I was eager to add to my list.

"No. They've had dead people in them. Yuck." Andy smiled. "I have a hotel maid's uniform for you. No one ever notices the person emptying the trash."

"When you get to the hotel, you're going in the back way. There'll be a maid's cart waiting," Jack said. These guys fit together seamlessly.

"And a marshal." Andy handed me the uniform, and they left.

The vest made my chest hurt even more. I ended up putting the vest on over my stretched out and now unraveling sweater. I was glad none of it showed under the maid's uniform.

I entered the hotel through the back door. The marshal who met me was in a maintenance uniform. "If anything, anything at all happens you get behind me," he said. "Any questions?"

"No. I just want to get to our room and lie down. My chest hurts."

"No fun getting shot." He nodded.

We took the service elevator to the top floor.

Howard was the only one still in the hotel who'd recognize me.

In the Presidential Suite, a policewoman changed into my outfit and left with the US Marshal for the reverse trip. If anyone were watching, they'd see two people come and two go.

I sat on the couch staring out the window. "You know it's kind of freeing being dead."

"How's that?" Jack asked.

"I can do anything I want, and it doesn't count."

"Interesting take on death. What're you thinking of doing that would count if you were alive?" He handed me a glass of water.

"I don't know. If I did something illegal, or mean, I'd end up feeling guilty. Not worth it."

50

He sat down and put his arm around me. I was careful not to press against his ribs as I laid my head on his shoulder. "Jack, who is Andy?"

"He's one of my team."

"You know you say that as if you were all still together."

"Once a team, always a team. We've been through a lot."

"I can tell. The way you questioned Lacey. I hope you never use that skill on me."

"Will I have to?" He smiled down at me.

"No. I'll tell you anything you want to know." If we were going to make it, one of us had to be always truthful. Perhaps, it would rub off. NO. A little voice shouted in my head. Stay positive.

"Anything?"

I shrugged. "I've led a pretty dull and uneventful life. Unless you count moving all over the world or the last three months. The only thing you'd be in danger of is dying of boredom."

"I think I'd survive it."

I finished my water and set the glass on the table. "When I was younger, I wanted to join the Air Force. I was going to be like my dad and live the exciting adventures he did when he was away. He told me it was like being a businessman working for a big corporation, the only difference was you got to fly planes. Nothing special." I glanced up at Jack. "That's not true, is it?"

"No." He got up and refilled my glass.

Had I pushed another button? I was going to have to remember not to ask so many questions. Of course, I wouldn't. I can't help myself. If I don't ask, my imagination takes over, and it knows no bounds.

Jack handed the second glass to me and sat down.

"If I ask you a question you don't want to answer, it's okay. I know I ask a lot of them." It used to drive Don crazy. "But a very wise man once said, 'if you get it out, Ens, we can deal with it.'" I did a terrible Jack Trace impression. It made him smile.

"What do you want to know? I'll tell you what I can," he said.

"It occurred to me in the parking garage that you know an awful lot about me, but I don't know much about you. Except you're an honorable man." I ran my fingers down his cheek. "Do you know how important that is?"

He held me. "You're so special. Why hasn't someone closed the deal with you?"

"I've never been that important to anyone." I looked away.

"March asked you to marry him and he came out here to try to convince you to go back with him." He tipped my chin up so he could look me in the eye. "He wouldn't do that for anyone else."

"Maybe, but he had someone on the side he wasn't willing to give up." That had been the story of my love life, a kind of I-want-you-for-show-or-money. The problem came when I wasn't the one they loved.

"He's a fool." He took my glass. "You're a curious mix of confidence and doubt."

"I'm not hard to figure out. I was that annoying kid in school who sat in the front row and asked the teacher questions no one else was interested in. The one with all the right answers and very few friends. I wasn't asked to homecoming or the prom. When I went to college, I got straight A's and," I wasn't going to tell him about my only college romance. It had ended more or less just like the one with Don. In humiliation. "I'm smart at academics and stupid at relationships."

"You aren't that way now. You have good friends and—"

What was I going to say? I do for now? But just wait, that will end. And there was that creeping doubt, that lie, that wouldn't leave me alone.

He got up and refilled my glass. He handed it to me as he sat beside me. I thought about his reaction to my simple question in the parking garage. I know a lot of people don't care for their middle names, but what was the big deal about not having one? It seemed like a good idea not to pursue it. "Last night. What did I do?" I set the full glass down. I'd float if I drank it.

"You got stoned off a rose."

"Something has been struggling to escape my subconscious all day. I keep having flashes of bits of conversation."

He looked away. "You were pretty stoned. Mostly, you passed out."

"I keep hearing Andy saying, 'It's Goddamn her. She's real.' It doesn't make sense."

I felt him tense. Not the good kind. "You're supposed to be taking it easy. I think we should call it a night."

"Not until I get an answer. Why did Andy think I wasn't real?"

"It's a story for another time. Right now we both need some sleep."

I knew there was no use in pressing for more information. Besides, I was exhausted. I kissed him goodnight and went to bed. Maybe I'd ask him again in the morning.

Chapter Eight

Long before the sun came up, I woke from another nightmare. Luckily, I hadn't awakened screaming. That would have drawn a lot of unwanted attention. I had to know Jack was okay. I peeked through the open door at him. He was asleep.

I hurried through my morning routine. Good thing I'd packed for three days. The problem came with tomorrow being the third day. I'd have no more *clean underwear*. The anxiety came straight from my mother. I can still hear her scolding me, "You never know when you might get rushed to the hospital." I smiled. As a result, I always have extras when I travel. I was pretty sure this situation wasn't going to resolve itself before I needed more undies. I'd see what I could do about the situation today.

In the kitchen, I found the mini hotel coffee maker. "Who only drinks two small cups of coffee?" I opened the half-size refrigerator. On the top shelf set two containers of yogurt, a package of fruit cups, and two bottles of juice. I smiled. That was about what had been in Jack's refrigerator the first time I stayed at his house.

Shots ripped through the early morning calm.

They didn't stop.

"Jack," I screamed.

There are three types of people. Those who run from trouble, those who freeze and those who run toward it. I'm in the category that puts me directly in harm's way. I raced toward Jack.

He stood in the doorway to my room.

"Jack."

He pivoted to face me. "You okay?"

"Yes," I said in a gasping whisper.

"Stay put."

I couldn't stop shaking. I couldn't breathe. I managed to nod.

He left me in the dead silence.

I figured we'd be moving out of the hotel today. They weren't going to understand any of this.

Jack came back in, "Doc, this way."

"What happened?"

"They found us."

"How?"

He didn't answer. He was already on his cell phone. "Andy, we've been compromised. I don't know how the hell they figured it out. Meet us at the Larch safe house." He turned to me. "Get your things." He was in command mode.

When that happens, it's wise to do as you're told and ask questions later. Much later. It isn't that I'm a little lamb who follows him blindly. It's more that I don't get shot at, routinely. Logically, he's the one who knows how to keep us alive.

I stopped at the door to my room. "Jack." Sprayed across the wall, between my room and the hall, were bullet holes. A lot of bullet holes. The bed I'd been in less than half an hour ago was peppered with slugs. Feathers from the pillows still floated in the air above the devastation.

"What's wrong?" He glanced around. "Son-of-a-bitch. Get only what you need."

I grabbed my underwear, toothbrush, nightgown and cosmetic bag. I can live without the rest for a while. I shoved it all in my purse.

As I walked past the bed, I began to shake again. There were so many bullet holes in the wall and mattress. It wasn't so much the close call—though that played a part—it was more that Jack and I had changed rooms last night. If we hadn't, he'd be dead right now. I dropped my purse, and everything fell out. The room he'd slept in had a direct view of the entry. It provided him a clear shot at the door.

"Doc, come on."

I shook it off, crammed everything back in my bag and whispered, "Later." I'm good in desperate situations. I'm not sure what's past desperate, but I was standing in the middle of it. They'd either been after Jack, or they knew he wasn't in that room. Both options sent my adrenalin levels skyward. This wasn't what Stanton had in mind when he told me to take it easy.

We hurried through the hall. People had come out of their rooms to see what had happened. "They really needed to be more paranoid," I said as I glanced back at the crowd looking at the bullet holes in the wall.

"Self-preservation won't occur to them until the police arrive." Jack opened the door to the stairway.

He called the police, as we rushed down the stairs, and out the service entrance. He explained what had happened and told them he'd be in touch when we were safe. In the garage, he opened the back door to his truck and moved his aid bag to the seat. "I want you on the floor. Stay down, no matter what." He handed me the gun he kept strapped to his ankle. "It's going to be okay."

One of Lois's toys squeaked as I settled on the floor. I dragged the stuffed bear out from under me and held onto it. Gun in one hand, toy cradled in the other.

He pulled the truck out of the parking garage, not at the breakneck speed I'd half expected, but as if he were going to work. No sign of urgency. Nothing more than the typical early morning commute.

The sky began to glow with the day's first light.

"You okay back there, Doc?" Jack asked as we left the smooth asphalt for a gravel road.

I could see the roofs of houses and leafless tree branches as rocks crunched beneath the tires. We had to be in an ally. We slowed and pulled into a garage. Jack shut off the engine as the door closed behind us.

The only window in the area was covered with yellowed plastic blinds. Inside, the place could have been a 1950's movie set. You know, the house that's staged, so the scientists know how things are affected when *the bomb* explodes. This could have been that test house. The only thing missing was the test dummy family. "Where are we?"

"A safe house," Andy said as he came down the hall into the living room.

In the living room, a small picture window looked out on a barren yard. No trees or bushes to block the view. "Doc, stay away from the windows," Jack said. To Andy, "Either they knew we'd changed rooms, or they were after me. Had to be me."

"Or the shooter didn't care which of you, he hit," Andy said.

"Only the three of us knew we switched rooms," Jack said.

"That's not exactly right," I chimed in. "The maid knew. I was putting my things in the closet when she came in to turn down the beds. She may not have known we switched rooms, but she knew who was sleeping in which one."

"More likely, they thought you were both in the same room," Andy said as he turned away.

Jack took out his phone. "Casey, I want you and Tony to question the night clerk and the maid from last night." He hung up.

"You didn't tell them what to ask," I said.

"They know," he said as he pulled Andy to one side. "If they get me, you know what to do."

"Jack. No." They weren't talking about him being hurt again. This was in the event of his death.

"Doc, it has to be planned for." I knew he was right. I wrapped my arms around my chest. If they got Jack, there'd be no hope for me on two fronts.

I walked up to Andy as my temper monster stormed out from behind her big red door in my head. "If we hadn't changed rooms I couldn't have saved Jack. If I hadn't gotten up so early, I'd be dead. Now." I straightened. "I want these people shot. Every damn one of them dead in the street. Do I make myself clear?" Andy's eyes were wide. "Good. I did not pull him out of that basement so some idiot can shoot him in bed. I've—I'm—Shit." I whipped around to face a surprised Jack. "And you play hell with my Hippocratic Oath." I'd done it, let my crazy loose before I thought. "I'm not supposed to want people dead." I walked away before I said anything more. Mentally I pushed the red door closed on my temper.

"She gets testy, sometimes," I heard the smile in Jack's voice.

"Yeah, I think I'm more afraid of her than I am of you."

"Wait until you see her mad."

"You two know I can hear you." I went into the back bedroom to try to stuff my stress into tight compartment in my brain.

I left the door open as I walked into the small room. "Someone's been shopping at the Salvation Army." A bare mattress and box springs sat on a scratched brass bed. They'd crammed a faded chair into the corner next to a table that doubled as a nightstand. The only decorations were a wood and brass lamp and a worn blue rug.

Fortunately, this place didn't smell like the last crummy house Jack and I had been in. That one had smelled of rot and blood. At least, this one had furniture to sit on instead of a filthy floor. A shudder escaped me at the memory of the nightmare I'd awaken from an hour ago as it replayed in my head. They'd killed Jack again. I had an uncontrollable urge to be sure he was safe.

I found him and Andy in the kitchen. Silently, I went to Jack and put my arms around him.

"Talk to me, what's wrong?" He held me tight.

I shook my head. I wasn't going to say anything in front of Andy. He left us.

"Tell me what's wrong," Jack said.

"I had another nightmare. That's what woke me up so early." Carefully, I laid my head on his chest. "I needed to know you were safe."

"Ens," he whispered as he held me. "I'd give anything for you not to have gone through that."

"It wasn't your fault." The memory of how close we'd both been to death in the library at his house on Christmas Eve still haunted me. "If only one thing had changed neither of us would be here holding the other. It's that basement."

"When we get through this, things will be normal." His voice held an *I hope* quality.

Our normal wasn't exactly... ordinary. "When we get home, you owe me a dance."

"Jack," Andy called. "The FBI is under the big evergreen on the corner." He pointed out the window.

"Is Brad with them?" I asked as I watched the van.

"He's on his way. He'll be here by noon," Andy said.

"I haven't made a great impression on him. First I steal his truck in October then I kept him up all night Christmas Eve with my phone calls."

"He understood. You know he was trying everything to get to you," Jack said.

Andy laughed. "I heard about the truck. I would have loved to see the expression on his face when you delivered two would-be killers to him." His manner sobered. "On Christmas Eve, we were trying from the Boise side too. We passed you on our way to Spirit Springs. You were right behind the snow plow."

These guys knew everything about everything. I'd have to get used to it. I'm not accustomed to a world where people have the ability to know what goes on everywhere all the time. My dad had been part of that world. His bag was always packed just at the right moment. For the first time, I wondered if I'd known the real man or the dad he wanted me to.

"Did you get the phone checked for me?" Jack asked.

"Yeah. There's no breach. I thought that was straightened out. What happened?"

"March."

"Why is that POS still making your life miserable?" Andy looked at me. "Oh, right."

I changed my mind. I wasn't going to get used to *it*. "You know, I don't like the fact that everyone knows all about me and us. I want some things to be private."

"Does she know who her father was?"

Jack shook his head. "Not a clue."

"What?" I looked from one man to the other. They weren't going to tell me. That wouldn't stop me from asking. "Exactly who was he?" I faced them, hands on my hips, determination at the forefront.

"Classified," was all Andy said.

I bit my bottom lip. This door had been slammed on me more

times than I cared to think about. So, I found a semi-comfortable chair. I'd downloaded a medical journal on trauma. I figured with Jack penchant for injuries, it would come in handy. I spent the next few hours reading. Finally, I snapped the cover to my Kindle shut, settled back in the uncomfortable chair, and closed my eyes.

Things from Saturday night were still disjointed. "Does she know?" What didn't I know? Apparently a lot, with Jack, Don, and now my dad. Who were these men Jack called? How were they connected? I recognized Andy and the US Marshal from the other night. They were in the picture in Jack's office. Now, it seemed they were all out of the Army but still connected.

Then there was Don. He'd told me he'd saved Jack's life. Why would you save someone, then make their life miserable? I laid my Kindle beside me, and it slipped to the floor.

Floor. "Jack," his name had come out too loud.

"What?" He looked over at me.

"I know when Don switched phones."

Jack glanced over at Andy.

"Don did have your phone out of my sight. It was when we were at your house. We were looking for it, hoping you still had it so we could locate you. He found it under your bed."

Andy left the window.

"How long did he have it?" Jack joined Andy.

"It wasn't more than a couple of seconds. The time between rings." I got up and joined them.

"Doc, I'm impressed you remembered at all after that night."

"Let's see." Andy took out his cell. Seconds later, Jack's phone rang. Then it rang again. "Three or four seconds."

"With the security on it," Jack's words became measured. "There was nothing he could do to it."

"Even if he had a lot of time he couldn't disable your ah, entry method," Andy pointed out.

"If he couldn't get into it, what was the point?" This didn't make sense.

"He wanted you to find me." Jack's eyebrows knit together. "But not too fast."

I took Jack's phone from him. I turned it over in my hand. "This isn't the phone I had that night. This one is different. Heavier, thicker."

"He switched phones," Andy said. "Why return it before he hacked into it?"

"The phone he gave me had your contacts on it. At least, they were all in code." This wasn't working out in my head. "He did everything he could to keep me from finding you. He," I shifted to face Jack directly. "If he'd listened to me, we would have found you that morning. That shit-headed jerk—" I took a cleansing breath.

"It's okay."

"Oh, really? It's okay? I don't think so. He had to know. How could he let—?"

"He wanted something that had nothing to do with my phone." He drew out his last few words. He glanced at Andy and nodded.

"Open your phone, please." I wanted to see the contacts.

He opened it and handed it to me. I pushed the recent calls. I found Brad's number. I turned it and showed it to them. "This isn't the same code for Brad."

Jack looked at me for a long minute. "You remember that?"

I nodded.

"Do you remember any of the other numbers?"

"No. Brad's was the only one I cared about that night."

"Do you have an eidetic memory?" Jack smiled.

"I wish. No, I just remember things. Usually patterns."

"What was the name of the officer who was in the emergency room after you were shot?"

I figured this was a test. I closed my eyes. "I couldn't see his name tag. He faced the door the whole time."

The two men looked at each other.

"I do not have an eidetic memory, just good recall."

Jack accepted my explanation this time. I handed his phone back to him.

"He couldn't breach the programming." Jack fell silent.

"You know as well as I do." Andy motioned to me. "To be safe, who have you called since?"

"You, Brad, Stan, Casey. None of the," He paused. "Others."

I didn't know who these others were, and I knew they wouldn't tell me if I asked. So, I didn't waste our time.

Andy nodded and looked at his watch. "Brad will be here in half an hour. Until then we all take the batteries out of our phones."

I popped my phone out of the case and removed the battery.

"Your Kindle, too," Andy said.

I retrieved it from beside the chair.

Jack popped out the battery.

Andy walked to the back door. "I'm going to go have a talk with the guys outside."

"Why doesn't he go out the front door?"

"You never let the enemy know where you are. Someone forgetting that has killed more than one good man."

Twenty minutes later, Andy returned. "We're silent." He tossed Jack his phone. "Except you."

"What did our friends have to say?" Jack motioned outside.

"The only electronics they'd picked up were our phones and Ensley's Kindle."

"The tech said they're clean. Here's your Kindle." He gave me the device and the battery.

"Don't we have something more immediate to worry about?" I wanted them to focus on who had shot up our hotel room.

"I'm afraid we've got another problem, and they're related," Andy said.

"That makes sense," Jack agreed.

I wanted to punch them both.

Chapter Nine

"Oh, for God's sake." Maybe it made sense to everyone else in the room, but not to me. "Stop talking like you can read each other's thoughts."

"Sorry," Andy said. "Old habit."

"Doc, let me see your Kindle."

I handed it to him and asked, "Who else could be after us?"

"If March—"

"Why won't he leave us alone?"

"You're underestimating how he feels," Jack said. "He came out here at Christmas to get you to go back and marry him."

How did Jack know he'd asked me to marry him, again? Had I told Jane before I left Christmas Day? Probably, I'd told her everything else. "If he loved me he would never have cheated on me with my supervisor. I was the one he'd take to parties. The one who could carry on an intelligent conversation. Someone who dressed up decently and didn't make a fool of herself. It wasn't love."

"From what I've seen, you clean up a hell of a lot better than decent." Andy put his hands up in don't-shoot-me-style. "Hey, just stating a fact."

"Thanks." That was sweet. "Jack—?"

"You're beautiful."

I smiled at him. "Thanks. But I want you to tell me why Don hates you so much. It can't be me."

"She doesn't know, does she?" Andy asked Jack.

He shook his head. "Amazing, right?"

"Will you two stop it?"

"I keep telling her," Jack teased.

I wasn't going to let this go. If there was any chance, Don March was coming back.

Jack's demeanor shifted as he put his hand in the middle of my back. "We'll be down the hall." He led me into the back bedroom and shut us in. He stared down at the floor as he leaned against the door.

When he finally glanced up, he said, "I was on a team right after I joined Delta Force. I was twenty-two. That doesn't excuse anything. It was a lifetime ago. We were under CIA orders. Don was an operative back then."

"I know Delta Force is tangled up with the CIA. I wasn't stupid when I went to those parties. I listened."

He looked up sharply. "Please, tell me you didn't hear something you shouldn't have."

I shrugged. "Probably. Like I said, I might as well have been one of the studs on Don's shirt. I didn't realize it because I didn't want to. He was always talking about operations going on here or there. He took me to a party he said was key to furthering his career." I shrugged. "I don't know why. The whole situation was wrong. It wasn't a party like the ones we usually went to."

"When was this odd party?" Jack's gaze was intent on me.

"Around the first of October."

He straightened. "That lousy son-of-a-bitch." All emotion drained from his face as he grabbed open the door. "Andy."

Instantly, Andy was there.

Jack's voice took on an urgent quality, "Tell me everything you remember about that night."

I started from the beginning. "It was on Saturday, October third."

The two men looked at each other then back to me.

"It was small, maybe fifty people, not the usual two hundred plus.

Don said it was to rid the world of a ghost. I remember thinking it was early for a Halloween party. If it was a Halloween party how could it be so important to his career?"

Again with the looks between them.

"Could he have said a phantom?" Andy asked.

I snapped my fingers. "Yes, he did say phantom. Tell me what's going on."

"Think back." I knew that tone. Jack had used it on Jane when he was trying to get her to remember something about a break-in at the B&B. It had a calm, hypnotic quality to it. "Did anyone talk about this phantom?"

"I don't believe in ghosts." We'd been through the whole other-worldly thing in October when I first move to Spirit Springs. The spirits all turned out to be human intruders or headlights through the trees.

"You better believe in this one, he's lethal." Andy pulled out his phone and left.

"You need to know the whole story." Jack shut the door again and leaned against it for a long time. He took off his Kevlar vest. As he leaned over and set it on the chair, I blinked. For an instant, he looked exactly like Don when he'd been in Jack's office. The physical resemblance was uncanny.

"It was when we were on a mission in Africa." Jack's face grew dark with the memory still haunting him. This story wouldn't have a happy ending. "Things had gone sideways. We were trying to get those girls out. With the drug dealer's guerrillas closing in on us, I made a hard decision. A life-changing one." He was silent as he looked past me. "My order took my best friend's life. I might as well have pulled the trigger."

The profound pain in his eyes made him look ten years older. Tears gathered in my throat.

"I'd have gone in his place—it was my unit—I should have. But I was responsible for all those people's lives, and I had a bullet in my chest." He went silent; his inner struggle played out on his face. "I lost five good men. The best. Dave Sullivan and I went through basic together. I was best man at his wedding. Godfather to his daughter and I killed him."

His words made my heart hurt. Tears blurred my vision and streamed down my face leaving behind cold, wet acid trails of agony. I kept silent, knowing there was more.

"His younger brother Jerry joined the Army a couple of years before Africa. Jerry blamed me for everything. I understood then, and I understand now why he'd want me dead." He gently took my hand. "Christmas Eve changed everything. The other man, the one we didn't catch, was Jerry Sullivan. He came to Spirit Springs to torture me to death. When he saw you trying to find me, he changed his plan. He wants me to hurt the way he has. That's why he's after you."

I reached up and touched his face. "I didn't know Dave, but if he was your best friend, I know what kind of man he must have been. He would have done the same thing you did to save those girls."

"You've got to understand how dangerous Jerry is. I can't let him get to you." He looked at me as if he were memorizing my face.

I closed my eyes. "We'll get through this as long as we're together."

Jack brushed the tears from my cheek then pulled me into his arms. "What did I do to deserve you?"

"I think it's the other way around. How was I lucky enough to find you?"

He kissed me. "You've been through too much."

I gazed up at him. "How do we resolve this?"

"I've never known anyone like you." He opened the door, and we went back into the living room.

I stopped him in the hall. "So much has happened since that party. I barely remember the drive out here. About the only thing I recall is the voice of the sheriff who called me every day." I smiled up at him. "He had a sexy voice," I whispered. "I figured he was about sixty with a potbelly. Imagine my surprise when *you* pulled a gun on me."

"I didn't recognize you."

"Why would you recognize me?" I watched him.

His hesitation lasted only a microsecond, but it was there. "From the picture, your dad had on his desk," he said.

"I'll let him know," Andy said as we walked into the living room. He stopped, his eyes on Jack.

Jack shook his head. "Now about this party. What did they talk about?"

"Like I said, so much has happened," I thought back. "Wait, one man laughed and said something about there wouldn't be any beaches in Maui soon. I figured he was drunk."

"Are you sure about Maui?" Jack asked.

"Yeah, they were all laughing. Drunk people end up doing stupid things. I tried to leave, but Don held on to me. There was no way to get away without making a scene."

"Any of them see you?" Andy asked.

"They all had to, I was the only woman in the room."

"Why wait this long?" Andy's brows furrowed.

"March." Jack stopped. "Think back, anything else you can remember?"

"Nothing I heard made much sense."

"Oh, it did to someone." Andy moved to where we stood. "If you can remember some of the things that were said, maybe we can piece the rest together."

"I'll try. It'll help if I can start at the beginning," I said.

"Start wherever you like and take all the time you need." Jack led me to the couch.

"The place we went wasn't the usual hotel or banquet room. It was in the country, like a country club. There weren't many people there and I was the only woman. I wondered at the time why Don brought me." I thought back to the chilly night. "Don didn't introduce me to anyone. That alone was odd. He was always taking me up to people and introducing me as *Doctor Ensley Markus*. I thought about asking him if he wanted me to wear my name tag from work so they could tell I was an MD." I didn't hold back my aggravation. "One man stayed in the background, always in the shadows. It was odd, every time I glanced around he was there. Watching me." The memory sent a chill up my spine.

"Describe him as best you can," Andy said.

"Tall, muscular, no distinguishing features. Regular to the point that he faded into the crowd." Both men were quiet. "He always remained in the background, and didn't mingle with the others in the room."

"If I asked you to leave and forget Spirit Springs and me would you?" Jack indicated the tacky room in the tacky house. "Or do you want to spend your life going from one shoddy house to the next?"

I faced him. "Okay, I can see this needs to be said. Again."

"I'll be in the other room." Andy passed me.

I grabbed his shirtsleeve to stop him. "You're staying. Jack doesn't seem to be able to understand this. Maybe you can explain it to him." I shifted my attention to Jack as I held fast to Andy. "I don't do things I don't want to do." I paused. Maybe this would help. "I wouldn't be here if this wasn't the only place on earth I wanted to be. With you." I glanced at Andy. "Is that clear?" I looked from one man to the other. "Good. Next time he says something truly dumb like that, I'm counting on you to remind him of this conversation."

In the kitchen, I grabbed my purse and sat back down in the uncomfortable chair. I rummaged past my underwear and nightgown until I found my notebook. I needed to gather my thoughts. The only way to do that was to make a list. I began writing. This was going to be a long one.

A knock on the garage door startled me.

"Doc, in the hall." Jack motioned toward the back of the house as he took a position at the end of the hall.

Andy went to the door.

I heard him swear. "We've been compromised. Again."

"Damnit." Jack took me by the hand. I grabbed my bag on the way out the garage door. "How?"

"We don't know. Alpha picked it up," said the black man dressed in jeans and a blue work shirt with a plumber's logo on it and Carl embroidered above the pocket. He was the maintenance man slash US Marshal from the other night.

We went out the back door, through the garage and into the plumber's van parked in the alley.

"Where to?" Jack asked.

"*Our* safe house," Carl said. He watched me. A white scar above his left cheek bone marred his handsome black face. "May I have your Kindle?"

"You're taking my Kindle? Why? You took the battery out."

"To be safe."

"Am I going to get it back?" I figured it was worth asking.

"No." He put it in a plastic bag that looked very much like an evidence bag.

"Listen, Carl, I have a lot of articles on it that can't be replaced easily."

"I'm sorry." He dropped my Kindle in a black satchel. He looked from me to Jack. "We have an update. They're after both of you."

"Fill me in, Casey."

"The intel came through a few minutes ago. The girl isn't the only target."

The girl? I was relegated to the status of *the girl*. The one in old movies who is completely useless and spends the whole film following the hero around, eyes wide with fear, ready to scream at the slightest noise. "Really, the girl?"

Jack was smiling. "She's a doctor."

Carl slash Casey looked surprised for a second. "Oh, right. Sorry."

"Would you like to see my diploma?"

"No, ma'am. I'm–"

"I apologize. It's been a rough couple of weeks." Make that months.

"Andy said you used to be with March," Casey said.

"Yes." I tried to calm my temper. I needed to change the subject. "Where are we going?"

"Need to know," Casey said.

"I figure since I'm going, I need to know." Behind me, I heard Andy snicker. He was next on my list. I took a calming breath. Mentally I held the red door to my temper monster closed. She'd had enough of a workout today.

Casey looked at Jack. "Sarge?"

"It's okay."

"We're going to *our* safe house."

"Fine." I decided if I asked where it was, I'd get another non-answer. If Jack was okay with it so was I.

I leaned against the van's side panel. The windowless vehicle had no seats in the back. Through the tinted windshield, I could see the sunny afternoon. I caught glimpses of massive trees lining the street. Boise's older areas are fascinating places. On the same block, there will be a huge old two-story home out of the early 1900's. Next door will be an eight-hundred square foot house set at the back of the lot. Then, a modern townhouse. Every street had its own collection of new and old dwellings.

We turned off the pavement onto a rough road. Probably another alley. We stopped behind a house with a second story. The brown siding and white scalloped trim around the windows gave it a gingerbread house appearance. "It's cute."

"It's reinforced," Andy said.

The garage door slid closed as Casey opened the back of the van. We stepped out into a clean garage. Clean as in nothing but our van parked on a dirt floor.

"This way," Casey said.

Inside, the house looked like someone's grandmother, no, great-grandmother, lived here. Right down to the knickknacks in the kitchen window. The laptop on the counter looked out of place. On the screen I saw a man, sitting at a desk, reading a report.

Chapter Ten

"Uncle Stan."

"Pumpkin, I'm sorry you're going through this on the heels of Christmas Eve. Kid." He glanced in Jack's direction. "Are you taking care of our girl?"

"Yes, sir." He put his arm around my shoulder.

Andy, Casey, and the driver stood behind us.

"Uncle Stan, what's going on?" I asked.

"Why did you go back to D.C.?" Uncle Stan had been in Spirit Springs while I'd been back east.

"I went to be with Sophie and her family." But he knew that. I'd told him when we talked.

"It had nothing do with Don March?" He watched me.

How could he think that? He knew I'd given Don back his ring. I reached up and laced my fingers through Jack's. "No."

"I wish you hadn't come back here."

"She had no way of knowing," Jack said.

"I've been checking into your kidnapping, Jack. I don't like the fact that Sullivan was there. I haven't been able to trace him. Alice Shaw's lawyer won't let her talk. March has been quiet since he returned to

D.C. So why the elaborate hoax? He had to know we'd figure it out." Uncle Stan shook his head. "It's not like him. All that trouble and—"

"What difference does it make where I went?" I hadn't taken my eyes off the screen. "And what does Alice Shaw have to do with what's happening now?" She was the woman who'd helped kidnap Jack.

"D.C. is where March's contact was coming from?"

Wait. What? "No, Don said his contact was coming from Mexico. It wouldn't make sense for them to come out here if they were both in Washington."

"It wouldn't if it was a legitimate contact. When you came back here, let's just say I've been dealing with some upset people who are putting pressure on some influential individuals and March is right in the middle of it." He shrugged. "S.O.P." He was supposed to be retired. Jetting around, playing golf, visiting old friends and being carefree Uncle Stan. The man on the screen was not carefree or retired. "It's going to take a while to sort this out." He frowned. "There's a hum of duplicity here. I don't like where it's leading. All of you be very careful."

I wanted to touch the screen. "Uncle Stan." My heart seized. "I can't be the reason anyone gets hurt." I held tight to Jack's hand.

"Before Alice Shaw quit talking, I found out Sullivan hired them. He scared her more than the thought of spending the rest of her life in jail."

"At least March kept the Doc safe." Jack pulled me closer.

"Stan," Andy said. "We're betting he's the hit man Lacey Harris hired."

"He may not be the only one out there. I've heard some puzzling rumors. As soon as I can nail down some facts, I'll let you know. Back to the party, tell me about the man who was talking about one of the operatives."

"He was short with brown hair, glasses, and an ugly mustache," I said.

"What else do you remember?" Uncle Stan asked.

"I asked Don about the man who kept watching me. He told me not to pay any attention to him. He was an eidolon. I remember having to look up the word. It's a phantom or a deception." I shivered. "It was Sullivan wasn't it?"

"Yes, you were at Sullivan's send-off," Uncle Stan confirmed. "Tell me about him, Pumpkin."

"Every time I looked up I saw him. He gave me the creeps." I paused. There was one more thing. "I saw him after the party a couple of times."

"What?" Uncle Stan and Jack said at the same time.

I felt Jack's hand tighten on my arm. "Where did you see him?"

"The next day, Sophie and I went to Sunday brunch. When we left the restaurant, I saw him across the street. I pointed him out to Sophie. Then, I saw him again the day they pulled my research."

The faces around me were a mixture of anger and concern.

"Kid." Uncle Stan's face turned grim. "It's time."

I think my heart actually stopped. Was I the one putting everyone's lives in danger? Could I stop all this by going back to Don? I squeezed my eyes shut. I couldn't. I wouldn't live my life with Don. "No," the word slipped out in a breathy whisper.

"Doc, what's wrong?"

"Is it me?" The emotions from Christmas Eve flooded back with such force I staggered.

Uncle Stan leaned forward in his chair. "What's going on? Pumpkin, are you all right?"

I shook my head.

Jack pulled his phone from his pocket as he hit a key on the computer. The sound went off as he walked into the living room. Uncle Stan had picked up the phone on his end. I was unable to take my eyes off them as they talked.

Jack looked over at me and nodded. "I'll have Brad get you all the information we have. – You know I will."

Jack returned to me. "Doc, I don't know how to tell you this." He took my shoulders, and I saw the regret in his eyes.

He was scaring me.

"Jerry Sullivan hates March as much as he hates me. That's why he's after you. He saw you with March and now with me. He figures he can make us both pay. You're the catalyst. I don't know what March was thinking taking you to that party. It was reckless and stupid. He *will* pay for it." Jack's words had a lethal finality to them. He let go of me. "I'm going to find out why he took you there."

"Jack," Uncle Stan said.

Jack had already punched a number into his phone. "March. Trace."

I looked up. Everyone's attention was focused on Jack.

"What the hell were you thinking?–You know damn well what I'm talking about. You took Ensley to Sullivan's *retirement party*. Were you trying to get her killed?–I don't care what you thought. He's come close to killing her twice in the past twelve hours. Is that what you're after? You can't have her so—?" Jack straightened. "You know as well as I do what Sullivan is capable of, you've seen the aftermath of his actions—what can you do from back there?—You know that won't work—sorry about the promotion." He had a satisfied smile on his face as he hung up.

"Well?" Uncle Stan asked.

"He thought if Sullivan saw her with him he'd leave her alone. I don't buy it. He had another reason. If I have to go back there and beat it out of him, I will. " Jack shut his eyes for a second. When he opened them, he asked, "Stan, have there been any attempts on your life lately?"

"No."

"Just the same, watch your back, Jerry Sullivan may be headed your way next."

"I don't believe March," Casey said. "Is he that arrogant or that stupid?"

I shivered. It was one thing for Lacey to want me out of the way, but a contract killer? "Is Sullivan that good?" I glanced from Uncle Stan to Jack.

"Yes," Jack said. "He doesn't want me dead. He wants me to suffer the way he has." Jack looked over at Uncle Stan. "It all makes sense, Sullivan wants March to pay too. It was his fault the helicopters didn't get there in time. Why only go after her out here?" His question was more to himself than any of us.

"I don't understand any of this," I said. "Why wait so long? That party was three months ago and Africa was over three years ago."

The tall man who'd been driving the van came back in. "Sarge, I have some information for you." The name on his shirt read Bob.

"I'll be right back." Jack walked over to Bob.

I turned to Uncle Stan. "You've got to tell me what's going on. I feel like the only child at Thanksgiving sitting at the kids' table alone."

"All I can tell you is I'm glad you got away from March. Ensley, you stay with Jack. Do you understand me? He's always been the best we have."

What frightened me most of all was Uncle Stan had called me Ensley. The last time he'd used my name I'd just fed the dog out of my mother's crystal Waterford bowl.

I heard Jack ask, "This a hundred percent?"

"Sarge, I checked it three times." He glanced over at me. "Is she the General's daughter?"

"Yes."

"She's," he turned his head and I didn't hear what I was.

I saw Jack smile.

Uncle Stan said, "I know how hard all the cloak and dagger is. I'm going to see what I can pull up on this end. Someone here knows something." His expression was touched with concern. "Pumpkin, you were with March then." His weak smile had me wondering if that was the real reason. "I've got some phone calls to make and some people to threaten. When I have something concrete I'll let you know. Don't worry about March." Someone handed him a sheet of paper. "Jack."

"Stan, we have a bigger problem. Sullivan was seen in Boise."

"I just got the information too. I'll see what I can find out on this end. Watch your backs."

The screen went dark.

"He was basically a sanctioned serial killer," Andy said. "They kept him on a short leash until he broke loose. That's when they forced him to retire." He took a deep breath then said, "I hate that guy."

"Why throw him a party?" That didn't make sense.

"If it were me, and I was a bucket of puke," Andy continued, "and I was about to be out of a job, I'd let those who were in that world know I was for hire. Why in such a public way? And who would have the juice to put those kinds of people together? I'd like to see the guest list."

Casey stepped forward. "I'd like to know, who'd want it known they were in the market for a hitman?"

»§«

Everyone knew what to do next. Everyone but me, so I opted to read. I found a bunch of old People magazines. Some of them dated back before I was born.

"I've got some supplies. Nothing fancy," Bob, the tall man from the Van, earlier said as he came in the back door with Andy. "Brad wants us to use new phones. Except for Jack. They'll be here in the morning pouch. I'll get them to you as soon as they arrive." He set a couple of grocery bags on the counter and left.

Andy pulled something from one of the bags.

"My Kindle. Thank you."

"We had the internet disabled, so I figured, I'd give it back."

I hugged him. "Thank you. This means a lot." I wasn't going to tell him I'd spent my days in D.C. reading. It had replaced Jack's cell phone as my lifeline. I hated the idea of needing a prop to hold on to sanity. It had worked so far, except for the nightmares.

"Had I known I'd get this response, I'd have gotten it to you earlier."

"Andy, how many kids do you have?" Jack asked as the other two men left.

"Just the two."

I smiled. "I bet they both have beautiful red hair and bright blue eyes."

"Want to see pictures?"

After fifty pictures of the most adorable kids ever, he ran out.

"Is anyone else hungry?" Jack called from the kitchen.

It was past noon and I hadn't had anything to eat. We'd been on the run all morning. We took the food from the bags.

"Bob brought a lot of fruit and veggies," I said as I peeled an orange.

"Bob?" Andy asked.

"That's what was on his shirt, and by the way, plumbers? Really? What is this? The Nixon administration?"

"I had nothing to do with it." Jack smiled.

"It sounds like Uncle Stan's sense of humor." I tossed the orange peel in the trash. "I don't like not having any communication." What if something happens in the middle of the night and we aren't able to call for help.

Jack held up a phone.

"Where'd that come from?" Andy asked.

"I picked Casey's pocket."

"That's going to piss him off," Andy said.

"Always does." Jack handed the device to me. "It's a burner. I don't want you without a phone."

Jack and Andy talked while I wandered around the house. On the windowsill in the kitchen, I picked up a pink glass slipper covered with dust. I brushed the dirt from it. In the toe, something sparkled. I tipped it and a crystal heart the size of a dime fell into my hand. It had a tiny hole in it, one you'd put a fishing line through so you can hang it. I bet at one time it had hung in this window. I held it up and let the sun sparkle through it. "Who used to live here?"

"A woman actually left it to us for a safe house." Andy smiled. "She was a mystery reader. The hall upstairs is lined with paperbacks."

If I asked how she knew to leave it to them, I figured I'd get a vague answer. I didn't ask.

I decided to take a page from Jane's book. I found a rag and started removing the layers of dust. I was having trouble concentrating, my thoughts stumbled around in my head. They fell over each other, only to struggle back up and trip again.

I ran my hand over the smooth wooden handrail to the upstairs as I climbed the steps. Andy was right, bookcases covered the wall breaking only for the doorways. My fingers made a soft thumping sound as I swept them along the spines. At the end of the hall, I entered a small bedroom.

The closet door stood open. I went to shut it and found an old suitcase in the way. Travel stickers from all over the world covered the front and back. I bent down and touched one from Italy. I smiled as Sophie's mother's words came back to me. "Ensley, you listen to Mama, you keep your head when you go back to the Idaho." I picked up the nineteen-forties style case.

My purse was crammed with things I didn't especially want to fall out in front of the guys downstairs. I set the antique suitcase on the bed and popped the latches. Inside the pink satin had elastic pockets around the sides and on the lid. This was perfect. I'd ask if I could use it. I snapped it closed and wondered why they hadn't taken the clothes or personal items from the closet. Guys. They probably wouldn't bother until they needed the space.

I went back down to the living room. "I found this upstairs. Do you mind if I use it?"

Jack looked up from the file he was reading. "You can have anything you like," he said and went back to reading.

I wondered why we were hanging around the little house. What were we waiting for? I'm not good at sitting on the sidelines. I wanted the person who'd shot up our hotel room. Only one way to find out. "Why aren't we out finding Sullivan?"

"He's the best at what he does. We can't go running around without more facts. When my sources have the information, they'll get to us and we'll act."

"I hope it doesn't take too long." Upstairs, I transferred my things to the suitcase. Back in the living room, I picked up the rag and began dusting again. I wiped the grime from a small box with a bouquet of roses inlaid on the lid. Rose. "Jack, does that rose seem too sophisticated for the kind of people Lacey would be involved with."

"Not if it's Sullivan." He laid the file down. "Your doctor friend was supposed to call me when the final lab report came back."

"Stanton should have an answer by now. Would you give him a call?"

"Why not?" Jack pulled out his phone and Stanton's card from his pocket. "Hello, Doctor Hayden, this is Jack Trace. She's fine, thanks." Jack smiled at me. "I'm calling to check on the lab results. I see. No, I don't give out my number. Use the one I gave you earlier." He shook his head as he hung up. "Nothing new."

I thought about that for a minute. "Maybe he's been busy."

"Talk to me, Doc."

I sat down on the couch next to Jack and curled up in the crook of his arm. There are times when I need human contact. Jack's touch is the best. "It isn't like Stanton to let a puzzle go. He almost went into research, too."

"Interesting."

"How are your ribs?"

"I'm fine." He lifted my chin. "I'm worried about you."

"I'll be okay. I'm having trouble concentrating. Stanton said the drugs would take a while to get out of my system. I don't like the feeling."

"You know you don't have to do this on your own. I'm here for you."

"It isn't anything I can't handle." I wasn't going to pull him any farther into my private hell. He had Sullivan to deal with right now. Besides, I'd done the research. It's what I'm best at. I had PTSD. At this minute, that wasn't the problem. "It has to be the aftereffects of the drugs." I hoped. Otherwise, it meant the PTSD was getting worse. I had to get Christmas Eve's nightmare memories into my long-term memory so I could deal with them. With the added grief of my dad's death, I wasn't certain I could do it on my own. It hadn't worked so far.

"What are we doing for dinner?" Andy asked as he walked into the room. "I'm not eating yogurt and fruit for dinner unless I'm forced to."

"We're going to have to tonight," Jack said without looking away from me.

"I have a source," Andy said. "Food delivered discreetly right to our door by a beautiful woman."

"Sarah?" Jack asked.

Andy nodded. "She gives ninja's lessons on stealth," he said to me.

Jack opened his phone and handed it to him.

"What sounds good?" Andy asked.

Jack turned to me. "Do you care?"

I didn't. I was still thinking about Stanton not getting to the lab report.

"Surprise us," Jack said.

"Who's Sarah?" I asked.

"Andy's wife."

"May I talk to her?"

Andy shrugged. "Okay." He waited. "Hi, Sweetie. Want to bring a lonely man and his friends some Chinese? Whatever you like. I will. There's someone here who wants to talk to you. Ensley Markus, Sarah Buckingham." He handed me the phone.

"Hello," I said as I walked away from the men. "I have a big favor to ask you. If you can't do it, I'll understand."

"What do you need?" Her voice was light and pleasing.

"Underwear. I didn't know we were going to be here this long. I can't wash them out, we move too much and hauling wet underwear around brings a whole new set of problems. Besides I have this thing about clean underwear."

"You, too?" She chuckled. "I can still hear my mother."

We laughed. "Must be a standard mother thing."

"Don't I know it? My little guys think it's a form of torture to put on clean clothes of any kind."

I told her what kind and size. "They come in packs of three. If you would bring a couple packages, I'd be forever in your debt."

"It won't be a problem. Anything else?"

Kevlar vest. "Yes. A couple of t-shirts. This vest is uncomfortable."

"I'll bring you what I used to wear."

I blinked. She used to wear a vest? Why? "Andy showed me pictures of your children. They're adorable." I walked back out to the living room as I thanked her and we said goodbye. I handed the phone to Jack.

When Sarah arrived, I was surprised. She was tall and graceful with raven hair and golden eyes. The four of us ate Chinese food from containers and laughed at Andy's stories about the kids.

At ten Sarah said, "I've got to go. Emily, our babysitter, has school tomorrow."

»§«

I slipped into my nightgown and new undies. The bed was soft but comfortable. I pulled the covers up and began tossing and turning. Like so many nights since Christmas, I fell into a fitful sleep. At some point, I fell sound asleep. Sound until the nightmare began.

I stood at the bottom of the stairs in that hideous basement on Christmas Eve. The walls ran black with slime. The smell of blood and rot filled my senses. In the middle of the room a single bulb swung from the ceiling. Underneath it, Jack hung lifeless.

This was a dream.

I had to wake up.

I had to get to Jack.

Blood covered him. Everything was drenched in his blood. It dripped from the handrail on the stairs, ran down the walls, and mixed with the dirt at his feet.

A man called from the shadows, "Not so pretty any more, is he?" It was the horrible man who'd tortured Jack. He bounced a police baton off his hand as he laughed.

I stepped onto the dirt floor.

Instantly, the dirt mixed with blood turned to mud. The mud rose up and grabbed at my legs. I fought against its demonic claws as I struggled to get to Jack.

Suddenly, I stood in front of him. I reached up to check his pulse.

I hadn't made it in time. He was dead. The kidnappers had made good on their promise. They'd cut him into pieces. "No!" The pieces struggled to get back together. To be Jack again.

"Ens, wakeup." A gentle hand brushed my face. "Wakeup. You're safe."

I struggled against the lie. He wasn't here. He was dead. Then, I felt the impossible. A kiss on my forehead. His kiss.

I fought to leave the basement. I was losing. The man who'd been laughing grabbed me. "No. Please."

"Ens, wake up." Strong hands gripped my shoulders.

I struggled back to the real world and opened my eyes. My heart pounded with the memory of him dead. I squeezed my eyes shut. "I'm sorry."

Jack held me. "Don't do this alone." He lifted my chin. "I'm here."

I battled to push aside the image of his lifeless body as I held on to him.

"Talk to me. It helps."

"I can't."

"It isn't a sign of weakness. I've been through it. If you don't let it out, it'll consume you."

"You?" Of course. "Africa." I settled into his embrace. "Lois is your support dog, isn't she?"

"Talk to me."

"I couldn't get to you. The basement floor was dirt. When I stepped down, it turned to mud—dirt mixed with blood. Your blood. The mud turned into claws. I couldn't break free. I was too late. You were dead." I pulled back. "I can't."

"I'm fine. I take a lot of killing."

"She okay?" Andy stood in the door.

"She will be."

"Good night then." Andy turned and left us.

I watched him walk away as a blast of images and snatches of conversation flooded back to me. "Jack."

He pulled on his t-shirt. "Ens, lay down."

I sat up, completely forgetting what I had on. It was more lace than silk. Hey, I like being a girl.

He pulled the blanket around me.

"Who am I?"

He studied my eyes.

"I'm not stoned. Andy leaving reminded me of that night in the hotel with the rose."

He started to protest, but I wasn't going to let it go this time.

"I saw the shocked expression on Andy's face when he walked into the lobby and saw me. I remember what he said when we got on the elevator. He said, 'Isn't that—?' and you said, 'Yeah, not now.'" I looked into Jack's worried face.

"It wasn't—"

"When I was laying on the couch on the verge of passing out he said, 'Why didn't you warn me? It's her. She's real. I nearly shit when I saw her downstairs.' So, who am I?" I waited.

He struggled with what to say as he held on to the blanket around me. He let go and rubbed the back of his neck as he stole a glance at the closed door. "We'll talk about it later. You need some sleep."

"Why won't you tell me?" I knew that tone. It was his you-have-to-wait voice, but not this time. "Tell me. I have a feeling it's important. Does it have to do with everything that's happening?"

"No. I'll tell you, but not tonight. We're exhausted and it's a long story."

"I'm going to hold you to that." I'd have my answer.

He pulled me into his arms and held me until I fell asleep.

A ringing cell phone woke me. I was still in Jack's arms. Which, by the way, is a great place to be.

"Trace. What?" He sat up pulling me with him. "We'll be right there."

Chapter Eleven

"What's wrong?" My mind was still warped in the fog of sleep and his warm embrace.

"Lacey's missing."

"That doesn't make sense," I said as I started to crawl out from under the quilt.

He stopped me as he held the blanket in place. "Get your stuff." He left.

I got dressed and packed my new small suitcase. It was perfect. I wouldn't need a bigger purse now, and I could grab the case in a second.

It didn't take us long to drive to the hospital. The streets of Boise are deserted at three in the morning.

Two police officers stood in the hall outside Lacey's room. Jack and Andy went to talk to them. I had an agenda of my own.

I figured since Stanton had been here last night at this time, he'd probably be here tonight. "Hello," I said to the nurse at the desk. "May I speak to Dr. Hayden?" The florescent lights above cast a sterile glow over the area.

"He left fifteen minutes ago. Right in the middle of his shift."

"Did he say why?"

"Is he your doctor?"

"Yes. He was here when I was brought in last night, and we went to medical school together." I didn't know if the medical school thing would help or not.

"Oh." She pressed her lips together. "All he said was to get someone in here to cover the rest of his shift. He left me short an ER doctor and this lab report."

"Is it for Ensley Markus?"

"Yes. She's in ICU." She checked her computer screen. "He's listed as the attending. That's not right." She refreshed the screen.

"I'm Ensley Markus, may I see it?"

She took off her glasses and looked at me through the tops of her eyes. "Like I said, she's in ICU."

"You can show it to me." Jack flipped open a wallet. It wasn't his sheriff's badge, That was clipped to his belt. He closed the wallet and put it away before I got a look at the contents.

"You need a warrant, sir." She pulled a folder from the desk below the counter. "I can't let you see it."

"Doc, your ID."

I pulled out my wallet and opened to my new Idaho Driver's License.

She handed the file to me. I opened it.

"Thank you. We'll give it back." He frowned as he looked over my shoulder. "I know what all these are." He ran his finger down the list. "The rest of these are above my pay grade."

"That compound." I pointed to one of the lines. "Was definitely not off any street. You can get the DMSO on Amazon. The rest of the drugs were laboratory grade."

"Is it a new designer drug?"

"Only if you want to kill your customers. Jack, you saved my life. If you hadn't gotten me here as fast as you did," I stopped and read the report again. "The narcotics were strong. But it's this drug," I pointed to the list, "That would kill the patient. A kind of failsafe." I leaned against the divider between the nurse's station and the hall. "You'd have to know exactly what to treat for or..." I laid the folder on the counter. "You'd better give that to the police," I told the nurse.

"If it's that complicated," Jack took the file and glanced at the report again.

I nodded. "Stanton had to be the one who put it together. The mixture had too many fail-safes for anyone to guess what to treat for. If you used the standard drug to treat some of the symptoms you'd start to cascade affect that would end up killing the patient. He had to know exactly what to treat for and what drugs to use, otherwise, I wouldn't be here."

The muscles in Jack's jaw clenched. He pulled out his phone, took a picture of the lab report. "I want Alpha to see this." He sent the picture to this mysterious Alpha whom I was pretty sure was Uncle Stan. "How well did you say you knew this guy?" Jack asked as he slipped his phone into his pocket and handed the file over to the nurse.

"Not as well as I thought. The Stanton I knew would never do this."

"I want to know why," Jack said as Andy came over to us.

"How is he," I asked.

"The cop will be sporting about ten stitches and a bad headache for a while."

I looked into the room where we'd talked to Lacey yesterday. The officers stood in the door blocking most of my view. They'd decided to keep her in the emergency area. It was the last place anyone would look for her. At least, that was the concept.

"What did you find out?" Jack asked.

"Only that someone got all the staff in the ward to the other end of the hall with a bogus call. When they returned, our boy in blue was on the ground, and Lacey was gone."

"We've got another problem," Jack said. "That rose was lethal."

Andy looked at me. "You were pretty stoned."

Jack had me explain what I'd learned from the report. "There's not going to be an easy way to protect against it. By the time they figure out it's more than a drug overdose, the patient will be in cardiac arrest."

"Alpha has the lab results," Jack said.

"How're we going to find Lacey?" That seemed important right now. "If they use that mixture on her, we can't get to her fast enough. It may already be too late."

"We've got to unravel the why, before we can answer the who part of the equation," Jack said.

I knew where I wanted to go first. "We need to start with Stanton. I have some questions for him. He could have easily let me die, and no one would have been the wiser." Why hadn't he? Was it because it was someone he knew? "It would have looked like a heart attack brought on by the drugs." Had Jack scared him that much? I explained that Stanton had left in the middle of his shift. "I can't believe this. I was at his wedding."

"Let's go," Jack said. "You have your vest on, don't you."

"Hey." I pulled him to a stop. "I want you in one, too."

"I'll call Casey."

"Kids, we need to get started," Andy motioned down the hall. "Does anyone know where this Stanton guy lives?"

»§«

Stanton's neighborhood set high above the valley in the Boise foothills. The houses were large and new. I wondered why anyone would live on a hillside overlooking the west end of the valley. It had to be sweltering in the summer. The homes along the steep, curved street were dark. All except Stanton's.

Andy rang the doorbell.

I held my breath. I didn't know what to expect. I couldn't decide if I was mad or hurt. We'd been friends. Classmates. I was struggling to keep my temper under control. Mad it was.

Bev answered the door. "Ensley." She looked at the two men with me as she pulled her robe tight around her.

"Bev, may we come in?" I didn't wait for her invitation.

The living room was a design project in progress. A tag hung from the back of an exquisite leather chair. "Where's Stanton?"

"I'm right here." Stanton entered, still in his scrubs. "I know why you're here. You have to believe me, I didn't know who they were going to use it on."

90

Jack clenched his fists. "That's not a great defense against a charge of attempted murder," his voice was skillfully controlled. When he gets this way, it's time to find the exits.

"You don't understand. I'm drowning in student loans, house payments, car payments, credit cards, and the kids' schools."

"So, you were going to murder someone?" Jack took a step toward him. "That was your answer?"

"Stanton," Bev gasped.

"Who did you sell it to?" This time it was Andy.

I moved back and let the pros take over. Besides, I was getting madder and that never ended well.

"Who are you?" Stanton managed to sound indignant.

That wasn't going to fly.

"I'm the guy who's going to kick your sorry ass if you don't give me the information I want," Andy said.

"I—" Stanton looked terrified. Good, he'd finally grasped the situation. "You can't threaten me."

"I can." Jack's voice had a menacing quality to it. "How would you feel if the woman—if your wife, was murdered because some piece of crap couldn't pay his student loans?"

"Any part of that make sense to you, high-speed?" Andy asked.

"I didn't know it was going to be Ensley."

I stepped into the mix. "And that matters, how?" This weasel wasn't the man I remembered. "If it wasn't me, it would have been someone else. Another human. Someone would be crying right now so you can have a new leather chair." I brought my fist down on the back of the chair.

"I didn't have a choice. I have bills to pay. I was going to lose the house. I had to do something."

"So your solution was to kill someone? Me. In what world is that even an option?" In the silence that followed, we could hear Bev crying.

"Who paid you?" Jack's composure has a way of making the air around him crackle.

I stepped back.

Stanton read the situation for what it was. Dangerous. "I treated a guy in the ER for a cut on his hand. He knew all about my situation. He offered me an insane amount of money to make a substance that was foolproof. Something that no matter what they tried, they wouldn't be able to figure it out in time." He glanced at me. "I'm sorry. I had no idea."

"And again, that's supposed to make me feel better?" My voice wasn't as controlled as Jack's and Andy's.

"How does an emergency room doctor have the expertise to put together a foolproof compound?" Jack asked.

Now that I thought about it, it made perfect sense. "Oh, he has all the skills he'd needs. He was first in our class in the lab, he was always trying new compounds."

Jack moved closer to Stanton. "You're going to do exactly what you're told." Jack motioned to Andy.

"They're on the way."

I hadn't noticed Andy making a call. Anger narrows my focus.

Jack didn't take his eyes off Stanton. "Here's how it's going to go, you *will* pick out this particular piece of garbage from the mugshots. You *will* tell the FBI agents all about the transaction. Finally, you *will* let them decide where to have your trial in State or Federal court. Is there any part of that you don't understand?"

Stanton's face had gone ashen.

Bev was sobbing uncontrollably now. A boy about six wandered down the hall rubbing his eyes. "Daddy, what's going on?"

Jack walked up to Stanton and said something meant only for him.

Stanton glanced at his son. Then squeezed his eyes shut.

"They're here, Sarge," Andy said.

I wanted to tell Bev everything would be all right. I knew it wouldn't. One desperately stupid decision and this family was ripped apart. Stanton's children would grow up without their father. Bev would be without her husband. Everything in his life destroyed and for what? I looked around the room. All for the pretense of affluence.

I knew nothing I could say would ease the shock and agony I saw in Bev's tear-filled eyes. If I said anything to her, it would only make things worse.

The boy ran to his mother.

Nothing ever touches one person. Events cascade through relationships leaving behind unintended consequences, altered lives, and broken hearts.

Out in the car, I slumped against the back seat. "Why do people make such bad decisions? They are, were, good people."

"Because honor and integrity aren't easy."

"You're a very wise man, Andy."

"Not me. Your dad."

Jack once said he knew, more than most, about my dad's honor. There was a strong bond between these men. Soldiers. A lifelong connection. It came from fighting and surviving together; burying their comrades; the terror of battle; of watching each other suffer; and with the good times, they shared.

Two FBI agents walked up to Stanton's house.

Andy pulled away from the curb, leaving behind the turmoil that would consume Stanton's family from now on.

All I could think about was Stanton and Bev. "It's all so needless. With a little common sense, they would have been just fine." I gazed out the window at the early morning sky. It was too early for even a hint of the bright day to come. Bright for some. I looked out the back window. We rounded a corner and the lights from Stanton's house disappeared.

"We'll get back to the safe house," Jack said. "You need some sleep."

"And I need to go home," Andy said. Instead of being welcoming, the gingerbread house appeared lonely. One dim light showed through the kitchen window. We circled around and drove down the alley.

Andy pushed the opener and the garage door slid up with slow deliberation. The headlights oozed under the door revealing the dirt floor and a body.

Jack and Andy were out of the car before the door was up all the way. I followed. I needlessly, checked for vital signs. The man propped against the back door was mutilated. All his fingers were broken, what was left of them. His face was battered beyond recognition. His shirt was shredded and blood marred it. His eyes were fixed and dilated.

Casey, the black man from the van, opened the back door. The body fell backward and landed at his feet. "What the hell?" He side-stepped the dead man.

"How long have you been here?" Jack asked.

"Ten minutes. I came in the front door. He had to have been here before I arrived."

Jack swore as he opened the man's wallet. "It's Quinn."

Casey took it. "Damn it." He flipped through it.

Andy pulled out his cell phone. "Brad, we've got a situation." He walked away.

"Who is he?" I asked.

"Quinn Large," Jack said.

That did and didn't answer my question. I figured pointing that out wouldn't help anyone. No, I needed answers too. "Who is Quinn and why is he dead in your garage?"

"He is, or was, the newest member of the team. He's been with us for two years."

"Oh." I decided it was time to step back and let them do their job. I moved toward the truck.

Before I had a chance to get more than a step or two away, Jack stopped me. "Stay close to me."

Andy came back. "This safe house is compromised. Brad wants us all downtown, now."

"Did you get the vests?" Jack asked Casey.

"I did." He went back inside and returned with two vests. Jack slipped his on over his t-shirt.

"Andy." Casey tossed him a vest.

Chapter Twelve

W e got in the car as the garage door slipped down, blocking the grisly scene from the real world.

"Shouldn't we notify the police?" I asked.

"I called my contact. They're on the way," Andy said.

I thought about that for a minute. He hadn't actually said he'd called the police. I decided that one of their agencies would take care of it.

"Do you have any information on Lacey?" Jack asked Casey.

"There's been no ransom demand. No contact of any kind. It doesn't look good. Stupid woman. What did she think would happen, dealing with that kind?"

"She had no idea who he was or what he was capable of." Jack asked, "Is Howard under surveillance?"

"He is."

A sudden chill ran through me. It had me asking, "Is the person who has Lacey the same one who did that to Quinn?"

"Yes." Jack turned the corner. The street curved around and became the central thoroughfare leading from the train depot, across the river, and down to the Capitol Building.

The hard sound of his 'yes' filled me with fear for Lacey. Had she met the same fate Quinn had? "Do you think she's dead, too?"

For a few seconds, I didn't know if he'd heard me. Finally, he said, "I don't think so. The question is why kill Quinn? It doesn't fit. Was he a loose end or in the way? If Sullivan was holding true to his old pattern, Quinn would be alive to take the blame for everything that's happened." He paused. "We've got a bigger problem. Much bigger."

"It's definite then, we have two factions working against each other," Casey said. "One is Sullivan, his pattern is too obvious. The other is going after him and taking out his pawns. I think your friend Stanton was lucky. My guess is he was next on the list to be eliminated."

"You two need to disappear," Andy said. "At least until we get this straightened out.

»§«

Brad had an office in the federal building tucked back behind the Capitol. Unlike the main artery in front, the street behind was narrow and dark.

I sat on the couch in the FBI office, and listened to the sound of men's muffled voices coming from the next room. I thought about Quinn and what he'd gone through. I shivered as Lacey came to mind. Was she suffering at the same hands?

Stanton and his family. Lacey. Their motives were all too common, money and love. So commonplace. Yet, the outcome so unexpected. The man behind it was after Jack and me.

I laid my head on the arm of the vinyl couch and took as deep a breath as my bruised chest, and the vest would allow. I closed my eyes and concentrated on relaxing.

»§«

I woke as the sun warmed my face. Someone had put a blanket over me. Jack. The room around me was silent. I hadn't expected to be alone. On the table next to me I found a note.

. . .

Doc,

We went to check on a few leads. Tony is there. Call if you need me.

Jack.

"Tony?"

"Yes, ma' am."

The tall man who'd been driving the van last night sat at the desk. "You guys are so quiet." His shaved head suited his bold handsome features.

"Habit." He licked his fingers. "I have zeppole."

"Be still my heart. Is it homemade?"

"Is there another kind?"

"Not according to my friend's mother." I missed Sophie and her... my other family. Her Italian mother had made it her mission to fatten Sophie and me up. She kept insisting men liked women with substance. Sophie and I were pretty sure they didn't. So we ate her mother's great food and ran every other day.

"I brought coffee." He pointed to a cup. "Jack said you like it black."

"I do. This is perfect." I sat down at the desk with him.

"These are filled with huckleberries." He pushed the container of round puffs toward me.

We talked about Boise and Idaho and ate dessert for breakfast.

"Sorry, you got shot yesterday."

I tried to move the vest off my injured chest. "It's an experience I'd just a soon not repeat."

"I hear that. Hurts like a son-of-a-gun." He smiled. "So, you're the doctor."

"I was a research physician."

"JPL," He nodded. "I heard."

"How do you guys know all about me? It's unnerving."

"Yeah, I bet. Sorry."

The door opened, and Sarah walked in. "Hey, Tony. Ensley, how are you holding up?" She had a bag in her hand. "You can't go around in a sweater with holes in it. I got you a better shirt for under your vest."

"It isn't very comfortable."

She held up the sack. "This will help." She popped a Zeppole in her mouth. "Mmm. Your mom is the best cook, Tony."

We went into the bathroom across the hall. "This is made to go under your vest." She handed me a t-shirt.

I pulled off the tags as she took out another shirt. "I guessed at the size. I hope it fits."

I slipped out of my sweater and the vest.

"Ouch. They got you pretty good."

"Three slugs right in the middle." I looked down, my chest was dark purple. "If Jack hadn't insisted I wear one of these," I glanced back at her.

She considered me for a long minute. "He's a good man. Don't let him talk you out of caring for him."

"He almost succeeded at Christmas. He broke my heart when he lied to me." Okay, then. This wasn't like me. I'm not *that person*, you know the one you have to wait in line behind because they're telling the grocery checker their life story. I'm the one who doesn't share anything. Now here I was divulging my most private feelings to an almost perfect stranger.

She handed me the t-shirt. "Be patient, he isn't used to having a woman around. Funny too, you'd think a guy who looks like that, would have women all over the place. He never has."

I remembered the night I'd made a drunken pass at him and been turned down flat. "I thought he had someone."

She shook her head. "I asked him once, you get to do that when you're one of the guys, and you're bold enough. He said he was only getting married once and he hadn't found the right woman yet." She watched me.

My plan was the same. I loved Uncle Stan, but I'd been around when he'd gotten a couple of his divorces. I'd seen firsthand the misery he'd gone through. I never wanted to put myself or anyone I'd loved enough to marry through that pain.

"If we can get past Christmas Eve—" I sighed and rested against the sink.

"Don March."

"Does everyone know about him?"

She nodded. "He's a rotten piece of work. Mama always told me to find the good in someone. No one is all bad. Right?" She shook her head. "He's one driven man."

"Sarah." I fastened the vest. "Why do Jack and Don hate each other so much?"

"That's a puzzle. All I know is it started a long time ago, after that mess in Africa it got so much worse. I don't know how much you know. Jack got a couple of commendations out of that mission. A Silver Star and a Purple Heart. Don took the brunt of the blame. It set his career back, and we know that's all important to him. Don was the one who didn't send the helicopters in time. He almost cost me Andy."

"I finally got the real story out of Jack about Africa." I squeezed my eyes shut at the memory. I gripped the edge of the cold porcelain sink. "It was almost too late. I almost didn't come back." I'd poured this much out. "He was coming after me." I swallowed hard. "If I hadn't come back when I did, we would have missed each other."

She smiled. "He would have found you. He's a strong man and a pain in the butt. Right?"

I laughed. Jack was proving to be a handful. "How long have these guys been together?"

"Seems like forever. Jack and Tony go back to the beginning. Andy joined the team ten years ago and Casey about eight."

"I saw Jack and Andy question someone the other night. They're good."

We heard a knock. "Doc, we need to go."

Sarah opened the door to Jack. She whispered something to him as she patted him on the chest. "Bye, Jack," she said louder.

"We found Lacey," he said as he watched Sarah walk away.

"Is she okay?"

He faced me. I knew by his expression she wasn't. "She's in intensive care."

I was processing that information as we walked down the hall.

Jack said, "We need to get you—"

"What? Somewhere safe? No. Last time we were split up it didn't work out well." I wasn't going anywhere. "I've got a vest on. I'm all right."

"We've got to talk to Lacey," he shook his head.

"How is Howard?" In all this, I'd only heard him mentioned once.

"He's okay. We have a man watching him." Jack stopped in the hall. "They sliced Lacey's face. It's slashed to the bone in some places."

"No. Poor Lacey."

"After everything she's done, you feel sorry for her?" Jack tilted his head.

"Yes. I don't know what monsters she's fighting, but she's lost in a frightening world of fantasy relationships and who knows what else."

Without a word he put his arm around me. "Stay close to me," he whispered.

To my surprise, Jack's truck sat outside.

As we got in, I asked, "Did they call in a plastic surgeon?"

"I don't know." He pulled away from the Federal Building.

"This is senseless. What did they think mutilating her would accomplish?"

"That's what we're going to find out," he said. A few minutes later we pulled into the hospital parking lot.

"Has anyone talked to her?" I asked as the doors to the ICU opened.

"A couple of detectives." Jack said. "She won't talk to anyone."

"I don't think it's a good idea if we're in there. Is Andy here?"

"I am." He joined us.

"Is she talking?" Jack asked.

"She wants to see Ensley."

"What?" That can't be right. "She hates me."

Andy shrugged. "Every time anyone tries to talk to her, she looks away and says she'll only speak to you."

This was lightyears past difficult. Lacey wanted to get rid of me so badly she'd hired a hitman. Now, she wanted to talk? Wow. Really? "How am I supposed to face her? What do I say?"

"I wish there was another way." Jack put his hand on my back and glanced over at Andy. "We need to know what she knows."

They told me what they wanted from her.

"I don't know. You guys are so good at this. What if I go in there and make things worse?" I figured her goal was to rail at me again. To tell me how she was the one Jack really wanted and I was the flavor of the month.

"You'll do fine. Focus and don't let her get to you," Jack reassured me. "Remember she's the one who asked to talk to you."

"I want ears in there," Andy said.

"We can do that." Jack pulled out his phone, pressed some buttons and Andy's phone rang. "All you have to do is keep this pointed toward her. We'll hear everything."

I slipped the phone in the pocket of my blazer. "I'll do my best." They'd pulled the curtain across the glass doors facing the hallway. I hesitated. Going into a patient's room wasn't the problem, Lacey was.

Still, I empathized with her. I knew how it felt to want someone and have your expectations shattered. My only college romance had been a lie. After a two-month whirlwind courtship, one of the most handsome men in my med school class had asked me to marry him. He wasn't Jack handsome or even Don good-looking. Still, attractive. I heard Phillip, my fiancé of fewer than twenty-four hours, and his friend, talking in the library.

His friend asked, "What'd she say?"

"Yes, of course." Phillip said, "I'm set. Ensley is brilliant. She'll make a mint. Face it, after last quarter, I'll be lucky to graduate."

"What about Julie?"

Phillip laughed. "Are you kidding? Ensley believes whatever I tell her. Besides, sex with her is vanilla. No, worse. I'm marrying the woman who'll be rich and keep the one I love on the side. Am I good or what?"

It ended up being or what. I'd walked around the stacks and thrown Phillip's ring at him.

It left me with an overwhelming sense of inadequacy. As if I were nothing more than a commodity, someone's meal ticket. The feeling came back to visit me when I'd heard Don refer to me as his doll. It wasn't exactly the same, but someone had used me. Again.

Even though the relationship between Jack and Lacey was imaginary and not a lie, I knew the hurt she must feel. It didn't excuse her. But I did understand. I stuffed the memory of Phillip back in its box and shoved it in a dark corner of my mind under some other garbage I'd learned to deal with. I wasn't going to let him intrude on my life one second longer. Don, I'd dealt with.

Jack was different. There was no way I'd further his career. From the looks of things, he had a lot more money than I did, he was the head of an incredible team and a sheriff. He hadn't asked anything of me, okay, patching him up didn't count. But he'd lied to me.

The officer at the door nodded to me as he pulled back the curtain to Lacey's room. I thanked him and walked in. "Lacey, are you awake?"

"Yes," came her muffled reply. The light over her bed shown down on the mass of bandages covering her face.

I'd try compassion. "Are you in pain?"

"What do you think? He nearly cut my face off," she snapped back at me.

"I'm sorry."

"No, you're not. Don't pretend." She gripped the bed rails causing her heart rate monitor to beep.

"Lacey, you didn't ask to see me to..." I was only making her mad. I went to her bedside. "You need to help us find the person who did this to you. Did you know they shot up our hotel room? If things had been different Jack would be dead right now. There would have been no way I could have saved him. That isn't what you want is it?" I hoped pointing out the consequences of her stupidity would get her to tell me what we needed to know. "When you let people like this loose, you don't know who will end up dead."

She turned her face to the wall. The action made her groan in pain.

Wrong tactic. On to straight forward. "You wanted to see me."

"A man came up to me in the bar before the party the other night. He said he knew what you'd done. How you'd taken Jack from me and he could get rid of you once and for all. He said he'd do it for five hundred dollars." She shifted and stared at me. "I asked him why so little money. He said he was just fired and needed the cash. I didn't care. Jack should be mine."

"Lacey, you know that's not going to happen." What was it going to take to get her to realize that?

"Yeah, and it's all because of you. If you hadn't come here Jack would be mine. I can't compete with you. You're beautiful and smart, and he was so close to your dad." She put her hand to her face. "That's it. He feels sorry for you and... and."

We both knew that wasn't true.

She sucked in a breath. "I know if I'd had more time he would've come around. You should have left with Don. He's more your style. He's a big shot and you're a doctor. What do you want with a small town sheriff?"

I had no idea how to respond. "Lacey, I'm sure you've had a lot more success with men than I have." God, Jack was listening to this. I put my hand over the phone in my pocket. I hoped it would block the sound.

"Oh, right. What do I care about other men? I want Jack. I see the way he looks at you. I've seen him kiss you. I want him to kiss me like that. I've watched him fall in love with you. Why you? Why not me? He's so happy now. I should be the one making him happy. And that great looking guy Don wants you too. What do you do for these guys?"

She'd asked me that once before. I didn't like it any better this time. "You know if you and Jack were going to be together, it would have happened before I got here."

"He saved my life. He told me to find a decent guy. He is that guy. The one I should have."

I understood. "He was doing his job." Maybe that would help her understand the situation.

"He didn't have to be so nice. That night he waited with me until my dad got there. The next day, he could have sent one of his deputies. Instead, he came. Didn't that mean he cared for me? It had to."

And... it didn't help at all. I wanted to warn her he was listening to her every word. This was awkward, far beyond the he-wants-you-not-me. I tightened my grip on the face of the phone.

"He did, but not the way you think. He was concerned for your safety, nothing more."

"It doesn't matter." She stared at the ceiling. "I thought if I waited he'd get tired of you. He hasn't. I can tell—he's changed—he loves you. He'll never want me now. All because you wouldn't leave with Don."

I wanted to turn off the phone. I had to get her off the subject of Jack. "Lacey—" She wasn't listening to me.

"I want him to love me the way he loves you."

I reminded myself I was dealing with a traumatized woman. She'd come to grips with the fact the man she wanted didn't want her. Now, because of her actions, she was disfigured. I uncovered the phone. "Lacey, I know someone who has contacts with the best plastic surgeons in the country. I'll see what she can do for you. I'm sure she'll recommend someone local who can help you."

"You'd do that for me? Even after I was going to have you killed?"

Good point. "We all do things we regret." I knew I'd be the one regretting it if the person she'd hired had succeeded. "Tell me who this man is and where we can find him."

"I don't know who he is. He came to me." She stopped. "He didn't tell me how to get the money to him. That's not right, is it?"

Great. Now she'd figured it out. "Did he do this to you?"

She began to nod then stopped. "Yeah. He kept asking me questions about you. He wanted to know all about you and Jack and you and Don. I told him everything I knew. It wasn't enough. That's when he started this." She put her hand to a bandage as she began crying. "Nobody's going to want me now. I'll always be alone."

I had one more question. "What did he look like?"

"He was about my dad's height, average, bald with a new scar on his left hand. The one he kept cutting me with. I'd know him if I saw him again. If I can see. They told me I might be blind in one eye."

"I'll contact the plastic surgeon." I left. She didn't know anything more and I couldn't take any more.

"You did great," Andy said.

"That was hard." I avoided Jack's eyes as I gave him his phone. "I don't know how you guys do it."

Jack glanced at the phone in his hand. "I hoped she wouldn't bring me up."

"I'm fine." I couldn't say it hadn't upset me. It had. A lot. How could he love me and lie to me? That lie hung there in the hallway between us. We were going to have to talk about it. That wasn't a talk I was looking forward to. I went to my go-to defense mechanism, and changed the subject. "He has to be the same one who approached Stanton. It bothers me that he didn't only ask about me. He wanted to know about you." I thought about it for a second. "And Don. If I was the target, why ask about you and Don?"

"Alpha needs to know," Jack said.

"I think we should tell Uncle Stan."

"She's guessing, right?" Andy looked at Jack.

Jack shook his head.

"Oh, come on," I said as we walked down the hall. "I can put things together. Okay, not everything, just the obvious ones. If he isn't Alpha why was he Skyping with all of us on the computer at the safe house?"

As we left the ward, Andy leaned close to me and said, "It didn't help to put your hand over the phone. We heard everything. I thought you should know."

Fantastic. I tried to take a cleansing breath and instantly regretted it. I put my hand to my chest. I was going to have to figure out a different anxiety reliever. The whole deep breathing thing really hurt. "Thanks."

In the parking lot, Casey came up to us. "Sarge, we've got another problem." He glanced at me. "Classified."

"It's okay," Jack said. "We're going to have to get her a clearance. What she doesn't know, she figures out."

"Okay, Sarge, but this is big. Someone deactivated our CIA code."

"What?"

This, I could fix. "Try A5595JB7."

All three men turned and looked at me.

"What?" I stared back at them.

"Doc." Concern filled Jack's eyes. "Where did you get that code?"

"It's Don's."

"Shit. Shit!" Andy raised his hand as if to throw his phone to the ground. He thought better of it at the last second.

"You shouldn't have that. Did he give it to you?" Jack's voice remained calm. It was easy to see why he was in charge. Every time things went south he was the rock everyone relied on.

I shrugged. "No."

He moved me around, so I faced him. "This is important. Where did you get his code?"

I remembered sitting in my car in the parking lot of the motel in Mullen as Don gave that code to the person on the other end of the phone. "When we were looking for you, he called someone and gave them that code to get the name from a license plate number." I'd been so focused on finding Jack it hadn't occurred to me how stupid it was for him to give his code out like that.

"That Son-of-a-bitch." His voice was firm, threatening. He let me go. "What's he thinking? People would torture you to get his code."

I took his arm. Every muscle was steel hard. "You're the only ones who know. Who else would I tell?"

Chapter Thirteen

"That's a career ender." Andy's anger wasn't as controlled. "He won't be able to talk or blackmail his way out of it this time."

"I'm sure he doesn't remember." I offered. "Don wouldn't have me killed. Would he?" He'd said that night he loved me, he missed me and wanted me to go back to D.C. with him. I didn't think anyone needed to hear that bit of information.

Casey stepped forward. "Honey, Don March is a very powerful, unscrupulous man. One who'll do anything to keep his power." He rubbed my arms. "You keep that vest on."

Jack drug Andy to the far end of the truck. Jack looked like he was about to hit something. "Casey, I can't believe this. Don asked me to marry him four months ago. Then again on Christmas Eve."

"How did a sweet girl like you get mixed up with a dirtbag like March?"

"I went to a New Year's Eve party with my brother. Cole introduced me to the man who used to be his handler, Don."

Casey's eyes grew wide. "Sarge, did you know March was her brother's handler once upon a time?"

"Yeah." Jack came back to us. "Where is Cole?"

I didn't need to tell him he was scaring the absolute shit out of me.

He knew. He reached out and rubbed my shoulders. His touch was rough with contained anger. He was as concerned as I was. "I don't know. I haven't talked to him in a while. I can call Cindy."

"No. Casey, watch her." His words were clipped. Jack and Andy walked to Andy's car.

"Excuse me," I was upset too.

Casey stopped me. "I haven't seen him this mad in years. Not a man to be messed with when he's angry."

"I've never seen him like this. I did see him face down a man who had a gun pointed at his head." I slumped against the side of his truck.

"What happened?"

"I shot him."

"Good girl." Casey smiled

"I don't understand your world."

He took the spot next to me. "I wish it were different, but it never can be for men like us. It cost me a wife. Takes a special woman to live with our brand of crazy. We can't come home and answer the question, "What did you do today, honey." Most of our work is classified. Andy, there is lucky, he has Sarah. She used to be, let's just say she understands."

I watched Jack as he and Andy talked to someone on the phone. "It's been a fascinating few months." I needed comfort, so I leaned against Casey's shoulder. "Why does this all keep going back to Africa? And Don?"

"A lot of lives were changed that week. We lost good friends, we saved those girls, but your dad and Stan Hofstadter lost their careers." He hesitated. "We rely on Jack to make the hard choices. The right decisions. There are times when it comes down to a tradeoff. Those tradeoffs weigh on you. Doubt creeps in, and you question if you've made the right choice." He watched me. "There was a time after Africa when I thought we'd lost your man there."

"Is he mine?" A seed of self-doubt kept gnawing at me. "I don't know."

"Oh?" Casey gave me a toothy grin. "Then he's not doing it right."

"I know someone a lot like you. He went through three wives."

"Yeah, how did you guess Stan was Alpha?"

"I've known Uncle Stan all my life. When I saw him on that computer screen, I knew he may not be in the Air Force any longer, but he was in charge of something. Then there's the fact that he comes to Spirit Springs regularly for poker games with Brad. You guys are all in one government agency or another. It can't be a coincidence."

"I can see you're going to be a problem. Way too smart for us poor boys."

I smiled. "Jack's one of the most intelligent men I've ever known. Do you know he has a passion for physics?" I nodded toward Jack. "He's so much smarter than Don, probably why Don hates him. You, Mr. Casey, can charm your way out of or into anything I bet."

"Doc, Casey," Jack called to us as he motioned for us to join Andy and him.

"You and I are going to disappear for a while," Jack said to me. "Brad has new documents for us."

»§«

I sat in the hall of the Federal Building, while the team met in Brad's office. I watched as the agent standing across from me scan the area every few minutes. First, someone tried to kill me. Then I was in ICU. Now I was disappearing. This wasn't exactly how I'd imagined the weekend going. I wondered where my beautiful dress was and Jack's suit. He'd looked so elegant at the party. I wondered if his missions had taken him to embassy balls and state dinners.

At the far end of the hall, a door opened and several people entered, ready for an ordinary day's work. Their words and laughter echoed down the barren hall as the door swung shut behind them.

The agent stepped away from the wall. "This way." He motioned to a door.

The office we entered could have been in any government building anywhere in the world. The only personal touch was a fake plant in the corner of the windowless room. It reminded me of my office in D.C. At least there, I'd had a window and a real plant. Sophie had insisted on it. She said they produced oxygen and kept the air fresh.

The chair in here wasn't any more comfortable than the bench in the hall. I got up and walked around looking at the photos of old buildings hanging on the walls.

"Ma'am, please don't go near the door."

"What?" I glanced at him.

"Top is glass." He motioned with his head. "Someone can see your silhouette."

"Oh, right." I nodded. "What's taking them so long?"

"I don't know."

It wasn't long before his walkie crackled to life. "Where the hell are you?" Brad was annoyed as usual.

"We're in room 408," my agent slash guard said into the walkie-talkie.

The door opened, and the men walked in. All of them Brad, Andy, Casey, Tony, and Jack.

Brad handed me a new driver's license and a credit card. The name on them read Ensley Allen. "I can live with that for a while."

"Good," Brad said. "Then we're all set. Right, Trace?" Brad stood there waiting for an answer.

"You know how I feel about breaking up the team."

"You have your orders. They'll have your tickets ready for you downstairs. Stay in contact." He fixed his gaze on me. "Call if you need me. I'll get to you this time. We all will." He left us. He never waits around for comments. He's like that grumpy man you can't help but like because you know he has your best interests at heart.

"What now?" I asked.

"You go get your tickets." Casey smiled and gave me a hug. "The Sarge has my number. I'm here for you." He left.

"Stay safe," Tony said before he followed Casey out the door.

"Ensley, you take care." Andy gave me a kiss on the cheek.

"Say hello to Sarah for me and thank her again." I hugged him back.

Silently, Jack and I went downstairs.

He opened a door with Transportation stenciled on it. Inside, a woman about our age sat behind a metal desk. Jack handed her several sheets of paper. "Mr. and Mrs. Allen you're flying to Seattle." She gave

Jack the tickets and pushed a new purse toward me. "They want you to leave the old one here."

I transferred all my things to the new bag. It had one large, cave-like compartment. I prefer one with as many inside pockets as possible. That way everything stays in order. At least they let me keep the old suitcase.

We turned to leave. "Mr. and Mrs.?" I asked.

"Don't worry. It's not permanent." His tone was sharp as he reached into his pocket and handed me a ring. I noticed he'd already put his on. I slipped the plain gold band on my finger.

This was not the man who held me while I slept last night. Outside, I stopped him. "What's wrong?" We stood in the middle of the stream of people going into work. They were forced to part around us as they made their way inside.

"This is serious."

"I got that part when some idiot killed the bed I'd been sleeping in, and when a mutilated body showed up on our doorstep."

"You don't understand. They split my team up. That's the best way to get us all killed, especially if we're dealing with Sullivan. He's crazy. He was the other man in the basement a couple of weeks ago. The one we didn't catch." He averted his eyes. "Now we have this mysterious second party. We know Sullivan's pattern. We don't know who is behind the other set of circumstances. There're too many players, too many unanswered questions, too many consequences if I'm wrong."

Molten fear seared my heart. "We'll be okay." I hoped. "Are the others leaving too?"

"They have their orders. Brad and Stan are doing everything they can to protect us." We walked against the flow of people. "I don't like running. It never works," he said as we stopped at the curb.

"Could it be Don who's behind the other group?" I had a feeling that particular wrong choice in my life would haunt me for a long time.

"I wish it was him." He shook his head. "I can handle March. We'll get it figured out, it isn't easy to hide from us."

A dark SUV pulled up and we got in. "Your bags from the hotel are in the back." The agent driving was my guard from earlier.

"Thanks, Clark," was all Jack said.

I laid the small case beside the others and sat down across the seat from Jack.

»§«

The airport swarmed with people arriving and departing. Some carrying skis, some with briefcases in hand, and others returning home with bags of souvenirs. Wives kissed their husband's goodbye or hello. Children ran to greet a returning uniformed parent.

We knew where we were going. The problem was what we'd find once we got there. The idea of going to a city like Seattle might work. We'd mix in with the crowd and become invisible. I'm good at invisible. I'd done it masterfully for a lot of years. Still, the city was unfamiliar and that would put us at a disadvantage. Most of all, Jack didn't like it.

Why hadn't they listened to him? Why breakup the team?

Brad had made arrangements for us to bypass security, they wouldn't understand about our Kevlar vests or Jack's weapon. Even with our arrival expedited we had to run to catch the nine o'clock flight. The action hurt my chest. It had to be more painful for Jack's ribs.

I was on my second pass through a discarded People magazine when Jack said, "This isn't what I wanted."

"I know." I remembered Bev earlier and how her life had been ruined by Stanton's ambition. I thought of Lacey and what she'd tried to do to me and how it had backfired so horribly. Then I thought about Sarah. I wanted what Sarah had. I wanted to tell Jack we'd be okay as long as we were together. Then I remembered his words when he'd told me we'd be pretending to be married, 'Don't worry. It's not permanent.'

He was right. Nothing lasted forever. The thought left me empty and cold. No, I felt like a shell, with nothing inside. No cold, no warmth, only a darkness that craved light. I looked at the panel of lights and switches, call buttons and air controls above. An airplane wasn't the place to talk. Maybe it was. "Jack," I whispered. "Talk to me." It always worked when he said it to me.

Finally, he said, "I can't keep putting you through this kind of thing."

I wasn't a hundred percent sure what *this* was so I went for the indisputable. "I thought we decided we were better together than apart." At least that's what I'd gotten out of our talk after I returned from D.C. "Are we going through that again? Because I can't."

"I have to think this through. Make a plan."

Got it. I couldn't read about one more super-colossal actress or look at another dress. I laid my head on his shoulder.

He took my hand.

»§«

The Fairmont Olympic is a dignified, gray stone, four-hundred and fifty room hotel. With all these rooms I knew we'd vanish into the background. Out front, a doorman in a long black coat opened the taxi door for me and set our luggage on a carrier. A planter filled with lush greenery buffered arriving visitors from the the city traffic beyond.

Inside, the grand lobby was decorated in gold and blue brocade couches and chairs. At the foot of a grand staircase, we passed a towering flower arrangement. I felt out of place in jeans and a Kevlar vest. Okay, no one could see the vest. Still, I knew it was there. I resisted the urge to straighten it.

"Mr. and Mrs. Allen, it's nice to have you with us." The clerk flashed us a patented smile and began to enter our information. "You're early. I'm sorry, your room isn't ready. We'll be happy to store your luggage for you if you'd like to go shopping or sightseeing." He turned his attention back to the computer screen.

"Thank you," Jack said. "My wife is tired, is there somewhere quiet we can get something to eat and relax?"

"Yes, sir." He wrote the names of a couple cafés on at notepad. As he handed it to Jack he said, "I have good news for you, your room has been upgraded to the Bridal Suite."

That didn't make sense. We'd expected a small out of the way room. I looked from the clerk to Jack.

"There's been some mistake," he said. "Who made the change?"

"No mistake, sir." The clerk smiled as he handed Jack a sealed envelope. "This came for you. With the gentleman's compliments."

The contents read:

Jack and Ensley,
Enjoy your short time together.
Don

"When did this arrive?" Jack asked the clerk.

The poor guy took one look at the expression on Jack's face and stepped back. "It was here when I came on shift."

"When did you get here?"

"Half an hour ago. Is there a problem, Sir?"

"We have a change in plans. Cancel our room."

Chapter Fourteen

My heart pounded so hard I coughed. The biting fear surging through me left behind a cold, unforgiving terror. The same horror that brings me screaming out of my nightmares.

Jack pulled out one of the burner phones we'd been given and dialed. "Stan, we have a leak, March knew we were going to stay here. —Yeah, we're gone.—No. I'm not taking a chance. I'm not—no, you're right. Thanks." He hung up.

Outside he said, "Pick a cab."

"The blue one. Why am I picking?"

"People have patterns they aren't aware of. They make subconscious choices all the time. They never take the first item off the shelf at the store, or they park by the cart return. Things like that."

Maybe if I analyzed my choices, I'd make better ones in the future. I glanced at Jack. Was he a good choice? So far, things had been terrifying and delightful, painful and pleasurable. Then, there was Don. Maybe I should become a nun. They don't have to deal with men. There were two problems with that option. I'm not Catholic and Jack's kisses. The Catholic part could be remedied. Jack could not. The nunnery was out. Totally out. "Interesting. Who would know how I chose?" I knew the answer before I got the whole sentence out. Don knew. "Why is Don doing this?"

He stopped and pulled me close. "Don isn't behind what's going on," he whispered. "He's taking advantage of a bad situation."

"What about the note?"

"That was payback." He took my hand. "For me, not you."

"I don't understand."

"It's twofold." He paused. "After you left, I went to see Jane. March was checking out. I reminded him I have contacts in D.C. When I talked to him earlier, I made it clear I knew he was up for a promotion. Looks like he didn't appreciate it." He smiled down at me. "March isn't behind the attack on Lacey or shooting up our hotel room. The problem is, if he can find us and he knows we're together, then so does Sullivan." He paused. "So does the mystery man."

The cab took us to a shopping mall.

"Why are we here?" I asked as we made our way inside.

"We're waiting for someone."

We bought coffee and sat down at one of the tables in the food court. People milled around, a couple of teenagers had taken a bunch of straws from a counter and were blowing the wrappers at each other. Mall Security was headed their way.

The vendors were all the main players you find in big malls. Hamburgers, tacos, Chinese, juice, cookies, and pizza. Early lunch goers were scattered around at the other tables. The noon rush wouldn't show up for another hour or so.

I sipped the last of my coffee as a cleaning cart stopped next to us. A woman in her fifties dressed in a maintenance worker's uniform said, "I hate these last minute arrangements." She tugged at her uniform as she took some cups from another table. "You'd think those idiots would get my size right. Everything you need is in the car. It's on level three, section M, next to the stairs. The license number is on the tag." She laid a key on the table but didn't take her hand away. "Trace, I want everything back. It better be in the same condition I gave it to you in. I don't care what Hughes says. Am I clear?"

"We'll do our best, Marilyn."

She nodded. "I'll hold you and bright eyes here personally responsible if anything is missing or broken." She moved to the next table.

I smiled. "You lose much?" I said as we made our way to the escalator.

"There was a slight misunderstanding over a car a couple of years ago. She didn't appreciate the fact that it was parked twenty feet off the end of one of the piers."

"I can imagine." That sounded like a story I wanted to hear. "Who was driving?"

"Casey." He smiled.

The car turned out to be an SUV. He opened the back hatch and tossed our suitcases in beside a FedEx box. Inside were our new driver's licenses and credit cards. My name was now Ensley Myers. Another first. I'd been three different people, and it wasn't even noon. We found two weapons. I took the smaller one. He put our old ID's in the box and sealed it.

After shutting the door, he said, "Ensley, I want you to," He stopped.

"Yes, sheriff." I stood in front of him with my arms crossed. "I do not like the fact that you aren't telling me anything. Am I supposed to take things on faith? Or do I get to be part of this?"

"You don't understand."

"No, I absolutely do not, because no one is talking to me. I feel like," I stopped. I was about to say something I didn't mean.

"What?" He watched me as if he were afraid of what I'd say.

"Like I'm not part of, of this. It's my life too. I'm capable of doing more than pulling foreign objects out of you."

"This is worse than you know." He pulled me into his arms. "We're out here on our own. I hate having the team split up. It's the beginning of defeat. I told Brad that before we left."

"We'll be fine." I hoped. "What do we do now?"

"How do you do it?"

"What?" I asked.

"You have the ability to take everything as it comes. I know you get frightened." He held me tighter. "You've been through so much in the past few months. I worry how much more you can take before you hit your limit." He let me go. "Right now, we need some clean clothes, and I want you to get rid of that big suitcase."

The agent who had driven us to the airport had brought our things from the hotel. That included my weekender case. "It's part of a set."

"Where's the rest of it?" His words sounded cautious.

"Spirit Springs. Why?"

"Where did you get it?" His voice held a note of please don't-say-it.

I froze. This was not happening. "Don gave it to me. It wasn't just a gift, was it?" He didn't have to answer. I knew. "Jack, I'd never thought—"

"When we get home, and I will make that happen, I want you to give me everything he gave you."

"I don't have much left." The memory of throwing all the things he'd given me in a box marked trash still made me feel like I was twelve. In the end, maturity had won out. "I sort of had a temper tantrum before I left D.C. If he put tracking devices in the things he gave me," I laughed. "He's tracking a lot of innocent people. I donated everything else. The only reason I kept the luggage was because I didn't have time to get more. There wasn't anything wrong with these besides the fact that Don gave them to me. I was kind of in a hurry to get out here."

"I can imagine your donations pissed him off." He smiled. "Let's get this done." He turned serious. "I don't want you to buy the pretty stuff you usually wear. Keep it drab. We're supposed to be an old married couple."

"Old married couples don't get that way by being drab." At least, my parents hadn't.

He looked away. "Give it a shot."

Instead of splitting up we went shopping together. Jack grabbed a couple pairs of jeans, t-shirts, and underwear. I took longer. I wasn't going to buy just any jeans. I coerced him into an Ann Taylor store.

"Ens, I thought we were going to keep it simple."

"We are, but life is too short to wear uncomfortable jeans. Besides the other store didn't have my size in t-shirts. I'll compromise, we can go to the department store so I can get something that will fit."

"Only if that store is Eddie Bauer." He pointed across the hall.

"That's fine if you take me to dinner."

"It's two thirty."

I draped two pairs of jeans over my arm. "I'm sure we can find something to do for a couple of hours. Besides." I leaned close to him. "They won't expect it." I pulled back and smiled at him.

"I'd like nothing more than to spend this afternoon wandering around with you, but we can't. We need to get your clothes and leave." He glanced at the entrance to the store. "I'm sorry. We'll have to catch something to eat on the road.

»§«

At a truck stop, we pulled all our new clothes out of the bags and I transferred my things to his duffle and my small suitcase. I zipped up the duffel as he asked, "Is everything out of the suitcase?"

"What are you going to do with it?" I handed it to him.

"I'm going to give him something to chase." He walked around the back of a semi. A minute later, he returned. "That should keep him guessing for a while."

The truck's license plate read Alabama. "Maybe he'll have a load for D.C.," I said.

"That is too much to hope for." Jack grinned. "Let's go. I don't like standing in the open."

Chapter Fifteen

J ack started the car. "Would you like to drive down the coast?"

"That sounds great." Maybe for the rest of the afternoon, the world would leave us alone.

"I promise things will be normal when we get home."

I reached over and put my hand on his arm. "Don't make promises you can't possibly keep. I have a feeling if we aren't out looking for trouble, it'll be actively searching for us." I left my hand where it was. "After all, it's part of my past that's playing more than a small role in what's happened today."

"Doc, we can never escape our pasts. The best we can hope for is to be wise enough to deal with the consequences when they catch up with us."

We talked and listened to the radio as the city dwindled into country. "Do you know what the odds are of one of my med school classmates ending up in Boise the same time I did? And that he'd be in so much financial distress, he'd make a lethal concoction that would be used on me?" I glanced out the window. "I don't. It's the fates conspiring. What I can't figure out is if they're with us or against us."

We drove along the ocean.

"I've always loved the Pacific," I said. "It's so vast and wild, it's like standing on the edge of the world."

"Will he know that?"

"Don? No." The late afternoon sun glint off the wings of the seagulls as they floated over the whitecaps.

Jack pulled into an overlook parking area. The surf below us threw itself against the rocks in a never-ending effort to break the shore. When the rocks refused to yield the wave flew up in a spray of frustration.

He shut off the SUV. "Right now, let's take a walk on the beach."

The desolate seashore wound along at the base of the cliff, and it faded into the mist. We stood wrapped in a cocoon of fog blocking us from the world outside. Giant black rocks lay just beyond the breakers. The ones close to shore, thrust out of the surf, remnants of an era lost to time.

The trees on the bluff above surrendered to the relentless wind. Their branches bowing inland with each brutal gust. Each time the gale ceased the branches straighten a little less.

I slipped my hand in Jack's and breathed in the briny scent of the ocean as gulls glided effortlessly on the invisible currents above. Their shrieks greeted every crashing wave.

I held Jack's hand tighter and leaned my head against his arm. I would definitely treasure our walk on this cold, windy beach. This island of peace in the chaos of the weekend would remain with me always.

Ahead, the cliff had collapsed into the sea, blocking our way. We stopped by a ring of blue-green tide pools surrounding a massive dark rock. I reached down and touched one of the tiny jade sea anemones. The water felt icy and pure on my hand. Instantly, the creature curled its grass-like arms back to protect itself.

When I stood, Jack pulled me to him and held me for a long time. "I need to tell you something."

The tone of his voice sent a thread of anxiety twining up my spine.

"I'm a soldier, a warrior. I've fought my whole life in one way or another. It's what I'm good at, who I am." He held on to me as if he thought I'd run from him. "My grandmother wanted me to go to college. I wanted to join the Army. We struck a deal. I'd go to college until I was eighteen, then I could do what I thought was best. She said I should have the chance to be a world-class physicist before I went off to protect the country we both loved."

"You would have been brilliant and probably the only scientist carrying a weapon," I said.

He grinned, then turned serious. "Right after I became part of Delta Force, my team and I were assigned to take care of a situation in Serbia. An operative had gotten himself in trouble. It was the first time I came in contact with March. His ambition had clouded his judgment. He was tangled in a situation he couldn't get out of without someone losing their life. They'd sent him after information. Had he gotten it, he'd have been a hero. But he wanted too much more. There were only two outcomes. He'd end up killing a lot of people or he'd die. I didn't give him a chance to make the choice. I had orders and I yanked him out of there. He blamed me for the failure of the mission and reported me. He told my superiors I'd been overeager. He didn't know I brought back the information they wanted. It didn't hurt his career. It was my promotion that gnawed at him."

Jack wasn't done.

"He blames me for a lot of things, things I had no control over. Situations he caused out of vengeance or ambition. Incidents I was sent to clean up. You know what happened in Africa? He wasn't responsible for the situation, but his hesitation ended up being a deadly one."

I wondered if Africa would ever fade. I knew on some level it was one of those events in life that lives with you always. In that dark place, you struggle to keep the door closed on.

"Not long after his extraction from Serbia, he requested I be sent to rescue a female agent. It was the first time I went out alone. Armed with only the information Don gave me, I went to get her. Either his intel was inaccurate or he lied."

Jack paused and his hazel eyes lost a little sparkle. "When I arrived, the federal police were walking her out of a cafe. They weren't taking her to jail. She was headed for a bad end. I was young. I should never have been on that mission. I had the expertise, but not the experience.

With all my contacts false or compromised, I had to devise a way to get her free and us out of the country. Alive. That's the time I had to dig the bullet out of my shoulder left-handed." He smiled down at me.

I remembered him telling me that my removing a slug from his shoulder without anesthetic wouldn't be as bad as that had been. I smiled back.

"We made it out. Don wanted her—us dead. Like so many other times, I can't prove it. All I know is what she told me the night we didn't think we were going to survive." He stopped. "When we got back, I confronted March. It was a mistake, he's a formidable enemy, but I was young and I was going to put the world right." He struggled with something more. "With March, it always comes down to a woman."

I averted my eyes. Why hadn't I seen it earlier? Oh, yeah. Don was only the second man I'd ever been with and the first one who'd openly cared for me, or so I thought.

"You were different." He lifted my chin. "You have to believe that. If you'd been like all the rest, he never would have gone to all the trouble he has to try to get you back."

We stood in silence.

Jack has built walls to keep the world at bay. I know when he comes up against one by the way he hesitates, and the struggle that plays out in his eyes. I'm not sure some of them will ever come down. He is trying.

My heart pounded so hard he had to feel it as he held me.

"He's never going away." Lines of concern gathered between his eyes. "I keep thinking he'll get tired of screwing with me. His efforts haven't turned out in his favor so far. If he isn't trying to make me pay for something, he's going to be after you." He held me in silence for a long minute, then he said, "Can we survive him?"

"Jack, I know now, I never loved him." It was my turn to hold him for fear he'd run away. Crying myself to sleep every night in D.C. had brought one fact starkly to the forefront. I love Jack. Loved him more than I thought was possible.

"We're good then?"

The lie of Christmas threaded it's way between us. Still I said, "We're good."

We stood in each other's arms without talking, watching the blue sky soften and melt into gold as the day slipped into night.

When we got back to the truck, he opened the door for me. I love it when Jack does that. It makes me feel valued and respected. I know that's not PC, but neither am I.

I stole a glance at him. There isn't much that's sexier than a man with good manners. "Thank you." I kissed him.

He smiled at me. He has the best smile.

As I climbed in the SUV, my new impossibly-large purse spilled. "What?"

"What's wrong?" He looked over my shoulder.

I pointed to the jumble on the floor. "That's not mine." I indicated a phone charger.

"Maybe it came with the purse."

"I don't think so. I have a bag that came with one, it had its own pocket that snapped shut keeping it in place. This purse doesn't have any compartments." I glanced up. "So, how did it get here?" I picked up the device.

"Did you leave the purse unattended at any time?"

"No. It's so big the airport police would have blown it up thinking it had a bomb in it." I set the bag upright. "The only place I put it was under the seat on the plane."

"The woman in front of you kept getting into her things on the floor. It wasn't there. Did anyone bump into you?"

"Both airports were crowded. I was jostled a couple of times."

"It had to be then. Is there anything else that shouldn't be there?" he asked.

In the dim light of the SUV's interior, I sifted through the rest of the items. "No, it's all mine."

As he motioned for me to get in, he whispered, "Don't talk."

That scared me.

"We need gas," he said as he turned the Explorer around and headed back the way we'd come.

As we retraced our route along the beach road, he reached over and took my hand.

»§«

Cars and trucks filled the first gas station we came to. He signaled for me to get out of the SUV.

Outside he said, "That device appearing is bad. Don finding us is one thing. I can't believe he'd hurt you. Me, in a heartbeat, never you. This is too well organized for a lone hitman. Sullivan is skilled, but his network is flawed and the information is slow getting to him." He glanced at the SUV. "We've got to get rid of the device and the SUV. I can't take the chance someone got into the SUV between the time we met with Marilyn and we left the mall."

"Jack. No." This was why he hadn't wanted to split up the team. We were out here without backup. "How are we going to disappear?"

"Ensley, I need you to," He stopped. Something caught his attention over my shoulder.

"Sheriff." I was pretty sure he was going to try to get me to go somewhere. I wasn't leaving and the sooner he figured that out, the fewer times we were going to have this conversation. "I will not leave. Do I have to call Andy so he can remind you of what I said earlier?"

"This is past dangerous." He continued to watch something behind me. "It isn't going to be like anything you've been through." He led me back toward the side of the convenience store.

I pulled him to a stop. "I'm not leaving."

"What if I can't protect you?"

"What if I can't save you?"

We looked at each other.

I wasn't budging.

He wasn't budging.

"You're impossible," he said as he pulled out one of the prepaid phones.

"Good. I'm glad we have that settled."

We walked back to the SUV. "We've been compromised. I'm changing things up. I'll let you know the details." He snapped the phone shut and set it on the sidewalk. He asked me to get him a cup of coffee.

I hesitated. He knew I'd find a way to be safe. He knew I'd call Brad. I knew he wouldn't leave without me.

When I came back out, he was standing by the SUV. "Doc—"

I looked up at him and waited.

He reached for my hand. "I need you with me. I'll never ask you to leave again." He went into the store. The door swung closed behind him.

I stood there stunned, holding his cup of hot coffee. It was more feeling than fact, the *I need you with me* had come out effortlessly this time. Did that assurance come with the promise of never lying to me again ... ever?

I watched him through the window as he paid for something. I needed to be certain I'd heard him right.

Before we got into the SUV he said, "This," His face held steady determination, "is what I want you to do and I don't want an argument. If things go sideways I want you to get out. If Sullivan finds us, I won't be able to hold him off for long with these cracked ribs." He brushed his fingers along my cheek. "I have to know you'll leave. That you'll call Brad and be safe. Do you understand?"

"I understand." This man was absolutely impossible.

"Good. Then it's settled."

"Right. I'm going to walk away and leave you to die." Maybe if I said it out loud, he'd hear how completely out of the question his request was.

"Ensley, I—"

"I'm not arguing with you, I'm only repeating what you said. I'll do exactly what you'd do."

"You're the most maddening damned woman."

"Oh? And how am I supposed to live the rest of my life knowing I let you die at the hands of some crazed killer? I saw what he did to you at Christmas, to that man we found in the garage and Lacey. You think I can add those images to the basement nightmare and come out sane? I'm waiting because I want to hear the answer." I managed a shallow breath. "What about you *needing me* with you?"

He went right past the *needing me* part. "Sullivan's worse than insane. I've seen the destruction he's left behind. "You leaving is a last ditch, an if everything goes south contingency." He stopped as he glanced in the direction he had earlier. "Get in the car."

I was about to point out that I don't take orders well, when I saw what had his attention. A man leaning against a car parked in the shadow of the building. A second man walked up and handed the first man a drink then he too leaned against the car and watched us.

Chapter Sixteen

The two men began walking our way.

Jack started the FBI car.

The shorter one reached under his coat.

"Ah, shit." Jack floored the SUV and headed straight for them.

They jumped to the sides.

I looked out the rear window. "They're running for their car."

"Stay down and hold on." He pulled out of the truck stop. "I don't know this area well enough to lose them. Damn it, why didn't Marilyn give me a car with GPS?"

"What do we do?"

"We make it so they can't follow us." He wheeled into an industrial area. "I don't want anyone hurt besides them." He pulled his phone from his pocket. Without looking, he opened it, told it to call Marilyn Baker, and handed it to me. "When she answers, tell her what's going on."

"Trace, what the hell? Since you're calling, I'm guessing they found you or you wrecked my SUV."

"Marilyn, this is Ensley Markus."

"Who?"

"Bright eyes," I said.

"Where the hell is Trace? Have you wrecked my SUV."

I grabbed the door as we slid around a corner. "No. We're being followed." I looked over at Jack.

"Damn it. Isn't anything easy with him?" she asked.

"Apparently, not."

"Where are you?"

I gave her the name of the town and the truck stop.

"What does he—?" The scream of the tires taking the corner drowned out her last word.

"Jack, what do you want her to do?"

"Put her on speaker."

I tapped the icon. The lights of the other car glinted off the outside mirrors. They'd caught up to us.

"Call the police." He gave her their license plate number. "Tell them there's a road rage situation. You might explain who we are, too."

"Got it. Hold on." After a few more scary turns, Marilyn came back on. "I have them on the phone. What intersection are you near?"

"We're leaving Kelly Industrial Park, we're on Placer headed west." He took the corner so fast I thought we'd go up on two wheels.

Jack slammed on the breaks as we turned back out on to the road we'd left minutes ago. The car behind us wasn't as smart. They hit the dip between sidewalk and street with so much speed they went air born. The impact caused them to fishtail and jump the curb. They result was a shower of sparks, scraping metal, and screaming tires.

Jack stomped the accelerator down hard leaving the others behind to gain control of their car.

"I don't like going this fast on a side street," he said as he kept the SUV floored.

I looked at the speedometer. We were going north of seventy. The guys behind us were going faster.

"How far out are the cops?" Jack asked.

Marilyn came back on, "They should be behind you any minute."

A few blocks behind the car chasing us, I saw the welcome red and blue lights of the police. "Here they come."

"Good. You two be careful and don't wreck my car." Marilyn hung-up.

Behind us, a police car pulled out from a side street blocking our pursuers as three more police cars raced by us headed for the excitement. "Why didn't they stop us?"

"Marilyn is excellent at her job. They knew we were the good guys."

Jack slowed to a reasonable speed. "One second you're doing seventy down a city street the next you're back to normal. You're astonishing." I was still shaking.

"No. Simply, well trained." He smiled. "Your tax dollars at work." He drove away as if nothing happened.

»§«

Half an hour later, we pulled into a used car lot. Under the high-pressure sodium lights multi-colored, triangular flags fluttered in the cold night wind. To my surprise, a man was waiting for us. When we got out, he called, "Sarge, what's going on?" The stranger walking toward us was easily six-six. He shook Jack's hand as he looked down at me. His ready smile offset the fact that he was enormous and intimidating.

"Ensley Markus, Ben Painter. Ben was with the team."

"How do you do?" I offered him my hand. His covered mine as if it were a child's.

"How's married life?" Jack asked.

"I'm going to be a dad. Can you believe it? Any minute. Scariest thing I've ever faced." His broad smile was filled with joy, but his eyes betrayed his apprehension.

Jack grabbed him and pulled him into a man-hug. "That's great. Congratulations to both of you."

"I'll do it. It's two-thirty, and I'm needed at home so let's get to it. I've got exactly what you're after." He pointed to a 1979 Ford F250 pick-up. I knew that only because it was printed on the windshield.

"Do we want something that old?" The black paint had long ago surrendered its shine to the ages.

"We do. No electronics in it. They can't track us," Jack said. "And I can fix it if I need to."

At least it didn't appear as old as Jane's truck.

"It belonged to an old guy," Ben chuckled. "Hey, at least it wasn't a little old lady."

The Ford didn't look like it would get us—I had no idea where we were headed.

"I thought about having it painted. The inside is pristine and the engine hums. You won't have to repair this one. The man was restoring it when his wife got sick. Said he was selling it to take her on a last vacation. I don't know if it was a line or not, I do know it's a great truck."

Jack looked at the price on the sticker. "Ben, I don't have enough cash. I can make a deal with you." He pointed to the Explorer. "Marilyn Baker want's that back in one piece." He smiled. "You know the drill. If she won't give you the full price I'll make it right."

"She's not going to be happy to hear from me. The last time I saw her she threatened to take Casey's and my next two paychecks to pay for that car that met a watery death."

They laughed.

"That was two years ago," Jack said. "But, no mistake, she remembers."

After all the papers had been signed we left the SUV and the phone charger with Ben and drove toward Portland.

Jack pulled out his phone. When someone answered all he said was, "Aspen." He hung up. "Now, we go to our people."

»§«

Ben was right, Jack's new truck was in good shape. In the morning light, the finish was more primer than paint. A new horse blanket-textured seat cover stretched across the bench seat. The spotless interior showed only a light coating of dust from sitting in Ben's car lot. The bed was longer than the one in Jack's new truck, but then this one didn't have a backseat. I moved the duffle bag around and put my feet on the floor.

I pulled my windbreaker around me as rain splattered on the windshield.

"Now that we can talk, and no one is following us, do you remember anything more about that last party?" Jack asked as he pulled into a convenience store. "First, I need some coffee."

"How are your ribs?"

"Sore," he said as we got out.

"No coffee. I want you to get some rest."

Inside he said, "Don't worry about me."

"You can't keep going like this and hope for the best."

"I'm fine." He took a couple bottles of water from the cooler and headed for the coffee.

He had to be exhausted. "Let me drive. You can sleep."

He ignored me.

Men. "Jack, let's find a motel. You need to rest so you can heal."

"Is there a motel around here?" he asked the clerk.

"The Blue Moon is up the road about three miles," he said and pointed in the direction we were headed. "I wouldn't stay in any of the ones closer."

"Thanks."

In the truck, Jack sipped his coffee in silence.

I wanted to get some things straight. "What's been bothering me is, if that party was to let people know Sullivan was now for hire on the open market," How could I phrase this? "If they were the kind of people who'd hire a hitman... why was Don there? Why was I there?"

"I've been wondering that myself," he said as he drove to the motel. "Either March is worse than I thought or he was there to see who showed up. It was irresponsible. If he needed a companion there are CIA agents available." He shook his head. "No. It doesn't track. They all knew he was CIA."

"Maybe he took me because we'd been seen together at so many functions."

"I don't think that party has anything to do with what's going on now. This is personal with Sullivan." He pulled into the parking lot of the Blue Moon Motel.

"What?"

"I'm worn-out. Even with your injuries you still function at full capacity."

"I wasn't drugged." He sounded tired no matter what he said. "Doc, let's get you somewhere you can get some sleep."

He pulled up to the office of the motel.

I put my fingers to his neck. "Your heart rate is faster than I'd like and you're pale." It was from stress, his injuries, and lack of sleep.

We found our room in the back on the ground floor near the exit.

I stretched out on one of the beds. Jack laid down on the other one. He needed sleep more than I did. I got up and sat next to him. "Take off your shirt."

For an instant he looked surprised.

"You're going to sleep and to do that you need to relax. Let me rub your shoulders."

Chapter Seventeen

I woke to Jack's touch. "Doc, there's a problem, we've got to go."

"Problem?" I looked at the bedside clock, we'd been asleep for five hours. I sat up and brushed the hair from my face. "What happened?"

"We have a missing man."

"Who is it?" Did I want to know?

"Quinn." He tossed me one of the power bars he'd bought earlier.

"Quinn's dead, isn't he?"

"That's now in question. Someone went to a lot of trouble to make the body in the garage look like Quinn. With the ends of his fingers missing and his teeth knocked out, they had to rely on DNA. Even with a rush it took a while."

He closed the motel room door behind us. When we were in the truck, he said, "I haven't told you anything that's classified anymore, but it isn't public knowledge either."

I knew they were still an active team, but for what agency? Only one way to find out was to ask. "Who do you guys work for?"

"There are questions I can't answer, things I can't talk about."

That hadn't worked, so I asked, "Where are we going?"

"Boise."

"Didn't we just spend a lot of time and effort leaving there?"

"It didn't work."

"Will the others be there?"

"Yes."

Outside gray clouds spilled rain on the world leaving everything clean and satiny. The wipers swept away the drops as they struggled to cover the windshield.

"I remembered something," I said. "We went to a party a couple weeks before the last one. I remember it because it was the night he asked me to marry him. Don picked me up late. It wasn't like him, he was always precisely on time. Almost as if he waited outside until the exact minute. That night he seemed nervous. As we walked into the party, he said, 'Ensley, this is an important gathering. I want you to be gracious to everyone.' Yeah, like I was ever rude. So why make a point of it that night?"

I unbuckled my seatbelt and moved next to Jack. "It was all normal until I heard a man asked Don about me." I sat a little straighter. "It was the same man in the brown suit with the ugly mustache. He didn't have it then, but I'm sure it's him." This was uncomfortable. I hated talking to Jack about Don, let alone relaying time I'd spent with him. "A little later Don brought me a glass of wine. He knew I never drank at those things. The only reason I went was because he'd told me it was critical to his career. His career..." He'd always been so concerned about his job. I put my hand on Jack's thigh. I stopped and mentally looked around the ballroom. "There wasn't anything out of the ordinary until we went outside. That's when I saw Sullivan. He was in the garden talking to a woman. She kept backing away from him. Finally, he took her arm and wouldn't let her go. I asked Don to do something about it and he said it wasn't any of our business. I told him I wouldn't walk away from a woman in trouble. I started down the steps, and he grabbed me back so violently I dropped the drink I didn't want. The glass shattered and the man looked up at us." I opened my eyes.

"What did the woman look like?"

"She was about Don's age, forty. She was several inches shorter than Sullivan, attractive with short blond hair. She didn't have on any makeup, and her dress was sullen black and ordinary, as if she'd gone out of her way not to be noticed."

"Shit." He pulled over to the side of the road and took out his phone. "Stan, the Doc saw Sullivan and Galveston together a day before he killed her. The man with the bad mustache was there. That has to be the connection." He gripped my hand. "Have you found out who he is? – Have you contacted Maui? – I see. I want that information as soon as you get it." He hung up.

The frown lines deepened between his eyes and the muscles tightened in his neck. "From now on, you need to do exactly what I tell you and no arguments."

»§«

We passed the *Welcome to Idaho* sign as Jack's phone rang. The rest of the burners lay silent in the duffle. He listened then hung up. "Change of plans. We're going to Emmett."

"Why?"

"We need to regroup away from Boise."

We turned off I-84 onto a two lane country road. A couple of miles later we found a gas station in a small town. I walked into the convenience store. I didn't want anything, but Jack was talking on his phone.

I knew calm may not be in our future. If we had one. I glanced out the large window at him standing by the truck. His head was bowed. It wasn't the prospect of the chaos that left me oppressively sad, it was the thought of that lie I couldn't let go of. Oh, I know he'd said it was so I'd leave and be safe, but it was still a lie. I swallowed the tears that threatened to choke me. I … we had to get it settled, but now wasn't the time.

I kept my gaze on him as if it were the last time I'd see him. He'd said he was a warrior. That wasn't right. He was a hero. The one who runs toward danger not away from it. The one who puts his life on the line for his country and comrades. But heroes don't lie. The air in the store became dense and hard to breathe.

I pushed open the door and walked out into the winter air. A piercing cold far below the temperature enveloped me. I glanced over at the aged truck, it looked stable and real. I felt as if everything I'd ever wanted was slipping out of my grasp. "None of this will last."

"I hope not." Jack walked up beside me.

I'd never get used to him moving so quietly. At least I didn't jump this time. I didn't have the courage to tell him what I meant. As he opened the truck door for me he asked, "What's wrong?"

"I... nothing.

He reached up and wiped a tear I hadn't known I'd shed from my face. "I know this is hard."

"It isn't the situation, I can handle that. I think." I indicated the truck. "It's ..." I had to wait, I reminded myself, this wasn't the time..

"You don't have to worry." He smiled. "I don't plan on getting shot. Is that's what worrying you?"

I put my arms around him.

"I wish you'd tell me," he said against my hair. "I can't help if you won't talk to me." He hesitated. "Don't keep things from me."

"I can't. I just can't."

He kissed me. "For now. When you're ready, I'm here." We got in. He started the truck but didn't put it in gear. "Stan found Maui." He stared out the windshield. "He's dead." He rested his hand on the gearshift. " It looks like Sullivan is working his way through the CIA." He didn't move. "I hope they don't send me after him. I can't be responsible for both brother's deaths."

It wasn't long before we pulled into a small community and into a strip style motel. The kind where you park outside your door. The rooms in a straight line marching away from the road.

"I'll be right back." Jack got out and went into the office. He returned and handed me a key.

"Keys?"

"Old school. Our room is at the end." He pointed to a Jeep that looked as old as our truck sitting near the back. "Andy is already here."

In our room, Jack shut the door. "Now. Tell me why you're upset. Besides the obvious, I know that's not it."

Right. Like I understood it completely. "I'm not sure I can."

"You know keeping it to yourself isn't doing either of us any good." He took my hand and kissed the palm.

There he went again, being logical and straightforward. I know from experience that people often times don't really want to know the truth. They say they do, but they don't.

"Tell me."

"Okay." I felt my heart rate elevate until I began to tremble. What if I told him and he said I misunderstood his intentions? What if I was pushing too hard? What if he wasn't ready? I was pretty sure my *rational switch* was in the off position.

"Ens?" He touched my face. "Talk to me."

"I don't want us to end before we get a chance to begin." The words rushed out. That's right, I threw everything right out there. I didn't bother to filter anything.

"What makes you think we'll end?"

"Because everything ends. I know there is no everlasting, no forever."

"You can't believe that." He glanced down at me, his eyes were dark with sadness.

"Do you know how many friends I've had to leave behind? We always promise to stay in touch and we'd be friends forever, in a couple of months the letters and calls became fewer and fewer until they stopped. Everyone moved on with their lives. I can't even remember most of their names. It hurts, but I know there'll come a time when I don't hear from Sophie any longer. Everything ends. Everything." I stopped short of saying we would end one day, too. I hoped that day wasn't close at hand.

I watched as anguish stole the light from his eyes. It was a hurt so deep I knew it was what was standing in his way. Finally, he said, "Not this time." He turned and left.

I stood there watching him leave. I felt the weight of his pain on my shoulders as it melted with my own hurt.

Seconds later, I heard a knock on the room next door. This man was puzzling. He stood there and said, "Not this time." Then he left. That was confusing right on the face of it. I mean, what the hell? What kept me from moving was the misery I'd seen in his eyes. Who had hurt him so deeply?

I kept remembering Brad's words on Christmas Eve, 'That was when he didn't have anyone to come home to.' Sarah had said to be patient with him, and Andy telling me it would be worth the wait.

I looked down at the gold band on my finger and remembered Jack's harsh words before he'd given it to me. "Don't worry. It's not permanent." Did he think we had a chance or not? He'd checked us both into all the motel rooms. Why was this so difficult? So confusing. There was so much I didn't know about, so much. Jack was the most complicated human I'd ever known. He'd come right up to the precipice of telling me how much he cared then he'd turn and walk away.

I took the duffle bag to the bed and took out my suitcase. My dress lay beneath it. Jack wanted me to tell him everything, but he kept his secrets and lies. I refolded the dress, and laid it on top of Jack's suit.

This weekend had started out so full of promise. We were going to a party that would bring money into the community and everything would be back on track.

It had been only five days since the bright winter morning when I'd returned to Jack. I sat down on the bed. Maybe this was our normal. If we were going to work, I'd needed to figure out a way to deal with the crazy situations and brushes with death. These weren't the typical dating hurdles, but this wasn't a standard relationship.

The door opened and Jack came in with Casey.

"Hi, guys." I did my best to smile as I stood.

Casey came over to me. "Has he been treating you right? If not I'm here for backup."

He made me smile. "He's doing his best."

Andy opened the door. "Jack, we still haven't been able to get in touch with Tony."

"Maybe something came up and he had to go out of town," I offered.

"He'd check in," Andy said.

"Are Sarah and the kids safe?" I asked.

"They're fine. Besides, no one in their right mind want's to mess with my girl."

Jack put his arm around me. "We found out who the man with the bad mustache is. He's Ronald Carter, he's one very lousy individual. Doc, tell them what you told me about the earlier party."

I told them everything. "I've been trying to remember more. I can't think of anything else."

"Carter. That's not good," Andy said. "Not at all. And Maui's death. Was it Sullivan?"

Jack nodded. "I don't like the element this adds to our situation."

"If this is Sullivan and Carter, it just got a whole lot worse," Casey said. "Any idea who Carter is fronting for this time?"

"What's giving me heartburn is that Sullivan has let himself be seen in such public ways." Jack said, "Why the conversation about Maui in front of an outsider? And if it was an ad for Sullivan's services, what was March doing there?"

I figured I'd remind them of what started this chain of events. "What does Lacey have to do with it all?"

"Sullivan found her the same way he found Stanton. It's how he operates," Jack said. "Why mutilate Lacey? That was useless and cruel. Half of it fits his pattern and half doesn't. Stanton and Lacey should both be left to take the fall for our deaths. Not in custody with alibies."

"Would he get injured and go to the emergency room in hopes Stanton would treat him?" I asked.

"He'd cut off a body part if it got him what he wanted," Casey said. "You can bet it wasn't by chance he showed up the night your friend was on duty. His error was not researching him well enough. He should have known you were classmates."

"First things first, we've got to find Tony," Jack said.

"Tony wouldn't let himself be taken without a hell of a fight." Andy paced. "We can't lose another team member." The sadness on his face was heart-wrenching.

The door opened and Tony walked in. "Sorry, I'm late. These old vehicles can be a pain." He stopped. "What?"

"I'm glad you're here," I said. All I'd been able to think about was finding him the way we'd found the Quinn look alike.

"We thought Sullivan had you," Andy scolded. "You forget how to use your cell?"

"My truck died for good this time." Tony shook his head. "Croaked right in the middle of a turn. I got out and damn near got run over. When I got up my cell phone was in worse shape than my truck. I had to hitch the rest of the way here."

A knock on the door drew everyone's attention.

Jack pulled his gun and held it behind him as he answered the door.

"This came special for the lady." A man in his fifties handed Jack a rose.

Chapter Eighteen

Jack closed the door. "Damn it." The flower's stem crushed in his hand an instant before he threw it against the wall.

I stood there stunned.

"He's a dead man," was all Jack said before he left.

All three of them looked at me.

"Ho-lee shit. Casey, watch her," Andy said as he and Tony followed Jack.

I clenched my teeth. "Are you the team babysitter?"

"I like it when you're the baby."

"You're so bad." I rolled my eyes at him. "Did Quinn join you guys about two years ago?"

He gawked at me. "How would you know that?" He smiled and shook his head. "It was when one of our team got married and left. He was the first man we lost to marriage. Might not be the last."

"Ben? I met him when Jack bought the truck. His wife is going to have a baby."

"No kidding? That's great."

"Jack didn't know about the baby either. I thought you guys knew everything."

"When Ben left he wanted out completely. We had to let him go.

It was hard, but he wanted a normal life. Looks like he found it. A kid." He grinned. "Wow."

"Casey, everything that's happened," I paused, "I feel like it's my fault somehow."

"Since you got here, things have been a little—" he sucked in his bottom lip. "Interesting. Your dad and that whole mess. You know he started looking into what ended up being the resort identity theft ring because my grandmother lost everything to that bunch? There were other military and government families targeted. Your dad was a great guy." He paused. "On Christmas Eve you have to know we were trying everything to get to you." He patted my hand. "I'm glad you came back. I for one, enjoy the eye candy."

"You're so funny." I hugged him.

Jack and the others chose that moment to return. "Hey, what goes on here?" Jack did his best to look disapproving.

"I'm making time with your lady." Casey laughed.

"Go find your own woman." Jack smiled at me.

"Let's go." Andy motioned toward the door.

We'd already been through three states and as many hotel and motel rooms. "Where are we going?"

"Back to Boise. Quinn is still feeding Sullivan information. That's why the rose showed up. He'll be expecting us to stay out of Boise," Jack said. "We'll meet you guys at the house."

I counted up all the money we'd wasted getting and leaving hotel rooms in the past day and a half. "I hope the government is reimbursing you for all the rooms we've abandoned," I said as we got in the truck.

"I'm more interested in getting Sullivan." He pulled me next to him.

I like older trucks they don't have that annoying center console. "Has Uncle Stan found out anything?"

"He's still checking into who hired Carter. I'm betting Sullivan is acting on his own. That's not what's bothering me. It's the whole feel of what's happened. I want to know who the second party is. The one who's following Sullivan around, sabotaging his efforts."

"Does this happen very often?"

He glanced over at me.

"This is so complicated. So many others—Lacey and Stanton —involved."

"Usually, no one bothers us. We aren't that important anymore."

Anymore? I had a feeling that wasn't strictly true.

»§«

We arrived first and to my delight we were back at the gingerbread house. "This is a surprise. I thought they knew about this house."

"Sullivan wouldn't expect us to return to Boise, let alone a compromised location. And if there's a leak in Brad's office they're going to expect us to go to the FBI safe house." He pulled into the garage and shut off the engine.

Inside I led Jack to a low back chair. "Sit down." I moved around behind him and began running my fingers over his tight neck muscles. "You're so tense. I can see why your ribs are sore. Take off the vest. I promise I won't shoot you."

He smiled and slipped out of it.

I moved down to his shoulders. I was sure he hadn't slept at all at the motel.

"God, that feels good."

"I took a class when I was an undergrad. It was an easy way to make extra money."

"You're full of surprises."

Something drew Jack's attention to the back door. He got up, pulled his weapon and moved to the kitchen.

When the door opened I was glad to see the team.

"What now?" I asked.

"We're going to plan," Andy said.

Since I didn't have a security clearance, or any idea how to participate, I decided to make dinner. Tony and Casey had gone to the grocery store. As I unpacked the food I felt like I was on that cooking show. What was it? The one where they give the contestants an unrelated assortment of food and tell them to make dinner. It looked like Tony and Casey had picked out their favorite things and hoped it would make a meal. One was hoping for nachos and the other wanted chicken and salad. They were getting chicken tostadas. It's one of the dishes in my limited expertise. I've gotten much better at breakfasts. Dinners, on the other hand, are still a short list.

Finally I called, "Dinner's ready."

Casey looked at the table and said, "Sarge, can we keep her? This looks like a real meal."

They ate every bite.

After dinner, Tony and Casey did the dishes. Andy talked on the phone.

I sat down next to Jack. "Events are all a jumble to me." I had to try to figure it out. We had to get to the discussion about *our* problem. "Who is Ronald Carter and what does it matter what I heard at that party? If they'd left it alone no one would ever know. Now all sorts of people know something happened." I thought for a second. "It was bad enough Don taking me there. What was the point of him making me stay in that room with all those men? And Sullivan, all I saw was him talking to a woman. Again, left alone I'd have dismissed it as a coincidence."

He put his arm around me. "March is worse than you know. Our theory is he put you in that situation, to force you to marry him."

I started to protest.

He put his fingers to my lips. "He's been manipulating people and events for so long he has a God complex. He gets what he wants by twisting a situation around until the person believes they have no other choice. He thought he could convince you the only way you'd be safe was to marry him. He didn't know you at all, did he?" He smiled and touched my face. "Overhearing what you did," He held me tighter, "Ens, these people are beyond ruthless. This is my other world. One I'd hoped you'd never get pulled into."

"Why me? There are a lot of women in D.C. who'd love being at those parties with all the influential people." I brushed my hair back. "Do you think he did it because he knew I was going to break it off with him?"

"Who did you tell?" Jack asked.

"Sophie, my dad, and Uncle Stan of course. Don had to know, I'm not great at hiding how I feel."

Concern lines formed between his eyes. "I know your dad was by phone, but what about Sophie? And Stan?"

"I called Uncle Stan. Sophie and I talked about it several times, but mostly in person."

"Where?"

"We're friends, we talked in different places. We talked about it at coffee and at work." What had Don done?

Jack was concentrating on me. "Your office was bugged."

"I thought so at first, too, but JPL was nutty about corporate espionage. They swept the offices regularly."

"On a schedule, right?"

"Yes, every Monday."

He smiled. "That works to catch the generic bugs. It doesn't work on a more sophisticated set-up. March would know to turn it off on Mondays."

"ie and I searched my office more than once. We didn't find anything."

"You'd be surprised how small they are. Usually they're disguised as something that's supposed to be there."

"Do you have any idea how annoyed I am? How dare he?" I wanted to strangle Don.

"An easier way would be to bug something he gave you." He glanced down at me.

The light came on so bright in my head I blinked. "Damn it. It might have been in anything. Did he have something to do with my research being pulled? I know the pressure came from outside the company." I took a deep angry breath, this time I didn't care how much it hurt. "Jack, my research was significant. It would have made a real difference. I'm not important. It was."

He put his fingers under my chin and lifted my face. "You're important to me." He got up and left me sitting there.

He stopped and turned. "Doc, did he give you your phone?" Jack took a step toward me. "Doesn't matter. He cloned it."

Everyone had focused their attention on me.

"No. If he'd been able to listen in when I was back in D.C., could he still?" I called Sophie all the time. If he was listening, I squeezed my eyes shut at the thought. I'd told her a lot of things I hadn't told anyone else. Ever.

Jack pulled out his phone. "Brad, send over a new phone for Ensley. March knew things he shouldn't." He listened for a few minutes then they hung up.

Chapter Nineteen

"Sullivan is going to be one sorry piece of manure when I get through with him. Do you have any idea how annoyed I am that my family is in danger?" Andy paused. "We don't have any intelligence on Sullivan." He turned his cell over in his hand. "Alpha and Hughes are tracing him separately. We should have something soon. I'm not holding out much hope for Quinn."

"Did Quinn have money problems like Stanton?" I asked.

"He'd never get a security clearance with money troubles," Andy pointed out.

"What about the identity theft ring? Could he have tapped into that and syphoned off money so Quinn didn't have a choice?" I asked.

"Andy," Jack said.

"I'm on it."

I was trying to make the situation fit a pattern. It wasn't working. "There's no logic to any of this. It's all so random. Why involve Lacey? I get Stanton, but not Lacey. He didn't need her. It would have been more effective if he'd sent the flower to my room. By the time you came to pick me up, I'd be dead."

"He wanted me to watch you die knowing there was nothing I could do to save you."

His words sent a shockwave of cold unrelenting terror through me. I wrapped my arms around me as if to ward off the tension I felt building inside of me.

"Involving Stanton was sloppy." Jack paused. "Involving seemingly random people is how he covers his tracks. It's the reason he's been able to operate all this time. The blame always falls on circumstances or someone else."

"Any luck on a new place, Casey?" Jack turned.

"We're looking."

Andy hung up his phone. "Quinn is at the airport. He checked in ten minutes ago for a flight that leaves in half an hour."

"That doesn't make any sense," Casey said. "Why surface now? He knew we'd find out where he was as soon as he popped up. Can we go ask him why real hard, Sarge?"

Jack smiled. "No. We're going to reserve a room in Leavenworth for him. I want some answers. Go get him."

"Jack." I went over to him. "I'm worried about you, I want you to get some rest." The five hours we'd gotten weren't adequate.

"I'm fine."

"You always say that. This time I get to play the doctor. I'm willing to bet you didn't sleep at the motel. Did you?" I pulled him back into the bedroom. "Lay down."

"Ens—"

"Quiet. I made good money giving massages. I bought a new car with my earnings. Pull off your shirt and relax." The bruises over his cracked ribs still lingered. I steeled myself against the memory that threatened to surface. I rubbed his neck, shoulders and back until he fell asleep. I covered him with a quilt and left.

In the kitchen area I sat down, "He's asleep."

"He's worried about you," Andy glanced across the table at me.

"I'm worried about him. He's been through a lot."

"So have you. This situation isn't doing any of us any good"

"I'm not concerned about me with you guys around." I paused. "Andy, you didn't see Jack hanging in that basement." I shivered at the memory. "I, I thought he was dead." As the pain from that night coursed to the surface I picked up the owl shaped salt shaker. She had tiny flowers in her hair—feathers. I turned it around in my hand. "I should have found him sooner." I glanced up.

That operation ran a lot smoother than this one has. My guess is he had a couple of months to get things up for Christmas. That's the way Sullivan operates, and that's what's making this so difficult. It's all off the cuff." He pressed his lips together as if he were holding something back. Finally, he said, "Jack's injuries were all superficial except for his ribs. He said the crazy husband broke those. He is the most physically tough man I've ever known." He smiled.

"I keep thinking about Don." I picked up the gentleman owl pepper shaker, he had on a cowboy hat. "He has all kinds of operatives who could do an exchange. Why Jack?" I remembered something. "I heard Don tell Brad he had special permission to have Jack do the exchange. Why would he need *special permission*? Jack is Special Ops. Right?" I hadn't gotten an answer out of Jack so I thought I'd give it a shot with Andy. I wasn't holding out any hope.

"All I can tell you is March is an ass, but he wouldn't get mixed up in something like abducting Jack or torturing him. Too messy not to mention the reprisals. Let's just say March isn't that stupid. I think he was out here to stop what happened. I can't prove it, but somehow March found out what Sullivan was up to." He gave me a sad smile. "He was here purely, out of self-preservation. And for you." He watched me as I sat there absently playing with the salt and pepper shakers. "My guess is he found out Sullivan was in Spirit Springs."

Like so many times before, I had the man who knew, right in front of me. He had a deeper connection to Jack than the other team members. All I had to do was ask. It hadn't done me any good in the past, but hey, I'm an optimist. Now, I had to work up the nerve. It wasn't that I didn't have the nerve to ask Jack, it was more the pain I'd seen in his eyes that had me backing off. That, and we'd only known each other since October, a little over three months. Mostly it was because I didn't know how to approach it, or what to say. "Andy." I looked down at the owls. I had one in each hand. I set them down on the multi colored Formica tabletop and brushed my hands over the fifties style kitchen table. My neck and shoulders ached with tension. I forced them to relax.

He hadn't taken his eyes off me.

"I don't understand Jack. He'll say something then walk away. It's confusing. It's like he's afraid." I looked up. I was aware that didn't make any sense. Jack was the bravest man I'd ever known.

He glanced at the closed bedroom door. "You have to let him take his time. He'll get there."

I turned the gentleman owl toward me. "I hope so. One minute I'm convinced he cares, then he says something and I'm sure I'm wrong." Jack was proving to be hard on my heart. We had to let things settle down. Then we'd have to face the lie from Christmas. Then what?

Andy thought for a minute. "Sarah told you to be patient. That's the best advice I can give you."

"What secret keeps him so distant? I know my damage." I brushed a few grains of pepper from the owl's cowboy hat.

Andy reached across the table and covered my hand with his. "I shouldn't tell you this, and if you tell him." He smiled. "But you won't. He's had a rough life. He's been kicked so many times." His eyes took on a somber quality. "If it wasn't for the support and love of one woman and her friends I don't know what would have happened to him. I wish you could have known her. She would have liked you." He patted my hand. "He'll tell you when he's able."

I smiled at him. "I can wait." Jack was struggling with demons. A conflict he'd have to battle alone at least until he... what? Trusted me? He had to. I know people think that because you have money everything is all Champaign and roses. They're blinded by the idea that all rich people are evil, or they have a romantic notion that they are charmed. They aren't able to take people as they are and not worry about their bank balance.

Jack wasn't the only one dealing with past loves gone wrong. I took the girl owl and brushed away the dust around the flowers in her hair. I had a couple of my own. This time I had to be sure. Christmas had brought one thing sharply to the forefront, there'd be no one else for me.

"Ensley?"

I drew my attention away from the owl salt and pepper shakers.

Andy's eyes remained intent as he watched me. "When he does I promise it'll be worth it." He went back to his tablet.

I thought about what Andy said. I decided my best course of action was to let life play out. I asked, "May I borrow your phone? I made a promise to Lacey. I need to call my friend Sandy and see what she can do." I positioned the two owls facing each other, but not quite touching.

"Lacey's not worth it, you know." He opened his phone he had it secured by his thumb print like Jack's.

"She's probably going to be in jail for a long time. I think that's enough punishment. She shouldn't have to go through life scarred."

"If we can prove she was a pawn she'll probably get off easy, if she does any time at all."

I sat on the couch and called my friend. "Sandy, how are you?" I asked when she answered.

"Ensley, it's great to hear from you. I wish you were closer, I'd love to get together." The excitement in her voice was contagious.

Sandy had been the anomaly in my life. We'd been good friends in college and she was one of the only people in my life who kept in touch with me. I hadn't done a very good job of it since I moved to Spirit Springs, but when this was over I would. "I'm in Idaho now."

"Great. For how long? Maybe we can meet in San Francisco. No, better yet the wine country up north. Let's make it a long weekend or maybe a whole week. How are you liking the potato state?"

I smiled. "This is an exciting place with equally thrilling people." I looked at the closed bedroom door. "I have a big favor to ask you." I told her about Lacey. "Sandy, I haven't seen her face, but from what I understand it's going to take a lot of work to put it back together. She may lose the sight in one eye."

"I can't believe you made anyone that mad. You've always been so easy going. What happened?"

"It was a misunderstanding. Believe it or not it was all over a man." I glanced up at Andy. He was smiling as he poured over the tablet in front of him. "I know. Unbelievable. Right?" I gave her the short version. The one without Stanton in it.

"That's some misunderstanding. Why help her after that?"

"She has enough to deal with. She maybe going to prison."

"Well, not that she doesn't deserve it. Trying to kill you. You've always been too kind."

"Is there anything you can do for her? Maybe the name of someone here who can help her?"

"I'll make some calls and see what I can do *for you.* I'll let you know what I find out. Keep that weekend in mind. I want you to meet Ryan."

"Ryan? The guy you were dating last summer?"

"Yes." Her excited laugh made me smile. "I'm engaged. The geekiest girl in our class is going to get married in June. He's a lawyer, and he's up for a judgeship. He's brilliant and handsome."

"Congratulations. That's great. When did this happen?" When I'd talked to her in September she'd been excited, but hadn't mentioned an engagement or a wedding.

"Christmas Eve. I'm still pinching myself. You should see my ring."

"We've got to get together before the wedding. If things work out I'll have someone for you to meet too." Again I looked at the door at the end of the hall.

"Tell me who."

"He's the sheriff of Spirit Springs."

"Oh, how romantic. A sheriff in a small town."

"Can you believe this?" Her voice bubbled with excitement. "The two girls who couldn't buy a date in college, with great guys?" We made plans to meet in May. I heard the hospital page in the background. "That's me. Got to go. Bye."

She'd been the one who'd talked me into staying in med school. Another choice, had it gone the other way, I wouldn't be here.

I gave Andy his phone. "Thanks."

"Ensley, I have something for you." He reached in his briefcase and handed me a new in-the-box Kindle. "Compliments of Brad and the FBI. Turns out these things don't appreciate their innards being messed with. Yours got a little ruined."

"Thank you and thank Brad. By the way, did Jack tell you about the battery backup we found in my bag when we left Seattle?"

"He did. If it got in there at the Boise Airport I'm not as

concerned." Andy glanced at the box in my hand. "If it wasn't Boise we're in a shit load of trouble. It means this is a lot bigger than we thought. I've been thinking and talking to Jack, we're checking on who is behind this other group."

"How would we find out who all is involved?"

He slipped his phone in his pocket. "We'll know pretty soon. Stan is working on it."

I swiped my finger across the bottom of the screen of my brand new device.

"Sorry about your lost articles." He motioned to the screen.

"It's okay, that was mostly temper. Everything is backed up to the Kindle cloud. If not, I've got them on my computer at home." I thanked him and downloaded everything again. It took a while to reorganize all the books and articles. When I was done I laid the Kindle on the table. "Jack told me about Dave Sullivan, Jerry's older brother. What does one thing have to do with the other? If this Sullivan wants to kill me so badly, why go after Jack?"

"Jack's right. He always is. If we can nail down the group following Jerry around undoing his efforts, we'll be able to solve this situation." His brow wrinkled with concern. "We'll wait to see what Casey and Tony get from Quinn."

"I wish you and Jack were questioning him. You're good."

He smiled. "We play bad cop, worse cop pretty well."

"And you do it—Andy, you're a genius."

"Can I get that in writing?" He grinned at me. "Just for the record how did I achieve this exalted status?"

"There was another man who wasn't supposed to be there. At the party I mean. He's a cop. Not a policeman, he's FBI. One of the guys who came up with Brad at Halloween. He stayed at the B&B. I didn't think the CIA and FBI played well together. Why was he in Washington with the CIA and Sullivan?"

"One of Brad's men? That's not possible." Andy pulled out his phone. He scowled. "Brad's not answering." A second later Andy left him a message. "We have another situation. Call me." He turned his attention back to me. "When Casey and Tony get back I'm going to Brad's office if he doesn't call back," Andy put his phone on the table.

"Go ahead. I have the .38 we got in Seattle. We'll be fine."

"I'm not leaving Jack." He shook his head. "It's better if we're both here."

"I understand, I'm not trained. You're a good friend." I was still having trouble concentrating. It's the reason I couldn't remember things the way I should. "What agency did this Sullivan work for?"

"He wasn't technically with *one*."

"So, what do an FBI agent, a bunch of CIA operatives, a shadowy man and I have in common?"

"That's the puzzle. You've got to throw Jack in there too." He paused. "I know where you fit in. "

I did too. "I've tried to put things together, but there's a hole. I'm not sure there are only two bad guys."

"It's a Gordian's knot."

The back door opened. Brad came in with his usual briskness. "I see you got your Kindle. Good. I won't have to hear about that anymore."

I held up the device. "Thank you." I hadn't heard anything until the back door opened. "You guys are all part cat."

He laughed. "I'm not as good as I used to be." He looked around. "Where's Trace?"

"He's asleep, and he needs to stay that way for a while."

"Are we Mom now?"

"Oh, bite me. You may be in charge of the team, but I'm a doctor." I stood and faced him. "He hasn't slept since we left Boise." I was convinced he hadn't slept in the motel room. "If he doesn't get some rest he isn't going to heal." Don't get me wrong, I like Brad. He was there for me on Christmas Eve. "I don't want any complications." Still, I wasn't going to let Jack suffer one minute more.

Andy stifled a smile.

Brad rolled his eyes. "Fine, but he's going to want to hear this. So you get to tell him why he didn't."

I heard Andy laugh.

We both turned and said, "What?"

"This is great. I love it when someone stands up to you, and she's so small." He laughed again.

"Buckingham, you're on the edge." Brad leveled his gaze on me. "Go wake him up. *Please.*"

Before I left the back door opened and Tony and Casey came in.

"Where's Quinn?" Andy asked.

"He's really dead this time."

I opened the door to the bedroom. Jack was snoring softly as I knelt next him. "Jack, wakeup." I kissed him on the forehead.

"Doc, I didn't mean to fall asleep."

"I meant for you too. You were exhausted. Do you feel better?"

He sat up. "I do. Thanks."

"Brad's here, Tony and Casey are back. Quinn is dead."

He pulled on his shirt as he walked into the living room. "What happened?"

"They found Quinn dead in a bathroom at the airport," Tony said. "Some little old guy nearly had a heart attack. I can't blame him, it was a nasty mess."

Brad massaged his temples. "That fits. I came to tell you we're up shit creek." For the first time Brad didn't sound like we were all on his last nerve. That sent a wave of concern through me. "Whoever is behind this is good. As in *you* good, Trace."

I looked at Andy. "Ensley remembered something from the Sullivan party. One of your men was there."

"Which Goddamn one?"

Brad has a tendency to get upset. He needs a vacation. "I don't know what his name is, he was with you in October," I said.

Brad shook his head. "How do you remember these things?"

"Because he was the one who helped Jack to the ambulance." I put my hand to my bruised chest.

"What's wrong?" Jack toward me.

"Did this all start then? Was he the one who was supposed to kill you before you got to the hospital?"

Brad frowned. "Trace?"

Jack looked from me to Brad. "It was Blake Bell."

Brad called his office. "Is Bell there? Do not put me on hold. Tell me where he is. Now."

Chapter Twenty

"We've got a more pressing problem," Casey pointed out. "Quinn wasn't just dead, he was tortured. Worse than the guy in the garage. Sullivan cut off more than his fingers. I don't know any who wouldn't break under that. I think it's safe to assume Sullivan knows everything Quinn did."

I felt sick. "How can one human do that to another?"

"Easy, one isn't all human," Andy said.

"I want to know, what was the point?" Jack said more to himself than us. "If Quinn was feeding Sullivan information, why sever the connection? Especially when he went to all that trouble to convince us Quinn was dead. Have we found out who the man in the garage was?"

"The coroner determined he was a homeless man."

"That brings up the question; why the charade?" Jack shook his head. "Brad, any ideas?"

"That was the other reason I came over. We found the connection between Quinn and the Markus operation. We've traced all of the names we got off Ralph's computer. Most of them were military, U.S. Marshalls, CIA, FBI and ATF and their families. They were trying to pressure them into cooperating. Quinn's mother was on that list. It took a while to find her, she remarried recently."

"U.S. Marshalls?" Casey said. "Hold on." He pulled out his phone. "Hey, Grams. In the past few months, has anyone approached asking you about me? No. Anything." He smiled. "No. I don't think that counts. I'll call you in a couple of days." He grinned. "Nothing. Unless you count a cold call about roofing."

"Why? It seems like a lot of trouble to go to for a few stolen identities," I said.

"Darlin', if you're going to hang around you need to think bigger. They weren't after a few bank accounts, they wanted classified information. Spending a million for land, some broken down equipment, and a few computers would be pocket change compared to what foreign countries would pay for the information. Your dad had only scratched the surface. Lucky for us, he was stubborn."

"But why in Spirit Springs?" I needed answers.

"Because they were stupid," Brad said. "They were so intent on the money, they didn't look into the town the way they should have. They weren't all idiots, they got us a few times."

Tony stepped in. "They thought they were moving into a dying small town in the middle of nowhere. They didn't know whose town they'd moved into."

"With Quinn dead, this place isn't safe," Brad faced Jack. "You've got to move. I know what you're going to say, Trace. I will not let this team be destroyed. You four have been the last ditch for too many people, and I, for one, am not letting this pile of excrement ruin that."

I could put those pieces together. They were still an active team. They were too practiced, too skilled, and too linked to a world few people knew existed. Plus, they had their very own safe house. These men were a lot more than just a team that left the Army. I wasn't a hundred percent sure they'd left the service. I looked at them with a new respect. The couple hundred questions rattling around in my head would have to wait for answers.

Before Jack asked, I went to the bedroom and got our things. I returned and set our bags by the couch.

"Quinn knew all of our safe houses. I'm not going to be happy if we can't use this place again," Tony said. "Reminds me of my grandmother's."

"Ideas, Brad?" Jack looked at him.

"Like I said we're up shit creek. Casey, you guys have any place?"

He was already on his cell. "No. Not on the phone. Meet us," He glanced at Brad. "Where do you want to meet my other boss?"

"Marty's Café. Casey, you, Andy, and Tony go together. We don't need a parade across town."

Casey shook his head. "We can't leave our vehicles here. What if we need them?"

"Take them." Jack grabbed our bags.

I looked out the rear window as the garage door slipped down.

I needed to destress. I couldn't think straight. Running was out. Jack's ribs and my chest wouldn't allow that much activity. I felt my breathing increase. I closed my eyes and concentrated on the memory of the ocean. In my mind we stood on the beach again watching the waves as they crashed ashore then receded. I smelled the salt water and heard the gulls above. On the horizon the sun slipped toward the water in a glow of gold. I felt Jack's arms around me. The truck slowed, turned and stopped.

"Doc, are you okay?"

I opened my eyes. "I needed to refill my glass."

"Your glass?" He looked concerned as he tilted my head back.

"I'm not stoned. Those drugs don't cause flashbacks." I smiled up at him. "It's going to sound silly."

"Try me."

I repressed a nervous laugh. I'd only said it out loud to Sophie. "Here goes. In my head I have a glass of optimism. I try to keep it full. It's broken a couple of times in the past few months. On Christmas Eve the glass shattered. Does that make sense?" Of course, it didn't. I figured I'd gone this far I might as well spill my guts. "I need a new glass. One that's—"

He was smiling at me.

"I know, I'm not very rational."

"When this is all over we'll get you a new glass."

"You don't think I'm crazy?"

"Oh, I know you are. You came back to me."

Someone knocked on the window. "You two going to sit out here or are you coming inside?" Brad hollered.

"I think he needs to have his blood pressure checked," I said as I slid from the seat.

"It's just his style," Jack said as we walked to the door.

The country style café was a long squatty building. If the setting were a little different, and the vehicles older, this would have been a truck stop from a fifties movie. White stucco walls and a red tile roof and gravel parking lot. The billboard high above read Marty's Country Café. At one time it must have been outside the city limits. No longer. There was a strip mall across the street, a motorcycle dealership next to the pawn shop on one side and a horse pasture on the other.

Inside, it had an old time feel to it. Not retro. More like the owner hadn't updated, ever. Booths lined both sides of the dining room. Gray strips of duct tape kept the foam from spilling out through splits in the fake leather seats. Jack's head was only a few inches from the low ceiling.

The team had chosen one of the tables in the back. We sat down and I picked up the menu. The knots in my stomach made everything on it appear unappetizing. I laid it down.

Tony and Casey were eating cherry pie, Andy and Brad were drinking coffee.

The waitress walked up as we sat down. "Do you know what you want, or do you need a minute?" She pulled a pencil from her apron.

"We need a minute," Jack told her. When she left he added, "Who's coming?"

"A woman in her late forties," Casey said.

"I don't like waiting around." Brad glanced at the emergency exit. "With all these vehicles we look like a traveling circus."

"There she is." Casey got up and greeted a woman at the door. He nodded. We watched as they talked.

Jack signaled the waitress and asked for the check.

The woman at the door gave Casey an envelope. She left and he walked back to the table. He handed the info to Jack. "Looks like we have a brand new place. Nothing in it yet, so we'll be sleeping on the floor."

Jack opened the envelope. "This will work. Good job, Casey," .

We left the small café. Tony and Casey each had a pie.

Jack turned back down State Street toward town. A few minutes later we slowed. "What the hell?" Jack said.

"Doc, get down as best you can." Jack moved over.

"What's wrong?" I scrunched down on the floor.

"There's an accident blocking the street," he said. "I don't like this. What are the odds?"

"Of an accident at rush hour?" I was halfway to the floor. "I'd say they were pretty good."

"Down." Jack motioned. "I don't like the fact that we've got to go through the North End with all the side streets and stop signs." He flipped on the blinker.

I wished we had his other truck. The floor in the backseat was more comfortable. "Jack, we can't go up there without your aid bag."

He smiled. "We'll get it. With any luck we won't need it."

We seemed to stop every ten seconds. "There's no way Sullivan knows which route we'd be taking, or that we'd be here at all. He couldn't know there'd be an accident," I pointed out.

"Unless he caused it," Jack stopped again.

"Is he that good?" This guy was beyond belief.

"I've seen him implement more complicated tactics. I doubt he was behind this. Too many side streets. I'm not taking any chances."

To avoid the clogged traffic, we turned down a side street, along with twenty other resourceful drivers. Jack pulled to a stop behind a line of cars at a stop sign.

The new safe house sat up in the foothills. We left the grid of the North End section of Boise and drove up the gently curved street to a secluded house at the end of a cul-de-sac. In the xeriscape front yard, a for sale sign rested against a large rock next to the driveway. I knew why it was still for sale. It was beyond ugly. The plants in the yard were all dead. There were no trees, only rocks and gravel giving the building an over baked appearance. It should have been hidden in the desert not perched in the foothills of Boise. There weren't many windows on the west side of the large adobe looking structure. As we pulled into the driveway Andy came around the side of the house. Jack punched the code into the box by the garage door. It slid up exposing another empty garage.

I was glad it was free of dead bodies.

When we were inside, Andy's phone rang. "Got it. Thanks." He hung up. "Jack, we have a new problem. Sullivan gave his credit cards and his cell phone to a bunch of homeless people. Charges have popped up all over the city. We don't have any way to trace him."

Chapter Twenty-One

I set our things on the floor of the empty living room. The inside looked as foreign to the area as the outside. I'm not sure where it would have looked at home. The red clay floor tiles were uneven and the walls were finished to resemble stucco. A large fireplace occupied most of the wall facing the street. The area looked more like a patio than a living room. It even had the smell of damp earth.

I decided to wander through the house while the men talked on their phones. Besides, it was most likely classified. Leaving would save everyone from the awkward moment when they asked me to step out of the room.

From the outside the house gave the illusion of being undersized. Inside the opposite was true. What made the place look small was the berm that covered the north half of the house. The courtyard in back was carved into the hillside and the rooms lined up around the terraced area. None of the rooms had square corners making it impossible to arrange furniture coherently. And anything you put in them would wobble on the uneven floor tiles.

The windows on the patio side were large with a view up the treeless foothills to the forested mountains to the east. "I bet this is pretty in the morning," I said out loud.

"I imagine it is." Jack stood in the doorway.

"I'm going to put a bell on you. One of these day's I'm going to have a heart attack."

"I'll try. How are you holding up?"

I rested my back against the cool curved wall. "I'll be fine. I'm concerned about Jane. She's probably wondering if I left her again. Is there any way I can call her?"

"It's been taken care of."

Of course, it had. "How long are we staying here?"

"We have a lead. If things work out we'll be on our way home tomorrow." There was an *I-hope* quality to his words.

"When you say things like that it makes me think you can see into the future."

"No. But I have a plan."

I walked over, put my arms around him, and laid my head on his chest. "Life around you is unpredictable."

"I know. I didn't plan it this way."

"It isn't your fault. Crazy people are everywhere. Between the two of us, we've accumulated more than our fair share of the unstable. It'll take some getting used to." I stretched up and kissed him. "That makes it all worthwhile."

He smiled at me. "You're—"

"Jack," Andy called. "We have a problem." Andy stood in the doorway. "There's been an accident."

Jack stepped into the hall. "Damn it."

We entered the living room. "What kind of an accident?"

"Casey and Tony were hit by an SUV as they were leaving the grocery store. They're okay, but Casey's car is totaled. Tony has a broken ankle and Casey needs a ride."

"It wasn't an accident, was it?" I asked, not needing an answer.

"Brad." Jack was on the phone. "Could this be Carter? Sullivan isn't after the team. – Good." He hung up. "It was an accident. A kid took the corner too fast, blew a front tire and rolled into them. The kids in the car are shaken and bruised, but fine."

Jack and Andy began talking about defense.

I walked out of the living room and up the stairs to a round bedroom. I stood in an empty space, in a vacant house, wearing a Kevlar vest, with a team of men downstairs who were stunningly skilled. They were ready to protect me from a crazed man. One I'd only seen a couple of times last fall. "Wow." I slumped against the wall. I didn't like being the damsel in distress.

Back in D.C., Cole, my brother, insisted I take Kenpo lessons. I'd have to find a place in Spirit Springs or Mullen to begin again. I remembered Jack telling me the only gym in town was at his house. I wondered if he had free weights. I'd didn't like the machines at the gym.

"Doc, you okay?" He joined me by the wall.

"Do you have free weights?"

He smiled. "Not on me, but at home, yes. Why?"

"I've decided I'm little better than useless. When we get back, I'm going to start lifting weights, and begin Kenpo training again."

"What brought all this on?"

"I want to be more than the girl in the Kevlar vest." I shook my head. "That sounds like a bad movie."

He smiled. "I can arrange to have you go through Ranger School if you like."

"First, I'd never make it. Those guys are formidable. Second, I don't take orders very well."

"I've noticed."

"What if something happens to you again? I'd be helpless."

"You knocked that woman out at Christmas without any trouble."

"I didn't do so well against her husband. If she hadn't pulled me away from her him," an involuntary shiver over took me at the memory of the sleazy degenerate.

"I don't want you getting hurt."

"So I'm supposed to stay home and wait. Should I bake cookies too?"

"I can't see that happening." He smiled at me.

"If one thing had changed at Christmas, we'd both be dead. You almost were."

"I wasn't injured that badly. It was mostly hypothermia and dehydration, the broken ribs didn't help. Besides, you handled yourself just fine. When this is over, there isn't anyone else out there who hates me this much. Well, not anyone who'll go to all this trouble. You won't have to deal with any more places like this one." He indicated the empty room. "No more safe houses, and no more living out of a duffle bag and an old suitcase."

He'd stopped short of saying I wouldn't need a Kevlar vest. I figured it would be a part of my wardrobe from now on. I made a mental note to get some larger tops.

»§«

Half an hour later, Andy and Casey came through the back door.

"I'm going to miss that pile of rust," Casey set a grocery bag on the counter. "That." He pointed at the sack. "Is what I was able to rescue from the folds of my busted ass car."

"You'll find another one. Casey, will you stay with the Doc? Andy and I have an errand to run."

"Of course." He winked at me.

Through one of the slit windows I watched them drive away. "What makes a man become so brutal?"

"What man?" Casey asked.

"Jerry Sullivan. His brother, Dave, was Jack's best friend. What happened to Jerry?" I sat down on the floor next to Casey.

He thought for a second. "For men like Jerry it begins with the thrill of the hunt. When the excitement fades, it becomes desire for the kill. They become so proficient they crave inflicting pain. When Dave was killed Jerry was a wide-eyed kid, out to save the world from evil. Losing Dave broke him and he went into that dark place no one comes out of the same. It changed him, he became a psychopath."

I rested my head against the wall and studied the ceiling. Jack said he and Dave had set out to save the world. "What happened to Jerry to make him become a vicious killer?

"Losing Dave hit us all hard." Casey went on, "He wasn't only Jerry's brother, he was his idol. It was a bad business all around. It ripped Jack up to the point" he hesitated, "like I said, we nearly lost him. I don't know how he did it, how he was able to pull out, but he had something to hold on to, something that kept him going. I for one, am glad he did. I don't want to have to go to all the trouble of breaking in a new boss "

"Why is this coming back after all these years?"

"You know you ask the hard questions." He looked away. "And I'm not sure I want to tell you."

"I know Jack thinks I'm the catalyst, but it can't be me. Can it?" I needed him to say it wasn't me.

He leaned forward. "I have my ideas, but that's all they are. Ideas." He watched me as if he were trying to make a decision. Finally, he shook his head.

Once these guys make up their minds there's no point in pressing them. "Tell me about this Ronald Carter. When I saw him, he had an air of profound superiority about him. That's the reason I remembered him from the earlier party."

"Our Mr. Carter is an intrigue. He has a lot of—not power exactly, more influence. Which can be the same thing if you know how to use it, and your hold is over the right people. He's the one who hires the right personnel, and coordinates the mission. Whoever hires him sits back and watches in anonymity." He let out a sigh. "I'd like to know who is pulling Carter's strings this time. Believe it or not, that's more troubling, because it's someone with as much money as they have hate." Casey's phone rang. "Hello—I don't like the idea." Casey looked at me. "Are you sure that's what he wants?—No, we're not leaving.—I understand—yes, we'll be there."

"What's going on?" I asked as Casey drew his gun and opened the garage door. Andy's car sat alone in the space.

"It looks like someone got Sullivan." We got in the car and he backed out of the garage. "A traffic accident." He drove down the hill.

"Another one?"

"I don't like this." He braked for a stop sign. "It's not like Jack."

I thought about that for a minute. "Isn't it a little too convenient, for it to all end with a traffic accident?"

"Stranger things have happened."

I sat back. There was something too easy about it. "Why are we going?"

His handsome black face twisted into a frown. "This wouldn't be my first choice, but that was Brad's office, and they want us at the accident scene. Maybe they want you to ID him as the man you saw at the party." He sucked in his bottom lip. "That doesn't track, we all know what Sullivan looks like." He pulled to the side of the road. "If he wants you to identify him we could do that at the coroner's office." He dug out his phone. For a long minute he stared at the device in his hand. Then he placed a call. "Jack's not answering." He hit end and slipped the cell back in his pocket. "Nope. Not going."

"What's wrong?"

"If it were me, and it is, and I had to answer to Jack if anything happened to you," he tilted his head and gave a grin, "let's just say I'm smart enough not to dance that dance."

"I don't understand. If it was Brad's office why aren't we going?"

"Because, it's a trap." He glanced in the rearview mirror then checked the street both ways.

"A trap?" An overwhelming sense of doom filled me. "Would Sullivan kill someone to get to me?"

Casey didn't answer. He'd dialed Jack's number again.

I took hold of his arm. "Would he?" I needed him to tell me I was wrong.

"Yes."

"Oh." I let my hand fall.

"He'd have to go through all of us first, and trust me he'd never make it through Jack. Broken ribs or not."

Chapter Twenty-Two

"I'm not chancing hanging around out here." He dialed Jack again. This time he got through. "Sarge, do you want us at the crash scene?—Yeah, that's why I'm calling." Casey pulled into the garage. "Got it. We have another problem, someone in Brad's office has our code word. Where do you want us?—What's it look like up there? Is it Sullivan?—Out." He turned the car around and headed back to the ugly house.

"Was it Sullivan?" I asked.

"No. It was his rental car, but the body wasn't his. Jack said he'd meet us here."

"Every time Sullivan sets up a person to take the blame, someone takes out the pawn. Is it Carter? And if it is, why?"

"That's an interesting question." He was silent as the door slid shut behind us. Then he said, "I think the big question here is why? If someone let Sullivan loose to do his worst. There'd be nothing but a body count, and a couple of innocents to take the blame. So who is our second party?" He pushed the opener again and backed out of the garage. turned away from the safe house. "Right now we're going to drive around aimlessly for half an hour. Jack should be back by then."

For most of the half hour we were both silent. I struggled to put things in order. Casey concentrated on the cars around us.

»§«

Jack met us in the garage. Casey went inside and I went to Jack.

"I'm going to ask you to do something." He held up his hand as I started to protest. "No. I'm not asking you to leave. It doesn't do any good." He traced my cheek with his thumb. "I want you with me."

This time the words came out easier. I smiled. We *were* making progress.

Andy opened the garage door and called, "The house is clear."

Jack and I walked inside. "If you say no I'll understand. I won't pressure you." He paused. "It's not going to be easy." Another hesitation. "I need you to call March." Before I could protest, he went on, "He isn't going to tell me anything. I want to know why he took you to that party."

I didn't hold out hope he'd tell me either. Besides, the last thing I wanted was to talk to Don. I'd spent my two weeks in D.C. avoiding him and his calls. "I don't know if he'll tell me anything, or if he'll even take my call, but I'll do it."

"I think if he hears what's happened, he'll tell you."

He had a lot more faith than I did. We stood in the baron living room. Jack asked, "Do you still have the burner phone Brad gave you?"

I pulled it out of my bag. "It may not be charged." I pushed the button on the bottom and the screen flashed on. "It is."

Jack held his phone up to mine. After he pushed some buttons he said, "I'll be able to hear what he says."

I could do this. I had to. I listened to the phone ring. Out of the corner of my eye I saw Andy and Casey watching us.

"Who is this?" Don snapped.

"Don, it's—"

"Ensley. I heard about what happened after the investors' party. Are you okay?"

Shaking my head I said, "If standing in the middle of a vacant house in a Kevlar vest can be classified as *being all right*. I am. Which brings me to the reason for the call." No. Forgiving him for Christmas Eve was centuries away. Shoving the anger away I continued, "I have questions I need answers to." I held my breath.

"What do you need to know?" He sounded concerned.

That surprised me. "Why did you take me to Sullivan's party in October?"

"I wanted to ask you to marry me. I still have your ring."

I gripped the phone harder. "But why take me to that party with those people? Why did you want me in the room with Carter and Sullivan? And why were you there at all?"

Silence.

"Yes, Don. I know about them. They've both been trying to kill me. They've almost succeeded twice. One of them shot me three times. The only reason I'm alive is because I had on a Kevlar vest."

"Ensley, I can't tell you. If you'll come home, I'll keep you safe. They won't bother you if you're with me."

That last part didn't sound like the man who upgraded our room in Seattle to be an ass. I moved to Jack. He put his arm around me. "Please, tell me why that party, that night, with those men?"

More silence. Then he said, "I was under orders."

I looked up at Jack. The muscles in his jaw were tight.

"Who ordered you to put me in this kind of danger?" This didn't make sense. "And even if they did, why would you?"

"I'll say this much, they aren't supposed to be after you. I can't tell you any more. This isn't a secure line and I shouldn't have said this much." He paused. "Let Trace know he can stop all this, and save you. All he has to do is resign."

"No. I will not let that happen." I held on to Jack and quoted Brad. "'He's been the last best hope for too many people.' I will not be the reason that ends." The deep breath I took hurt on two levels. The bruise on my chest sent sharp pain radiating through me. It was nothing compared to the agony that screamed through my soul. I would not be the reason Jack gave up what he did. My breath now came in labored gasps. I had only one question left. "Who ordered you to take me?"

"I can't tell you that. If Trace cares for you, he'll send you back to me."

Jack's hand tightened on my shoulder.

"Don, no one sends me anywhere I don't want to go. If you knew me, really knew me, you'd know that. Thank you for what little information you gave me, us. If I end up dead, know that you're the one who could have saved me." I hung up and stared at the device in my hand as I began to tremble.

No one said anything.

As always, when I ended a conversation with Don, I questioned my sanity. I looked up at Jack.

He was shaking his head.

"Am I stupid? Why didn't I see him for what he was? He'd rather let me die than let me go. I've never been this, this... "

"Loved?"

"He doesn't love me. If he did, he'd," I stopped.

"He'd do what I'm doing." He left me and walked out of the house.

I stood there, openmouthed. He'd done it again. Said something significant, then simply walked away. I didn't understand. I looked at Andy and Casey. Their attention was focused on the back door.

Had Jack just said what I thought he said? Did he love me? My heart pounded so hard, the bruise on my chest ached. I knew I loved him, no matter what I'd said to Jane. There'd been no fooling Sophie or Mama in D.C. they knew the truth. I figured Jane did too. I even knew the moment it had happened. It wasn't logical and it sure wasn't how I imagined it would be.

What do you do when one of the most important things in your life happens? I figured standing there wasn't it. Going after Jack wasn't it either. I chose to watch Andy walk toward me.

I'm not certain what I expected him to say, it wasn't what he came out with. "Do you have your vest on?"

"Yes." He already knew that.

"Good. Keep away from the windows." He scanned the room. "Stay by the fireplace. You'll be out of the line of sight." He led me to the hearth. "The stone will stop any bullets coming from the street side." He walked back to the kitchen. "Casey."

"I'm watching," he said as Andy closed the back door.

Casey sat down beside me on the hearth. "You know if they keep leaving us like this we're going to have to start going steady." He winked at me.

"I," there were words out there. I wasn't able to pick out the right ones.

"Yup. Looks like you're permanent."

"I," words still remained beyond my reach.

He glanced at the closed back door. "I've seen Jack make split second decisions, ones that saved all our lives. He's struggled through a lot growing up. I know people think that if you have money you don't have problems. We both know that's not true. This is different." Another glance at the back door. "He'll get this worked out, too."

"I can wait." I'd told Andy the same thing. Had there been someone in Jack's past who'd hurt him so deeply he wasn't able to trust a woman? I had to change the subject. "Are you okay?"

He tipped his head to one side.

"The car accident."

"I've got a couple of bruises, but nothing like those kids." He gave me a half grin. "They'll be okay, until they have to face their parents."

"I can imagine. Is Tony okay, besides the ankle?"

"He's stronger than he looks. He'd be here if it weren't for that boot on his foot."

"Were you able to rescue any of the groceries?" I was babbling. I knew he had.

"I did. Some of them are forever embedded in the folds of the Bat Cruiser."

"Bat Cruiser?" I smiled. "Casey, you're so funny."

"Hey, it's big, black and wide. Or, it was. It looked like the Batmobile without the fins."

The back door opened and Jack and Andy walked in.

"Doc, we need to talk."

Chapter Twenty-Three

Jack threaded his fingers through mine and guided me upstairs.

My brain churned in confusion. I had no idea what he was going to say. Half of me was afraid he was going to say I'd misunderstood him. The other half was afraid he'd say I hadn't. It didn't make any sense, but what had lately?

He stood watching the sunlight crawl across the uneven floor. "I know I'm not doing this right. I'm not used to having a woman—" He rubbed the back of his neck. "This isn't the place or the time. We need to concentrate on getting home alive." He kissed me and left.

The kiss was *that kiss*. His goodnight kiss. The one that kept me tossing and turning.

Why had he brought me up here for those few words? He could have said them in front of everyone. I smiled. It was the kiss.

Now I had time to worry. I'm a world class worrier. My imagination has a tendency to spur on the process. I can envision all sorts of things. Crazy things. Things that aren't remotely possible.

He was right. It was more important to survive this and make it home. I sat down in the center of the floor. I needed time to think. I thought about my call to Don, and the party. I remembered Carter. He hadn't wanted me in that room. So he hadn't been the one who ordered Don to take me. The real question was, who had? I hadn't gotten the answer to who'd directed him to take me into that room. Damn it.

Was it someone in the CIA?

Oh, God.

I vaulted to my feet.

My brother. "Cole," his name came out in a gasp as I felt the terror surge through me.

Dread filled every cell in my body as I stumbled down the stairs.

Don had control over Cole. Was he safe? Had Don sent him on a suicide mission?

I missed the last tread and staggered into the living room.

Jack was on the phone. "Stan, we've got to find out who ordered March to take Doc to that party." He looked up at the sound of my faltering steps. "I know. I will." He hung up.

I nearly collided with Jack as I said, "Cole." I pulled out my phone. "I'm calling that P.O.S." I had Don's number punched in before anyone could stop me.

Jack pushed a button on his cell.

"Hello, Ensley."

"I need you to tell me where Cole is." My voice faltered.

"He's on assignment."

"Where? I need to know he's okay. Please." I heard myself begging. The last time I'd pleaded, it had been when Jack was missing and it was to the same man.

"All you have to do is come back here and I'll keep you and Cole safe."

"Extortion? Oh, hell no." I have a limited number of irrational switches in my brain. It's pretty much a bad idea to flip most of them. Big red pissed off switch flipped. My ugly temper monster burst through the door I keep her locked behind and raged out. "Don, you owe me, and you know why."

"You know that was—Is Trace listening to this?"

"I'm only going to say this once. You will tell me where my brother is and swear to me he's safe. If you don't, and anything happens to him, your life won't be worth," I grabbed for a thread of self-control and missed. "You mess with mine and you will pay for it. Got it? Good. Now, where is Cole?"

Silence.

I'd gone way, way too far. Vaguely, I wondered if his phone was tapped and if there was a law against threatening a CIA POS."

The silence spread through the phone connection and into the room around me.

Jack took my cell and hung it up. Into his he said, "March, this is a secure line. I've never seen anyone this mad." It always amazed me how he was able to stay so calm. "Even you have to understand he's all the family she has left." He paused. "You know I have a higher security clearance than you do, so tell me where he is." It was Jack's turn to listen. "Thanks." He hung up. He pursed his lips. "Might not be a good idea to call him again for a while." He pressed a contact on his phone. "I don't trust March, I'm double checking his story."

When he hung up I said, "I have to know, is Cole okay?"

Jack wiped a tear from my cheek. "He's safe and he's going to stay that way."

"Thank you. He said if I went back there, he'd keep Cole and me safe. He wouldn't do anything to put Cole in danger, would he?" I put my arms around him.

"No."

"You're not going to tell me where Cole is, are you?"

"No."

It didn't matter. If Jack said he was safe that was all I needed.

"Doc, threatening a man like March can backfire on you."

"I don't care."

"You might someday."

I thought about that for a minute. He was right. What if Christmas Eve happened again? "I have Uncle Stan, Brad, and the guys."

He smoothed my hair back. The sadness on his face had me regretting what I'd done. "On Christmas Eve, they couldn't get to you. I know you would have found me on your own. What if you need him in the future? Really needed his help? It's never wise to make enemies."

"I don't have your ability to remain calm. No matter how hard I try, I'm not always rational."

"Your crazy button gets pushed." He smiled. "You're strong. March is going to be a problem for us for a long time." Then he asked, "What does he owe you?"

"It doesn't matter."

"It does to me. Tell me."

"I can't." There was too much humiliation attached to it. I lead him back upstairs. When I was sure no one could hear us I told him all about Beth, my department head, and Don's affair and his lame excuse for his actions. "I don't know how many others there were. He made me feel inadequate."

Silence.

Finally, he said, "I'm sorry." We stood in the center of another lull. The quiet pressing in around us. "You'll never have to worry about that again." He stopped short of asking me again if we could survive Don. He had to know we could. If ... if only it wasn't for the lie.

»§«

As the three men stood in the kitchen, Jack's phone rang. "Trace. What—No. I'm not leaving Ensley here alone.—I don't like it.—No, I understand. We'll be there." He walked over to where I was reading and knelt beside me. "Doc, I've got to leave."

"I'll be fine. No one knows we're here and as long as they don't drive a truck through the wall, they won't be able to get in."

"They're sending an agent. He'll be here in fifteen minutes." His manner turned from somber to grave. "I'm leaving you with the truck." He took out his keys and put them in my hand. "I don't want you here without a way to escape." That all too familiar worry line formed between his eyes as his mouth tightened. "I've been given orders. Damn it. Andy, you and Casey go. I'll catch up."

"You can't do that," Andy said. "I'll wait."

"You guys argue long enough and the agent will be here. Don't worry. I can manage for a few minutes. I have the .38."

Jack didn't move. "If this works out, we'll be on our way home in the morning." He kissed me, then pulled out his phone. "I want you on the phone with me until the agent gets here."

I took out mine. A minute later, I heard the garage door open and shut. Almost immediately, the back door opened and Jack walked back in. "To hell with it. They can fire me. I'm not leaving you."

I was pretty certain they weren't going to fire him, whoever *they* were. I wasn't sure what they'd fire him from or that they even could.

When my guard arrived, it was the same man from the hall at the Federal Building before we left for Seattle.

"Kevin Clark, Ensley Markus. Keep her safe. Understand?"

"Yes, sir." He smiled.

Jack turned to me. "You'll be fine."

"I don't know where you're going or what you're going to do, just promise me you'll be careful."

"I will."

Again, I heard the garage door open and close.

"I'm going to check outside," Kevin said. "It shouldn't take more than a few minutes."

"Thanks."

If I had time to myself, I could take a quick shower. As I entered the bathroom I realized I had two problems. No towel and no soap. The soap was in my bag. The towel would be tricky. I was going to have to bring one with me next time. I headed for the kitchen. Surely, those guys had bought paper towels or napkins. I hoped they'd bought two of whatever.

I heard a crash in the garage. Had something happened to Kevin Clark?

I took out my .38 and pulled open the door, and stepped onto the concrete floor. Kevin stood by the open garage door. "Kevin?"

I felt a sharp sting in my neck.

Chapter Twenty-Four

I threw up.

In all the TV shows and movies, they show the drugged person waking up with a slight headache or with no side effects at all. Ah, if that were only true. I have a list of things I truly and completely hate. Throwing up is one full notch above crying. I've been doing a lot of crying lately. Usually about Jack. So much for being the stoic girl who keeps her feelings to herself.

I threw up again as my head shrieked with pain. To make matters worse, my hands were secured behind my back. I wiped my mouth on my shoulder. I rolled over and bumped into something. No, someone.

I knew that raven hair. "Sarah?" She didn't move. She lay crumpled on the floor next to me. I nudged her as I scanned our surroundings.

"No. Please. Not another basement." I fought against the pain in my head and the memory of Christmas Eve.

I opened my eyes. A crack ran across the stained concrete floor to a rusty drain. At least, this basement was dry and didn't smell like rot and blood.

Sarah groaned. I turned back to her. She was still unconscious.

I struggled to sit up. My stomach threatened a full scale revolt as my head pounded. I took a deep breath, which caused my chest to hurt. "Great." My vest was gone. So was my blazer and my over-the-vest t-shirt. At least I still had on the undershirt. I saw my blazer and t-shirt in a pile by the stairs.

Whoever was after us now had the advantage.

I managed to avoid the mess I'd made on the floor as I jostled my unconscious companion. "Sarah. Sarah. Wake up."

She moaned. A rivulet of blood had dried on the side of her face. Jack told me she was Mossad. She'd know how to get us free. The problem was, if they were able to take her I didn't stand a chance.

A shudder rushed through me. This could not be happening.

"Focus." I took in the area again. A few boxes, the kind you keep office records in, were stacked in one corner. To one side sat a discarded printer and a broken desk chair. There had to be a commercial enterprise above us. Maybe they didn't know their place of business was being used as a prison. If I made enough noise, they'd hear me.

I started yelling. The more I yelled, the more my head hurt, and the more I wanted to throw up. It wasn't long before the door at the top of the stairs opened. Either we'd be saved or I'd find out who was holding us.

The man who walked down the steps wasn't from a business. He wore jeans and a Kevlar vest. It wasn't Sullivan. First, I knew what he looked like, and second, if it had been him, I'd be dead on the garage floor where Jack would find me.

That meant this was Carter's man, and he wanted Jack dead. This guy was trying to draw out Jack.

I watched the man walk toward us. He was tall and lean with a large weapon in a shoulder holster. His dark hair was pulled back in a ponytail, accentuating the long scar running down his neck. It couldn't have missed his jugular by more than a few millimeters.

"Will you shut up? No one's going to hear you except me, and you're pissing me off. Not a great idea."

I had to convince him to untie me so I could help Sarah. That would give us a chance to escape. "I need to help Sarah. She's bleeding.

Untie me, please." I added the please because I have good manners. Much better than his. I'd never tie anyone up and throw them in a basement.

"Who cares? All I have to do is keep you alive for the next group. Then, you won't be my problem." He went back upstairs.

Next group? The good news was, he was going to keep us alive. Then what? I had to get my hands free. "Sarah, can you hear me?"

She moved her head.

"Sarah, wake up. We need to get out of here." I hoped she didn't have a concussion. I looked around. The only one who'd been throwing up was me. That maybe good news. If she'd been unconscious for a while, it wasn't. I bumped her with my shoulder. "Sarah, wake up. We're in trouble."

"Andy? What?"

"It's Ensley. Sarah, wake up."

She blinked at me, then looked around. "What the hell? Where are we?"

"Does your head hurt?"

"Yes."

"Do you know where we are?"

"No. Do you?"

Good. No confusion and her speech wasn't slurred. "What happened to you?"

She struggled against her bindings. "I got a call about Daniel falling at daycare. I went to get in the car and bang." She brushed her face against her sleeve. Then she saw the blood on her shirt. "Damn it."

"Any ideas what to do next?"

"Let's get these ties off first. Turn around." She fought with my bindings. "You throw up?"

"Yeah. I was drugged. Again."

"I hate when that happens."

Finally one of the plastic ties came loose.

"Did you see anyone before you passed out?" she asked.

"Only the FBI agent who was supposed to be guarding me. He

stood there, watching as someone stuck a needle in my neck. Which, by the way, hurts." I rubbed the sore spot at the base of my neck. "I tried to attract attention. All I got was an annoyed man with a big weapon," freeing her hands. "Ponytail."

She rubbed her wrists. "Ponytail?"

"He didn't introduce himself and he had a ponytail. So, Ponytail." I scooted away from the mess on the floor. "He wasn't very sympathetic."

"I'd like to know who we're dealing with." Sarah rubbed her wrists. "We've got to get out of here before our men come after us." She smiled. "That won't end well for this guy. Andy has a temper."

"I've seen Jack come close to getting mad twice. Once, when they blew up his truck. At the time, that was more important to him than the bullet in his shoulder." I rolled my eyes. "Boys and their toys. The maddest I've seen him was when he found out I had Don's CIA code."

"Jack's a force to be reckoned with when he's mad. Wait," She blinked and her eyes got wide. "Don March's security code? Do not say that out loud again. Shit. If the CIA finds out … What was he thinking?"

"Jack asked him why he'd given his code in front of me when he called him."

"This keeps spiraling into a dark ugly hole." Sarah glanced at the steps.

"I think I know who the people upstairs are. I don't understand why," I said as I followed her gaze.

"Who are they?" she asked.

"Have you ever heard of a man named Ronald Carter?"

The door opened at the top of the stairs. We moved around so it looked like we were still tied up. Ponytail and another man came down the steps.

The newcomer had greasy hair and a couple weeks growth of scraggly beard. Ponytail was lean and hard while Greasy-hair looked as if his only exercise was hoisting a bottle of beer.

"You know, I'm not stupid," Ponytail said as he walked toward us. "Since you're both conscious, you're both free. Am I right? Doesn't matter." He held up my phone. The one Jack had copied to his. He watched me as the device burst apart as it hit the concrete. To complete the destruction he brought his boot down on the already destroyed device. "Trace can't track you, now."

I struggled to keep my face neutral. I knew I hadn't succeeded. I never do.

He smiled. "Ladies, we're taking a ride."

I know what that means in old movies. I was hoping he wasn't a film noir fan.

Ponytail grabbed my arm and yanked me to my feet as Greasy-hair jerked Sarah to hers.

"May I at least put my clothes back on?" I indicated my blazer and t-shirt.

"Go ahead."

I left the vest behind just in case Jack found this place.

» § «

Outside the car window, the desert flowed by in an unchanging ribbon. One knoll of sagebrush looked pretty much like the last. Everything gray and desolate.

"Where are you bad boys taking us?" Sarah asked.

"Shut up," Greasy-hair snapped. By the way he smelled, he'd showered the last time he'd shaved. Weeks ago.

Sarah and I looked at each other. This time, our captors hadn't taken any chances. They'd secured our hands with more zip ties behind our backs. Which, by the way, hurt. At least they'd buckled our seatbelts.

I remembered Jack telling me this wasn't going to be like anything I'd been through. He was right. I knew I was going to die—we were going to die. There'd be no finding us out here in the middle of nothing.

"Sarah," I whispered.

She shook her head.

I swallowed hard against the inevitable.

Ponytail had turned off the freeway onto a paved county road long ago. We left the pavement for dirt and gravel. The old sedan wasn't equal to the desert road. With no way to brace ourselves, every jolt tossed us around. The seatbelts only kept us from hitting the roof.

We were close to the mountains on the west side of the valley and a long way from Boise.

We dropped down off the rim we'd been traveling along. This area was exactly like the last: flat, and desolate. The only hint of life was a building off in the distance. Several minutes later, Ponytail pulled to a stop by a weatherworn barn.

He opened the back door, snapped open Sarah's seatbelt and, in one swift motion, grabbed her and threw her to the ground.

Greasy-hair pulled me from the backseat. Unfortunately, he didn't let me go. "What are they going to do with them?" he called to Ponytail. He wasn't as tall or as muscular as Ponytail, but he had strong hands that dug into my arm.

"You're getting paid not to care."

Greasy-hair drew me close with his dirty fingers. "I thought maybe while we waited." He made smooching noises.

"Go right ahead." Ponytail glared at him. "When Trace catches you, and he will, if he leaves you alive. You'll wish he hadn't."

"Oh, yeah? I've got a gun."

"Idiot. Have at it, if you're feeling lucky. I'm talking billion-dollar-lottery lucky."

"What about that one?" Greasy-hair pointed to Sarah.

"You have a death wish? This one'll kill you herself and if she doesn't, her crazy-ass husband will rip your arms off and beat you to death with them. Hire a hooker." He scanned the sky. "I wish they'd get here. Damn it, I knew this was a bad idea." After he checked his watch he said, "We've got a while to wait. I don't like it. I want this over with so I can get out of this state. Hell, I'm leaving the country. You can hang around and wait to die if you want. Taking them is not going to sit well with Trace and Buckingham." He touched the scar on his throat. "Trace doesn't have much of a sense of humor when he's pissed." He pointed to me. "And trust me, this is going to piss him off."

"How long before they get here? And who are *they*?" Greasy-hair asked.

"The less you know, the longer you'll live. Let's get these two in the barn."

The men pushed us forward. The weather-beaten structure didn't have any windows on this side. Next to the building was a large tank.

Wordlessly, the men closed the door behind them. Inside hay was baled and stacked along one wall. There were two doors. The set of garage-sized double doors we'd entered through and, one regular door at the far end. The walls were all windowless and weather-beaten. The frigid wind raged through the gaps between the wallboards. I wrapped my arms around me. "Ponytail said they were supposed to keep us alive. If they leave us in here in this cold, we're not going to be in great shape."

"There has to be a way to keep warm." Sarah paced around as she took in our new jail. She paused as she looked at a pump in one corner. "Let's pull the bales around, maybe we can block some of the wind."

We tugged the bundles, they had to weigh a hundred pounds each, into a u-shaped enclosure. It should help. I remembered the night in the mountains above Spirit Springs when Jack and I had faced a night in freezing temperatures. Then, we'd been able to start a fire and hold each other for warmth. "Sarah, I don't like the fact Ponytail knows Jack and Andy. I wonder if the guys they're waiting for will know them, too." I went over to the pump. On the ground, next to it, lay a large wrench. I picked it up and dropped it on one of the bales. If I got the chance, it would make a great weapon.

Sarah shook her head. "This is bad. We've been transferred twice." She sat in the shelter of the bales. "And there's another move in the works. After that, we'll be on our own."

I felt the last slivers of hope slip away. It was one thing to be held in a basement in the city. Now, if we escaped, with these guys, and the desert, we'd never make it back.

After hours of shivering and being miserable, we heard the sound of a helicopter.

"Sarah?"

"I hear it. This is bad."

How would Jack find me now? And Sarah? She had babies at home and Andy.

Chapter Twenty-Five

Our first set of bad guys opened the door and led us out into the cold, bleak area surrounding the barn. Two men got out of the helicopter. The pilot took Ponytail aside as the second man unloaded something from the aircraft.

I watched Ponytail and the pilot exchange words. Ponytail kept shaking his head. Finally, he walked over to Greasy-hair and handed him an envelope.

Greasy-hair looked over at us and nodded.

Ponytail stood motionless as Greasy-hair got in the car. He watched as the vehicle zigzagged through the sagebrush toward freedom.

I felt my shoulder muscles tighten as our only mode of transportation bumped toward civilization. I couldn't fly a helicopter. Maybe Sarah could.

The man headed our way pointed his assault weapon at us. You'd think after you have a gun pointed at you five or six times it wouldn't be as scary. It's still as terrifying as the first time.

"Inside. Now." He motioned to the barn.

Ponytail was bad enough, but these guys were different. They had the hard unsympathetic presence of mercenaries. Men ready and capable of doing anything and not worrying about the consequences. Ponytail stood head down watching the fire as we were shoved back inside.

My imagination took the opportunity to run wild. Were they going to take us up in the helicopter and throw us out when we got high enough? No. If they were going to kill us, they would have by now, and skipped moving us out here. I hoped being alive wasn't temporary.

I struggled to put the pieces together. They'd found the safe house. That meant there was another leak. The image of Agent Clark standing in the garage as I was drugged answered that question. Somehow they'd gotten Jack, Andy, and Casey out of the way in order to get to me. But why Sarah? Was she added insurance? But insurance for what?

I knew Jack would find me. For now, I held on to that hope with both hands. "Sarah, what do we do?" I said as the door banged closed.

"There's a lot of nothing out here. The only ranch house I saw had to be twenty miles back." She paused. "I know we aren't going out of the country, at least not with these guys. Helicopters can't fly that far and they wouldn't chance stopping for fuel with us on board." She looked at the closed door and shivered. "I have no idea what the range of their helicopter is. It depends on how far they flew to get here. I'm willing to bet they didn't take off from a sanctioned air strip."

"Something has changed," I pointed out.

"Good point," she said. "Ponytail wasn't supposed to stay." She glanced at the door. "I wonder what altered their plans."

"I think it's more of a *who* changed things. Was it Jack and Andy, Sullivan, or Carter."

»§«

One of the double doors opened. "Get out here." Ponytail motioned to us.

The other man, not the pilot, pointed his weapon at us, "Right here and don't make any trouble." His angular features gave him a ruthless appearance. What gave me the shivers were his soulless eyes.

They were almost black. He was massive. His head appeared to sit right down on his shoulders. No-neck said, "Sit and shut-up."

At least we were warm. I glanced over at the barn and the large rust-colored tank next to it. I wondered if it held water or fuel. With the well inside it was probably gas.

The pilot who'd talked to Ponytail earlier, was solid and lean, like a snake. Dark hair and the shadow of stubble on his face gave him an evil look. Mr. Evil. At least, his stubble looked as if it was on purpose.

"Sarah—"

"You were told to shut-up." Mr. Evil shoved the barrel of his rifle against my back.

In the late afternoon gloom, we sat by the fire. I was hungry and thirsty which equaled grumpy. "Are you going to give us something to eat or at least water?"

"No." It was No-neck.

"So, you're going to let us starve?" My stomach had recovered from earlier and I hadn't eaten since breakfast.

"What the hell do I care?" Mr. Evil said. "You." He motioned to Ponytail. "Get them back in the barn."

Okay, that was pointless. Don't get me wrong, the warm was great while it lasted. Still, it was odd.

Ponytail lead us toward the double doors.

As it turned out Sarah was as cranky as I was without food. When we got inside she whirled around, brought the palm of her hand up to ram it into his nose. He ducked and swept his leg around knocking her's out from under her. She hit the ground. I grabbed him in an effort to keep him off balance.

It didn't work. He cast me off as if I was weightless.

It gave Sarah time to regain her feet.

"I'm not in the mood for you two." He didn't take his eyes off Sarah. "I'll give you some advice. The people paying us want you alive. So, knock it off. It's not going to do you any good to try to escape. I'm a hell-of-a lot nicer than those two." He shoved his thumb over his shoulder. "So, if you know what's good for you, don't try this on one of them."

193

Nice wasn't precisely the word that came to mind. I watched one of the double barn doors slammed shut behind him.

"That didn't work out well." Sarah brushed the dirt from her jeans.

"We've got to get out of here."

"We can't do anything until an opportunity presents itself." She sat on one of the bales of hay. "If we can catch one of them off guard, we may have a chance."

"Ponytail was ready for you." I took the spot next to her.

"I won't underestimate him again. He was fast and strong. I can't compete with that."

"So we wait?"

She nodded. "Unless you have something else."

"Sorry, I have no idea what to do."

Sarah looked at the door. "I wish they'd give us some water. I skipped breakfast. I won't do that again." She grinned. "Not when you two are in town."

»§«

The door opened. "Out here, both of you." No-neck motioned with his weapon.

We followed him outside. These two had come prepared. They had a decent camp set-up. No tent, good, maybe we wouldn't have to spend the night in that drafty barn. Camp chairs, a small cooler and a couple of backpacks were around the fire. Off to the side, I saw the unmistakable brown wrappers of MRE's. Maybe they'd share them with us.

"Here." Ponytail handed each of us a bottle of water as he motioned for us to sit by the fire.

I was shivering so hard I almost missed the rock allotted to me. I twisted the cap off the water. "This isn't drugged, is it?"

"You want it or not?" Mr. Evil asked.

"I don't want to be drugged again." I held the bottle.

"Drink it or throw it in the fire, I don't give a shit." Mr. Evil rolled his eyes.

I opted to drink it.

They let us stay by the fire. I figured that was about as kind as they were going to get. The good news was, we got some water that wasn't drugged.

Something zipped by me. It sounded like a giant mosquito. Then another zipping noise. I looked around. Everyone lay on the ground. "What?"

"Ensley, get down," Sarah shouted.

Ponytail pulled me over.

"What was that?"

"That, Cupcake, was a bullet." Ponytail lay next to me. "Trace is going to be pissed enough if he finds us. I don't want to face him if you're hurt and definitely not if you're dead."

"Thanks." If their fear of Jack was another reason they were keeping us alive, it was fine with me. With the three bad guys here, the question now became; "Who's shooting at us?

"Someone who doesn't want to see the sun set." It was Mr. Evil. "Right now I'm not missing a payday because of them. Get them in the barn."

Ponytail ran us inside.

"If we're lucky," Sarah said as he shut and secured the door. "They're too busy to worry about the back door. It's flimsy, so we can break out that way."

Seconds later, we knew it wouldn't be our exit. Something on the other side kept it solidly shut.

"Get behind the bales. If they start shooting, the bullets will go straight through the walls. The hay should stop them."

My preference was not being shot at all. "If the shooter is Sullivan, how did he make a living as a sniper?"

"He isn't trying to kill anyone. Yet."

Gunfire ripped through what was left of the late afternoon.

Outside, someone yelled, "What the hell?"

A second later a car crashed through the double doors. The vehicle hit the hay bales we were hiding behind. The impact pushed us and the hay back. Fortunately, crashing through the door and hitting the bales had absorbed most of its energy. The bad news was the vehicle was on fire. Now our problem was the blazing mass between us and the only opening.

Sarah hurried to one of the door-less walls and turned her back to it. She was about to kick one of the boards out when I yelled, "Do you smell that?"

"Gas."

It wouldn't be long before the flames ignited the gas fumes. "Stop. Not there." If I ever saw my brother again I was going to give him a big kiss. He'd drummed into me to always take in my surroundings, find the second exit, determine a baseline, and form a plan of escape. I'd done the first three. It was the plan part I was struggling with. "The gas tank is on that side. Over here." We raced to escape before everything exploded.

The fire now filled the front half of the barn. Fortunately the driverless car had angled to the side of the barn away from the gas tank. Unfortunately, that side of the structure was now fully engulfed. It wouldn't be long before the flames met the fumes and we were blown to hell.

I kicked out more boards. It confirmed my worst suspicions. Outside the dead grasses around the barn were a blaze. A sagebrush burst into a column of flame.

We were out of time.

"There's no way we can get through that or the smoke—" I started coughing. Stepping back I bumped into the pump. Of course, water. I had no idea how to get it to produce.

Smoke now filled the barn as the flames crawled up the walls to the roof. My throat burned with each breath. "Sarah." I choked. "Do you know anything about pumps?"

She stumbled toward me. "Pumps? Hell, yes. I spent my summers on a Kibbutz. Thank you, Mother." She grabbed the wrench and had the water on in no time. Our only problem now was how to aim it.

A piece of the roof fell.

Another volley of shots rang out. This time, it had to be Mr. Evil and company. We could hear the report of the weapons. The sniper was either too far away or he was using a suppressor. Then we heard the unmistakable plink of bullets striking metal.

He'd hit the gas tank.

The water seeped under the wall and around our feet. I heard the sizzle of dying flames. I was choking and my eyes were watering so much I was almost blind. We squeezed through the opening in the wall.

Outside, we were now in a good news, bad news, worse news, which culminated in an, oh-shit situation.

Good news, the smoke should attract someone's attention. Bad news, we were both soaked to the skin and it was cold and getting colder. The worse news, we had two assault rifles pointed at us. The oh-shit part was the leaking gas tank.

In a few seconds; either the roof would collapse and the gas tank would explode, or the flames would ignite the gas and the tank would explode.

Either way, we wouldn't have to worry about the cold or the guys holding the guns.

The bad guys realized our predicament. Mr. Evil grabbed Sarah's arm and Ponytail took mine. We ran down the road. Panic was the only thing keeping me on my feet.

The concussion of the shockwave knocked us all down.

Behind us, the barn was now a smoldering skeleton. The blast had scattered burning wood for a hundred yards and put out most of the fire in the center. Fortunately, we'd made it a hundred and twenty yards. The helicopter hadn't fared as well. Several burning boards surrounded it. I hoped it would blow up, too.

"Watch them." Mr. Evil scrambled to his feet and ran toward his ride. As we gained our feet, more shots zipped through the after blast quiet.

This time, I recognized the whizzing noise and hit the ground with the others.

Ponytail rolled over holding his bleeding shoulder.

"That sniper is going to pick us off one-by-one," I pointed out.

The helicopter had taken off. At least the fire was spreading away from us. So, we wouldn't have to find the stamina to outrun it.

"Someone's got to see that," Sarah whispered.

"All I know about range fires is they move fast. I don't know how much fast I have left in me," I said. "Maybe it'll burn toward the guy shooting at us."

The gunfire had stopped again.

"What's with that guy?" I asked. "First, he fires as if to kill us. Then he stops. It doesn't make sense."

"Shut up. Our ride is back." No-neck waived his weapon in a get-moving motion.

Ponytail struggled to his feet. Between the bullet wound in his shoulder and the concussion of the explosion, I knew he was in distress.

The unmistakable plink of bullets hitting metal reached us as the helicopter took off again.

"Over here." No-neck shoved Sarah to the side of the road. "In the ditch."

It wasn't so much a ditch as it was a dent in the desert. We all slipped down the side.

Sarah brushed away the gravel sticking to her forearm. "This is going to hurt." A mat of blood formed where the tiny rocks had ripped her skin.

My wool blazer had held up its end of the bargain by protecting my arms from the gravel. Unfortunately, it hadn't provided much padding between my chest and the ground. My outside t-shirt was torn and my palms were bloody. I watched the fire gain strength as it burned away from us. The knees of my jeans were ripped and I could feel the sting of scraped knees.

I went to where Ponytail lay. "Be still." I pulled back his jacket and shirt.

I didn't want to tell him, but he wasn't going to last long if his friends didn't get him to a hospital.

"Which one of you is the doctor?" No-neck shouted over the sound of the incoming chopper.

Super. They were going to demand I preform a miracle. I hoped their first aid kit had more than Bactine and Band-Aids. If that's all they had, Ponytail wouldn't make it. "I am."

Minutes later, we got lucky. Mr. Evil was able to land. When we were back in the air, No-neck pointed his assault rifle at me. "Do what you can for him." He slipped on headphones and we did the same.

I asked for the first aid kit and was given a small aid bag. "That's going to help a lot. I don't know how much I can do. I'm so cold I can't feel my fingers and my palms are scraped and bloody." I looked at them in the light of the cabin. "And they have rocks in them." No one cared. The helicopter banked away from the fire and gunman.

"I need a flat surface that isn't in the path of a fire, or moving, and where no one is shooting at us." I figured that was a lot to ask for.

Ponytail lay on the floor as I rummaged through the aid bag and found some trauma clotting pads. They'd stop the surface bleeding but not the arterial. My only other option was to apply pressure to the wound while we were in the air. Risking anything more with all the movement would kill him. His subclavian artery had been nicked. The slice was big enough that he could bleed out. Everything he needed was in a hospital and not in the back of a moving helicopter. I didn't see them getting him to one in time. This guy wasn't as lucky or as tough as Jack.

The thought of Jack made me feel better despite the circumstances. Whoever these guys were, they weren't as good as our side. Would our guys know to look for us out here? No. Logic would keep them in Boise, not send them into the desert. When the fire was reported the team would have a better chance of finding us. If we were still there.

Sarah needed to be back with her boys, all three of them. All I had to do was figure out how to make that happen.

"When the sun goes down someone will see the glow from the fire," Sarah said.

"So what? You're not there." No-neck smirked at us.

"No. Your camping gear is though." I pointed out. "I bet your name is on some of it. I know I'd mark mine if I had good stuff."

The two men in the front seat looked at each other. "We're not that stupid," No-neck said without turning. "Besides the fire will destroy everything."

I glanced out at the desert below. The barn and everything around it was a giant campfire. If there had been a clue as to where we were going it was now ash. I couldn't look at Sarah.

"I need a firm surface so I can stabilize Ponytail enough to get him to a hospital."

"Do the best you can," Mr. Evil snapped.

"He needs a hospital." That should give them something more to think about.

"You're it, Sweet-stuff," Mr. Evil said.

The man on the floor next to me stirred. "Lay still." The compress was soaked with blood. I changed it.

In the growing darkness, we saw where the fire had burned out into the desert, leaving behind the smoldering barn. Dotted around the area were islands of vegetation completely untouched by the blaze. In the center, the flames were renewing their acquaintance with what was left of the barn. Its timbers jutted up like blackened fingers grasping for help.

"We can't get down there now," No-neck said from the passenger's seat.

"There's a spot over there." The pilot pointed upwind from the charred area. "The shooter is on the other side if he wasn't blown up."

I glanced at the wounded man. I wanted to help him, but I didn't dare until we landed. The clotting pad was beginning to help. There was too much damage, he needed surgery. Surgery I couldn't preform in the back of a helicopter. Moving or not.

The chopper bumped down and the rotors grew quiet. "Either one of you have any medical training?" I asked.

"No," Mr. Evil turned.

"I've got to have help, or he's going to die."

"You help her," No-neck said to Sarah.

"If I can get the bleeding stopped, he has a slim chance," I told Sarah.

"What do you want me to do?"

"Hold the clotting pad tight against the wound."

It took a while, but we got the bleeding stopped. Ponytail was unconscious, but breathing. For now, that was as good as it was going to get. I pulled a blanket around him.

No-neck and Mr. Evil stood by the back door watching the fire burn away from us.

» § «

The sun had trudged toward the western mountains. The shooter had either given up, or chased off by the fire. That idea was more hope than reason.

"Why haven't we gotten our instructions?" Mr. Evil grumbled. "I wanted to be out of here before dark."

"What about those two?" No-neck asked.

"Zip tie them to the seats."

"That's not going to work with these two. I know the tall one can get out of them no problem."

"If you tie me up, I can't help your friend." I didn't want to be zip tied again. My hands and wrists were sore enough. "I'd like a chance to get the gravel out of my palms."

"Handcuff them. Tight." Mr. Evil shrugged.

"That's not going to hold them, either," No-neck said. "We only have one pair."

"Handcuff the tall one's hands above her head. The other one won't leave her behind." Mr. Evil pointed out. "Besides, they're smart enough to know if they leave, either we'll find them or the sniper will. Their odds are better with us. At least, they know we want them alive." Mr. Evil walked over and unplugged the microphone from the radio.

No-neck secured Sarah.

"We aren't going to last in these wet clothes," Sarah's words were pushed out between chattering teeth. "Let us stand by the fire to dry off."

He snapped her handcuffs closed.

I watched the two men make their way toward the remnants of the campfire. "Do you think someone will report the fire?" My blood sugar was low and I was cold.

"I don't know. I do know this is uncomfortable." Sarah shifted. "I've got a handcuff key in my pocket."

"You carry a handcuff key?"

"Habit." She shifted and I reached in her pocket. "If we're lucky, there's some food in here. Or, at least, water. Let's take advantage of them being gone."

I unlocked her handcuffs. We searched through the cabin for anything to eat or drink. All we found was one bottle of water. "It's better than nothing." We split it three ways.

I helped Ponytail take a drink. "Who are you guys?" I asked.

He turned away. I saw the familiar silver clip on his jean pocket. I reached down and took his knife. I needed it more than he did.

"Do you know who's behind this?" it was Sarah.

He didn't answer.

Outside by the fire, the men kicked at the still smoldering boards in an effort to stay warm. Why wasn't the sniper shooting at them? Was he only after Sarah and me? That didn't make sense. If he was, he'd be shooting at us in the helicopter.

"Where are they taking us?" Sarah prodded Ponytail.

"Lady, I'm not telling you anything. Those guys would kill me and if they don't, Trace and Buckingham will." His voice was raspy and soft.

"How about if I put my foot in your shoulder?"

I couldn't believe her. "Sarah, you can't do that."

"If it will get us home, I can." Her eyes held a fierceness that left no doubt she would.

From his expression, Ponytail was convinced too.

"It could kill him," I said.

"Oh, like that would break my heart." She raised her foot. "Tell us what we want to know."

He shifted away from her and winced. "I don't know anything. Hell, I'm not supposed to be here. This wasn't the deal." He gasped. "The operation changed. My part was to get you here. They were supposed to take you off my hands."

"Take us where?" Sarah demanded.

"I don't know. I don't think they know. Why else would they be hanging around here. My part was to get you to the drop point. I was supposed to get paid and leave."

"You have to know more," I said. "Who hired you?"

"It was all through a third party. I figured if they went to all that trouble, it was better I didn't know. Besides, the money was good." He winced and put his hand to his shoulder. "Not good enough for this."

"Why do this if you're so afraid of Jack and Andy?" It didn't make any sense.

"I needed the hundred thousand. It was supposed to be easy money. In and out with no trail."

"We may never see our families again." The realization of my words cut straight through my heart. I looked at Sarah.

She shook her head. "Do you have any idea how upset I'm going to be if I don't get back to my guys?" She nudged him with her toe. "My foot in your shoulder will be the least of your problems."

"She will. You don't come between a mother and her children." Especially, not this mother.

"I don't know any more. I needed money. It sounded like an easy payday. I should have known better by the amount they offered. There isn't a paycheck big enough for me to face Trace again."

"Mister, you have no idea what kind of hell will rain down on you if they hurt either one of us. Dead will be your best option," Sarah said.

"Oh, I know." He turned his head. "How the hell do you think I got this scar? Trace damn near killed me. He will, this time." He looked up at me. "Cupcake, I don't know who the hell you are, but to pay someone a hundred thousand just to get you out of town," he paused as the pain on his face intensified.

"You need to stop talking." I changed the clotting pad, then searched through the bag for some pain medication. I kept telling myself he'd pulled me down when the sniper began shooting, and he'd helped me get away from the barn, that deserved sympathy. Not a lot, because if it weren't for him, I wouldn't be here. I gave him a shot of the only pain medication in the bag, then I held his head as he drank the last of the water. I wanted him to survive, to face Jack and Andy.

Off in the distance, the fire stretched out in a semi-circle. The flames glowed yellow in the growing darkness. Now, our only hope rested with the person who saw the fire and cared enough to report it.

"Sarah, we've got to do something. Anything to get away."

She leaned closer. "We need to keep them here. That fire is our only hope of being found." She slipped out the door.

Chapter Twenty-Six

They found what they were looking for and brought it back, shoving it in a storage compartment.

Sarah hadn't had time to get very far away. She had turned off the lights in the cabin before she left. As the men approached, they weren't able to tell we were one person short. Mr. Evil walked up and switched them back on. So much for not noticing Sarah was gone, and for not being a target.

"Where is she?"

"She went to find a bush." Hey, it sounded reasonable.

"You've got one minute to get her back here." Mr. Evil waved his gun in the air.

"Find her yourself." I didn't want to go wandering around with the sniper still out there. He'd gone to too much trouble to give up and leave. Besides, he'd set his ride on fire and aimed it at the barn.

No-neck leveled his weapon at me. "One minute."

I didn't want to end up with a bullet wound, so I put my attitude back in my pocket. "Okay." I hurried in the wrong direction. "Sarah?"

No answer.

I hoped she was a long way off.

If only one of us survived, I wanted it to be her. I only had the potential for a happy ending. She already had hers. I'd do everything in my power to help her get away. I hurried out into the desert away from the sorry excuse for a road.

"Sarah." Nothing. Good. If she'd set right out, she might be a mile away. Depending on how rough her path was. I stopped. What if the sniper had her? "No," I whispered. There was so much out here to be avoided. One group intent on keeping us alive and one man out there equally determined to kill us. I wasn't going to think about the wildlife.

I could do this. I had too much to lose not to make it.

"Hey, get back here." The beam of a spotlight skimmed across the sagebrush.

Great. This guy was supposed to be a professional and he was out here holding a bright light, making himself a target.

I heard him run up behind me. If my jeans weren't stuck to my bloody knees I'd be able to outrun him. As it was, I was struggling to walk. No-neck grabbed my arm and snapped me around. "What the hell are you trying to pull?"

"You told me to find Sarah." You idiot.

"If she isn't here in one minute we're leaving her. We'll see how long she survives."

"Damn it, they want them both," Mr. Evil shouted. "Find her."

"How long has she been gone?" No-neck tightened his hold on my arm.

"Ouch." I pulled against his pitiless grip. "A while."

"How long?" He shook me hard.

"I thought you guys were professionals." I wasn't making any progress getting free. "With all these lights on, that sniper can zero in on us."

"The lights," No-neck yelled.

Mr. Evil flipped them off.

Idiots. "You aren't going to find her."

"Oh, we will," No-neck said.

With my busted-up knees, I couldn't move very fast. As it turned out, my feet only occasionally touched the ground as he pulled me toward the helicopter.

No-neck threw me down. "Where the hell is she?"

"I thought you weren't supposed to injure me." I massaged my arm where he'd held on to me.

He jerked me up like a rag doll and slapped me. "Where the hell is she?"

I pressed my hand to my bleeding lip. "I don't know!" This guy was as mean as he was strong. I got the distinct feeling he didn't care if I was still breathing when we got to our destination.

He raised his fist.

I pulled back and braced myself for the blow that never came.

"Stop," Sarah shouted.

"That's more like it." No-neck lowered his fist. "Now get back to the chopper."

They shoved us in the back with the wounded Ponytail.

The men in front slipped on headphones. Sarah and I followed suit.

"This is starting to make me itchy. Why the hell haven't they contacted us?" No-neck asked.

"I don't know. What I do know is we aren't staying here." We took off.

Below, the fire's beacon burned bright as it shrunk into the night.

How could Jack find me now? In the ink black night I had no way to pick out landmarks or even tell in which direction we were going.

We weren't in the air long when Mr. Evil said, "We can't chance going any farther." We touched down. "We won't have enough fuel to make it back to the refueling station."

"At least we're away from the shooter and the fire," No-neck glanced outside.

I liked the idea of not being shot at, but I missed the warmth of the fire. Mr. Evil switched on the overhead light. Poor Ponytail was unconscious. Under the circumstances his vital signs were decent. I lifted the bandage. The bleeding had stopped. With him out I was able to repair the artery enough to release the clamp. At least he wouldn't lose his arm.

I sat back on my heels. I could see how the Stockholm Syndrome could affect someone. I felt sorry for Ponytail, he'd helped me. "No one is all bad," I whispered. Then I remembered No-neck. Okay, he was.

I added Ponytail's jacket to the blanket covering him. "You guys have any more blankets? He needs to stay warm."

Mr. Evil went to a compartment and pulled out a sleeping bag. "Here."

I unzipped it and covered the man on the floor.

Sarah scooted next to me. "This isn't good."

I got that part, but I asked, "Why?" anyway.

"Somewhere something has gone wrong," she said. "First, they kept, Ponytail, here. You heard, Mr. Evil, wonder why they hadn't gotten word where to go."

"Could it be the sniper?"

"I think that's part of it," she lowered her voice. "There's another man out there." After a quick glance around she continued, "I think he's the reason the gunfire has been sporadic." She glanced out into the darkness. "Someone is chasing the sniper. What concerns me is if those two don't get their orders soon they may decide to cut their losses, kill us, and split."

That brought a whole new urgency to the situation. How long could those two wait? My guess was not long. "How far away do you think the fire is from us?"

Out of the side of the aircraft, we could see the glow in the distance. "It's deceiving at night. I don't know. I can't take a guess without knowing how fast the pilot was flying."

I could almost feel Jack out there looking for us. I hugged my arms to my chest. I knew it was the cold, my hunger, lack of water, and my over active imagination. Still, the idea gave me hope. I remembered how hard it had been a few weeks ago to find him, and then the area was defined by the blizzard.

"Sarah..."

"I'm scared too. You have to know they won't give up. Andy will go to hell and back to find me." She put her hand on my arm. "He'll be following Jack the whole time."

"Hey, you two get over here," Mr. Evil called. "I'm not missing a payday if you two are dead."

The fire they'd built was a mix of comfort and dread.

I checked Ponytail before I left the helicopter cabin. He was still unconscious.

When we reached the fire Mr. Evil said, "We have spaghetti with meat sauce, or beef stew." He motioned to a duffle bag. "Help yourself."

I wasn't going to ask why the change of heart. I was too hungry. I opened the brown plastic container. With help, I heated the spaghetti. I was glad I'd chosen the meal that required the least amount of chewing. My teeth hurt where No-neck had hit me. When I was finished I felt a twinkle of hope return.

"May I have one for Ponytail?"

"Yeah," Mr. Evil said. He stared at me for a minute, then said, "Take the other beef stew. I don't like it."

Evidently, No-neck wasn't speaking to me. Good.

Before I opened the package I went to see if he was even awake. I opened the door and got in. "Ponytail, are you awake?"

"Yeah."

In the end he felt well enough to eat. I wasn't going to let him die if I could help it. I wanted him in jail. Hey, I'm not *that* nice.

Sarah and I helped him to sit-up.

"I have an idea," she whispered. "Those two seem to have relaxed a little. I'm going to leave."

"You can't. What if you get lost?" I don't mind telling you, I felt different about her absence this time. First, we didn't know where we were. Second, I was not excited about being left behind.

"I won't. I can see the fire." She pointed out into the night. "If I can get back there and Andy and Jack find it I can lead them here."

"What if they leave before you get back?" I felt the threads of panic begin to weave through me.

"They won't leave without me. You heard them, whoever they're working for won't pay for just one of us." She hugged me. "It'll be okay. Wish me luck."

"Good luck," I whispered as she vanished into the night.

»§«

The quiet was broken only by the sound of the crackling campfire. I stayed in the cabin. It was cold, but I didn't want to draw attention to Sarah's absence.

"You know her leaving it isn't going to work," Ponytail whispered.

"She was Mossad."

"Cupcake, I know exactly who she is. You're the puzzle." He angled toward me. "Saving me was a bad move. You should have let me bleed out, then you'd only have to deal with those two."

The matter-of-fact tone in his voice was a sad caption to his life's picture. "I couldn't do that."

He lifted his hand to his shoulder. "You know, Trace is probably going to kill me."

"No, he won't."

"You're right, he'll just send me to jail for the rest of my life." He let out a sigh. "Doesn't matter, I'm tired of this life anyway. The simple truth is I'm one misstep away from a bullet in the heart. A few inches lower and it would have been tonight."

I reached out a sympathetic hand, then pulled it back. Ponytail was wrapped in a hell of his own making. Was this the life Jack had chosen, too? No, he was the one trying to stop men like these.

A bullet shattered the window above me.

"Get out of here," Ponytail yelled at me.

I scrambled out, then turned to help him. "Goddamn, woman. Save yourself." I helped him slide out and lay on the ground by one of the skids. "Go."

The zipping sounds filled the frigid night air with another wave of terror. I crouched down and ran for cover. Between my sore knees and the dark, I was doing more stumbling than running.

I made an outcropping of rock only to find No-neck waiting. "You." He grabbed me. "I've had it. It's going to cost us more to fix the chopper than we're getting paid."

I struggled to pull free.

"Oh, no you don't. The other one is gone, so we aren't getting paid now. I'm taking it out on you." He raised his fist. "This is going to hurt."

No-neck fell to the ground.

I stood face-to-face with a man dressed all in black and wearing a balaclava.

"You're with me now."

Was this the man who'd been trying to kill us? No, those shots had come from the other side of the helicopter. Was he here to save me? That wasn't playing much better than my sniper theory. If he was my rescuer he wouldn't be alone.

"Come on." He signaled me to follow him.

Maybe the others were around here somewhere. "Is Jack here?"

No answer.

I stopped. If he wasn't with Jack that meant he was another bad guy. I couldn't go. I'd been handed-off so many times I felt like the object in a child's game of Hot Potato.

The man turned. "You've got one choice if you ever want to see," He paused as if choosing his next words carefully. He stepped back toward me. "Home again."

"Who are you?"

"Honey, I'm your last best hope."

I froze. Those were the words Brad had used to describe Jack and his team.

The man again motioned for me to follow him. "Come on. The sniper is going to figure out you're gone." He walked back to where I stood, in the shelter of the rocks. "It's hard enough staying away from Sullivan. The longer we debate, the worse our chances are." He pointed toward the helicopter. "Those two are angels compared to Sullivan. He's a sociopath."

Enough said. I hoped I wasn't trading one crazy for another. At least this man, despite his terrorist appearance, had disposed of No-neck.

The region we were in was as flat as the area around the barn. "Keep down," Mr. X said. "Those bullets go a long way."

A few minutes later, we dropped into a dry river bed. He stopped, slipped out of his backpack, opened it, and pulled out a jacket. "Put this on." He hefted the pack to his shoulders and began walking.

"Thank you," I whispered.

The sound of the helicopter taking off made me grateful I wasn't with them.

We skirted along for what seemed like forever. Every now and then, he'd stop and listen. Then he'd pull out night vision goggles and check around.

I was happy not to hear the zip of the sniper's bullets. "Where are we going?" I asked as we stopped for the third time.

"We're going back to the burning barn. If your friend is as smart as she's supposed to be, she'll be there."

"You know Sarah?"

No answer. But I hadn't expected one.

Now it was up to Jack to find us.

Chapter Twenty-Seven

"Jack?"

"Yeah?" Forces had pulled Doc into my covert world. I'm used to being the target. She isn't. I wanted my hands around Sullivan's neck. Doc was the innocent in all of this. If he wanted revenge, fine. I'd face him one on one.

"Sarge, you planning on breaking the steering wheel."

I glanced down. My knuckles were white and the muscles in my forearms were hard and aching. I'd managed to relax them when we pulled into the cul-de-sac.

Ahead, the garage door to the ugly mud colored house stood open. I crushed down on the gas. The breaks screamed as we slid to a stop in the driveway.

Kevin Clark, Doc's guard, sat on the garage floor rubbing his head. I slammed the truck into neutral, jammed on the emergency break, and threw open the door. "Andy, check him." I pointed to the agent. I drew my weapon and eased open the kitchen door.

Nothing.

The main floor was empty.

No sign of a struggle.

Upstairs the same.

"Get Brad here." The kitchen door banged closed behind me. I grabbed the FBI agent from the garage floor and pulled him up close and real personal. "What the hell went on here? Where's Ensley?" I tightened my grip on his collar. "You were to protect her at all costs." I shook him. Hard. "Talk."

"Sarge, he can't. You're choking him," Andy turned to Clark. "If I were you, I'd squeeze out something while you can."

"Talk," I grasped his shirt so tight it ripped.

I heard the sound of a car pulling to a stop. It had to be Casey.

Clark struggled to get the words out. "We—"

"Sarge, he's turning blue," Casey pointed out.

"Fine." I let him go. "What happened?"

"I heard a crash." He rubbed his neck. "I opened the door and someone hit me. I just came to." He took a step back.

"How long after we left did this happen?"

"Five maybe ten minutes." He put his hand to the back of his head.

I glanced around. "Casey, tell Brad, Ensley's been gone for two hours."

Andy walked over and began going through Clark's pockets. He held up a phone. "Shall we see who you've been calling on the taxpayer's dime?" He hit redial. "No answer. I'll have Tony get a name to go with this number."

I drug Clark inside. I would have tossed him in a chair, but there weren't any, so I threw him on the floor.

"I want a lawyer." Clark struggled to his feet.

Andy pushed him back down. "A lawyer? He's going to have to find you." To me he said, "Jack, Sarah isn't answering her phone." He kept his eyes locked on Clark. "My wife *always* has her phone. She hasn't picked up Colin from preschool. She's *never* late to get the kids."

Clark struggled to sit up.

"Stay put." Casey held him down with his foot. "You know better than to make a bone headed move like that." He held up his hand. "If I were a betting man, I'd lay out decent money you know who stole our women." He pointed to Andy. "His fuse is short." He jerked his thumb toward me. "His is burned down to nothing. So the way I see it, you've got one minute before I get out of their way."

I pulled out my phone. "Stan, Ensley and Sarah are missing."

"What? How did that happen?"

"An FBI agent flipped on us. Get me a full background check on Kevin Clark. I want to know how tall he was in the sixth grade. Everything. They're going to need it for the trial, if he lasts that long." I glanced at Andy. He looked as scared as I felt.

"On it. This guy smart enough to tell you everything he knows?"

I focused on Clark. "I'm about to find out."

"I'll have something for you in a couple of hours." Stan paused. "Don't kill him."

"I want information not a body count, yet." I hit the end bar.

"I know how you guys operate. I have rights," the idiot on the floor whined. "I'm a federal agent."

"You're a *federal* mess I'm about to clean up," Casey said. "Rock, paper, scissors to see who goes first?"

"I say we let Trace and Buckingham have a go at him," Brad said as he stormed in the back door.

I took Brad aside. "Does he have money problems?"

"You called Stan." It wasn't a question. "We'll coordinate and report to you." Brad turned to his former agent. "Clark, seriously, man? You've been around these guys long enough to know they'd catch you."

"I didn't have a choice."

I walked up to him. I wasn't going to let him know how pissed off I was. I was pretty sure it wasn't a secret. "As I see it, you have two choices. You can talk to Buckingham or you can talk to me. Your choice."

Andy came up beside me. "From where I stand, it all comes down to what you want in a cast."

I swear Clark tried to make himself smaller.

"For Jack here it's the love of his life."

I started to protest.

Andy shot me a glance. "Deal with it. Everyone knows." To the worm on the floor he said, "With me it comes down to the love of *my* wife, the mother of my children. So pick."

"Sir." Clark pleaded with Brad. "You can't let them–" He scooted away and bumped into Casey.

"If it was my wife, I'd have shot your ass already," Brad said. "You're on your own."

Casey shoved him with his foot. "Start talking."

My cell rang. "What have you got?"

"Sarge," Tony said, "I located Ensley's cell. She's—what the hell? It just went dark."

The muscles in my chest cinched tight. "Did you get a location?"

"The best I can do is an area."

He gave it to me. "Let me know if it comes back on." I knew it wouldn't.

Casey grabbed Clark from the floor. "What do we do with this?"

I yanked Clark away from Casey. "Who took Ensley?" I hadn't raised my voice. It works much better when I don't.

"I... I..."

"Give me the name." I curved my fingers around his collar bone. He dropped to his knees. "Now." I pressed harder.

He cried out in pain as he tried to pull away. "Stop." He reached up to pry my fingers loose.

I let go. "Last chance. Talk."

"I don't know his name. He was six one or two, lean and hard, dark hair in a ponytail. He had a long scar running down his neck." Clark traced a line down the side of his throat.

"Pierce," Andy said. "He knows better than to mess in our business."

"You made it real clear we didn't want to see him again," Casey said.

"Brad," I called.

He leveled his gaze on Clark. "I want to know who Pierce is working for."

» § «

216

The area was bad enough. A door to door in a neighborhood would take days. Taking them in a house would be a mistake. We stopped in a mostly vacant area. It had once been the car shopping destination for this part of the state. When the connector went through the dealerships took the opportunity to move to the west end of town. The acres of tarmacs that once held hundreds of new and pre-owned cars and trucks had become a dead scape of weeds, cracked asphalt, and trash. The vacant buildings in the middle of the pads were now a canvas for gang tags.

I stepped out of the FBI SUV and took in our options. The hotel was out. Too many witnesses. Pierce would hold them in a secluded place. There were a couple of office buildings. They were out, too.

This section is in the process of finding a new identity. Down the street was a new recreational park and corresponding businesses. There were only a couple of locations suitable for Pierce's needs. We needed to canvas the area for witnesses. It was going to take time. Time we didn't have.

I called one of the local cops I knew. "Christensen, Jack Trace. Busy right now?"

"What's up? And is it going to get me into trouble?"

"I have two missing women."

I heard a door close. "That's FBI land."

"They're here. We're running out of manpower and time. Bring some of your guys to the Main Auction? And, Chris, this is off the books."

"We'll be there as fast as we can."

It took Chris and two of his buddies half an hour to get to us. By that time we'd cleared the largest building.

"I owe you," I said as I shook his hand. I explained the situation and we split up into three teams.

I kept my team together. It's always best to search with men you know. We went to the kind of place I'd choose to hold someone. The traffic sounds from the overpass would mask any noise. I motioned for Andy and Casey to go around back. With everyone in place, I went in the front.

Shouts of, "Clear," came down the hall.

From the back Casey called, "Basement."

We met at the back of the building.

I held up three fingers.

Casey grabbed the knob. Andy stood ready to fire.

Silently, I counted down to one.

Casey jerked open the door.

I went first.

Lying near the foot of the steps was a crushed cellphone and a vest with three slug marks in it. Doc had been here. The only other things in the area were some file boxes, a discarded printer and a broken desk chair. Someone had thrown up in the center of the floor. The rest of the area was empty. I holstered my weapon.

Grabbing the phone and vest, I turned the cell over. It was hers. The stand on the back was missing and one corner was chipped. I stared at the crushed phone. "Time to play hard." I raised the phone to slam it against the concrete wall. I hesitated and instead slipped it in the pocket of my jacket. "Casey, have Tony find out who owns this building."

"On it."

I took the steps two at a time. I was going to have a conversation with Clark.

Andy hurried after me. Brad saw us coming, and opened the SUV door.

I grabbed Clark and pulled his ass from the backseat. "I'm out of patience."

"When that happens," Andy said. "It never ends well, for the other guy."

I didn't say a word. I didn't have to.

Andy stepped back. "Hey, do you know how hard it is to get blood out of clothes?"

Clark's eyes were wide. Good. I raised my fist.

He gave an odd cry just before he started talking. "Pierce came to me the day after Doctor Markus was shot. He said all I had to do was feed him the address of the safe house you were going to be in today. Honest. That's all I know. I didn't have a choice."

The fear in Clark's eyes had me asking, "Why not?"

"He had pictures of my wife's office, the kids' school. He said they knew exactly when my family was home." Clark's voice raised an octave. "He said if I didn't give him the information they'd kill my family." He looked up at me. "My wife and kids. You have to understand."

"Why didn't you come to me?" Brad broke in.

"I couldn't take the chance." He let his head fall forward. With his hands cuffed behind him he looked pitiful. "I think they have someone else in our unit." He looked away. "I can't prove it, it's a gut feeling."

"Someone has devoted a big chunk of time and money to get all this in place this fast." I stopped. Who had we crossed lately? No one with the kind of domestic organization it took to pull this off. I shoved my emotions to the side. Still, I could feel my heart pounding.

I walked around the outside of the building for the third time. I'd turned over every rock and piece of trash twice. It had been four hours since Pierce had taken Doc.

I stopped at the corner of the building. What had I missed? I put the timeline together. Pierce had to stake out the building. That meant someone saw him. I hoped Chris and company, along with the FBI agents would have something for me.

I went to the truck. "Casey, any luck on who owns this place?"

"I have him on the phone." He handed it to me.

"Hello, this is Sheriff Jack Trace, we have a critical situation. Two women are missing. Has anyone contacted you in the past few days about your office building on Main Street?"

"I got a call a couple of days ago. I told him, I was out of town, and to call me next week and I'd show him the place. He said he would. Since you're calling, I'm guessing he won't."

"Did he give you a name?"

"He did, I've got it written down here somewhere. Here it is. Bob Wilson."

"Did he call you on your cell phone?" I held my breath.

"He did. Hold on."

I waited an eternity. Finally, he came back on. "The number he called from was, 952-555-1957. Does that help."

"Yes, sir. Thank you very much." I repeated the number to Brad.

"On it."

Chapter Twenty-Eight

"The number's turned off," Brad said.

"Get Pierce's phone records." I knew it was a burner, but we were down to long shots. Pierce hadn't planned this. He's a decent adversary, but he played in the minor league and this was the all-star game.

Andy took me aside. "I don't mind telling you I'm scared."

I nodded. I couldn't say the words out loud. There was only one hope for Ens and Sarah, we had to keep our emotions restrained. I tried to steel my spine, but it felt like Jell-O. "The person behind this has juice. Enough to hire a mercenary on short notice to kidnap two women." Good, women. Not Ens and Sarah, just women.

"That mean's one thing, the person behind this isn't local." His face turned red with anger. As quickly all the color drained away. "That lowers our odds of finding them."

I looked away. "If I were planning this, I'd have a series of blind drops. Each contact would know only their segment. Nothing before or after. Only drop points."

"Something like that is hard to setup in a week." Andy rubbed his face with both hands.

"We've done it. All it takes is enough money. The good news is, with that kind of speed comes errors. All we need is one slipup. Nothing significant, anything will do."

Right now I had a call to make. It rang. I didn't know if March would pick up. Another ring. He had to tell me how he knew this would all end if I resigned.

"Trace, what do you want now?"

"You haven't heard then. And here I thought you were tuned into everything." I didn't bother to hide my sarcasm.

"What have you done now? Is Ensley okay?"

"I won't know that until you give me some answers. Who wants me to resign and why?" I pretty much knew why. There were a lot of bad people behind bars because of us.

"I'm not at liberty to say."

"My God, this is Ensley. Is your career so important to you that you won't lift a finger to help her? Save her." I had one thing left to say. "Deliver a message for me. Tell *them* I will find her and then I will find *them*."

"Find her? What the hell is going on?"

"She's been kidnapped." I could almost see him getting to his feet. "Still no answer for me?"

"I'll call you when I know something." The line went dead.

Another FBI vehicle pulled up and Tony got out. He hobbled over with his tablet. The document on the screen was Pierce's phone bill. "The last few calls were to someone named Gus Lawson. Our Mr. Lawson has his phone on." Tony flipped the case shut. "Brad's office is tracing it. We should have a location in a few minutes."

Chris and his friends drove up. "All we got was from the guy at the repair shop. We were lucky to get that in this area. The owner said he saw an old gray beater Toyota with a blue front quarter panel parked there this morning." Chris leaned against his car. "Sorry, man. That's all we got."

"Thanks. It helps." I shook his hand and thanked him again. A minute later Chris and company were gone.

"Got the location," Tony said. "I texted it to you."

Brad, Tony and Casey escorted Clark to jail while Andy and I went in search of Lawson.

No surprise, the address Tony gave us was a dive bar. One of the cars parked in front was the busted-ass gray Toyota with a blue front quarter panel.

This area too is in flux. The bar was across a diverted portion of the Boise River from a line of new condos and a golf course. No exit that way.

When the city widened the street they'd taken most of the bar's parking lot. Behind the single line of parked vehicles was a dark green shingled building. The fence and shrubs once gave the deck privacy. It had a nineteenth hole feel to it.

Now, the fence was board bare and most of the plants were dead or dying. Only a couple of large cottonwood trees remained healthy. Through the holes between dead plants and the board bare fence, I could see large multi-paned windows facing a deck. Where once diners had enjoyed the serenity of the lush green course across the waterway tree roots had pushed the patio bricks out of place making room for weeds.

It took a minute for my eyes to adjust to the dim, smoky atmosphere inside. The once elegant interior was now battered by time and more than a few fights. The stately dark wood was now scratched and the finish worn.

The large mirror behind the bar was cracked with one corner missing.

I noted the exits. The front door, out the patio doors, and through the kitchen.

"Pierce isn't here," Andy said. "but I didn't expect he would be."

The owner of the gray beater wasn't hard to spot. "There's our man," I indicated the crowd around a loud drunk. We went to the bartender. "How long has the guy in the corner been here?" I asked.

"Half hour. He's a regular." He nodded toward the crowd. "He handed me three hundred and said to keep the drinks coming." He glanced from me to Andy. "You guys cops?"

"Yes." I took out my sheriff's badge and Andy flipped open his ATF shield.

"I'm not surprised, he's one slimy bastard." He wiped at the clean bar top.

We went to talk to the scum in the corner. "Gus Lawson?"

"Yeah, who are you?" He downed a shot, then leaned forward.

Again we pulled out our identification. The crowd left before I could get my badge back in my pocket. Gus sat alone holding an empty shot glass. The sight of our badges had him pushing back from the table. "I don't know anything."

"That's real interesting," Andy said. "We haven't asked you *anything*."

"Let's go," I took him by the arm.

"Are you arresting me?"

"We're taking you in for questioning," Andy pulled out handcuffs. "We'll see what happens after that."

"I'm not going anywhere." He let his jacket fall open. Stuck in his belt was a revolver.

We both drew our weapons. "You have a permit for that?" I asked.

The sound of chairs hitting the floor, and patrons running for the door almost drowned out his words. "It's an open carry state."

"With two fingers lay it on the table." Andy motioned with his .45.

"No. I—"

"Two fingers, on the table, now." It was pushing six hours since Pierce took the two women. I was out of patience. "Or do you want to see how it feels to have two big-ass holes in you?"

He laid the gun on the table.

Outside, we put him in the back of one the FBI's SUV. I was sorry the instant I got in the driver's seat. This guy's stink filled the whole damn vehicle.

"Hell man, roll down your window," Andy demanded. "When was the last time you got near soap and water."

"Hey, *man*, I'm homeless."

"With the money you've been throwing around, you could have spent a buck on some soap." Andy rolled down his window as he took out his phone. "We're coming in. You might want to put us in a room you can hose down when we're through."

I smiled as I glanced in the rearview mirror. Andy was talking about the stink. The guy in the back was sure we were going to beat the hell out of him. Right now I was leaning in that direction.

They put us in a standard interrogation room. With everything set, camera rolling, recorder on, I asked, "Were you with Pierce this morning when he kidnapped two women?"

"I didn't kidnap anyone."

"Where did you get all the money?" Andy leaned against the wall.

"I got paid for a job." Gus's eyes darted back and forth between the two of us.

I leaned my fists on the table. "Must have been some job. We counted ten thousand dollars. Minus the three hundred you gave the bartender. By the way, he said to say thanks for the tip."

Gus gaped up at us open mouthed.

Andy walked around the table and sat on the corner. He straightened the collar on Gus's torn jacket. "Care to tell us how you earned all that cash?" He held onto the collar.

"I really needed the money."

I nodded slowly, "So you kidnapped two women." The sound of my fist slamming against the table echoed through the small room. "Care to know who they are?" I paused for a split second to let him think about how mad I was. "The tall one is his wife. The other one is mine." I let him think Doc was my wife. Just her name running through my head sent a wheeze of pain through me.

He gulped. "You're Trace?" The words squeaked out.

"I am."

His hand trembled he reached for his neck. So he knew how Pierce got his souvenir. Good. Now we'd make some progress.

"I didn't know what he was going to do. He came into the bar yesterday and asked the bartender if he knew anyone who could help him get some cargo out to the desert, and keep their mouth shut. I figured—."

"Where?" Andy pulled at his jacket.

"You can't do this." He pointed to the camera in the corner of the ceiling. "They have everything on tape. They'll arrest you." He pried at Andy's fist.

"This is how it works here," I came around the table and sat on the other side of Gus. "We don't work on the grid. We're what you might call Very Special Ops. We have our own rules." I indicated the camera over my shoulder. "No cameras, and no witnesses." I let that soak in. "Now. Where are our women?"

"You can't do this," his words were salted with the reality of his situation. "I'm not saying anything more until I get a lawyer."

Andy let go of him. "I'm done. He's yours."

My turn to play worse cop. I pulled out my Benchmade Infidel, a black double-edge dagger. Their logo is a butterfly. I enjoy the irony and it's a great blade.

I held the knife directly in front of his face and let the black blade slide out. *Slide* is a little misleading. It thrust out the end lightning fast. I got the desired response. He jumped so hard he nearly tipped his chair over. "Let's see how close I can come to your carotid artery."

In response Gus passed out.

"Ah, shit," I said and put my knife away.

"You might try a little softer approach when he wakes up," Andy said. "And by the way he pissed himself."

The door opened. "Damn it." Brad waved his hand in front of his nose.

Andy and I set the unconscious man in a chair and leaned him against the table. So the janitor could mop up.

It took a few minutes before Gus came around.

"Now then," I said. "Are you ready to talk?"

"You won't let him slit my throat will you?" Gus appealed to Andy.

"You helped Pierce kidnap my wife, what do you think?"

"I'll tell you what I know. Just don't kill me." He ran the back of his hand across his dry lips. "Can I get some water? Please."

"You want a steak too?" I asked.

"The water's fine."

The smell of urine and body odor was beginning to make my eyes water. I motioned to the observers on the other side of the window. "Talk. Where are they?"

"Mister, I can tell you where I left them, but I doubt they're still there. A helicopter landed just before I left."

I felt the muscles in my neck contract and my heart hammer. All the reason in the world won't help you when you have the taste of real fear in your mouth.

I couldn't look at Andy. I could hardly breathe. "Where did you leave them? Exactly."

Chapter Twenty-Nine

We pulled up to our office on base. Inside, we grabbed our uniforms and went to the head.

Tony was grounded. He was trying to get clearance to use a couple of Blackhawks. It was taking too long. I checked my watch. The sun had set. Without the helicopters we wouldn't have a chance to find them tonight. They'd be gone by morning, if they weren't already. I'm not a cynic, I know the odds, and they weren't in our favor.

Andy followed me to the head. "Jack, we need to talk."

Casey stayed in the outer room.

"Not now."

"Yeah, now. We're going to get them back. We have to believe that. I'm not going through life without Sarah." He glanced away. "The other night when I saw Ensley at the hotel, I couldn't believe it. At the hospital, you scared the crap out of that doctor. Hell, you scared me." He pulled on his pants. "I know she's your future. Don't look at me like I have lace on my jock. It's true."

I fastened my Kevlar vest over my busted ass ribs. "After Glory," I shoved my arm in the sleeve of my shirt as I averted my eyes. "I want to trust Ensley," I slumped against the wall as I zipped my shirt. "What if she cheats on me the way Glory did?"

"Glory's life plan didn't include an Army sergeant. The most important thing in her world was her." He buckled his belt. "The only smart thing you did then was follow your grandmother's advice and not tell her about your ah, money situation." He stopped and waited for me to look up. "How many times has Ensley stepped up to save you? And," he folded his arms, "you've known her for all of what now, four months?" He shook his head and sat to pull on his boots. "You really think she's going to wake up one day and say she's changed her mind? Hell, I know better and I've only known her for few days."

I've survived things that would kill most people, but this, she scares the living shit out of me." I knew why. I loved her too much. The only time she' hadn't stood by me was when I'd given her no choice. I'd lied to her. I could still see the look of anguish on her face, the pain in her eyes. Heartache I'd put there. "She left me once."

"She came back," he said as he secured his belt. "Now, let's go find our women."

The Blackhawk crews were finishing their safety check.

We were out over the Mt. Home desert in no time. I hoped we weren't too late. If that helicopter had taken them to another location we were up shit creek. We would find them in time.

This part of Idaho is vast and empty. The area west of the Owyhee Mountains is home to a volcanic field. There's nothing there, but towering rugged peaks, and a few hearty souls. It isn't a place I'd head with two unwilling women.

We had only a general direction. We flew straight for the area. It wasn't long before we spotted the glow of a range fire.

» § «

I kicked a smoldering chunk of wood. They weren't here.

The larger timbers of the structure still burned. Dead center of that barn were the remains of a car. Around us, the fire still crept out into the desert.

"Sarge, over here," Casey called. He stood over a melted cooler, a couple of burned camp chairs, and the remains of two backpacks. One of the packs had been pried open.

"We aren't going to get anything out of those." I tried the other one. It was useless.

"Sir," one of the soldiers called. "Over here."

The three of us joined him.

"I've been around helicopters for a while now, those." He pointed to the ruts in the ground. "Are the marks from the skids from a medium sized chopper. I'd guess one with a backseat. Thing is, the depressions aren't deep enough. I'd say they stripped it down pretty good, or they're out of fuel."

"Thanks." I said. "We've got to—"

"Sir," Sloan the chopper pilot called as he came toward us. "We've been called back to base."

"Who gave the order?" This was bad news. Without the Blackhawk we were not only grounded, we were sightless.

"We have a missing plane. Twenty people on board. I'm sorry. They've called in all the search aircraft. You can come back with us."

"We're not leaving."

"Yes, sir. I'll leave you all the equipment I can. I don't know how long we'll be gone. I'll send a hummer back for you."

"Thanks. Good luck finding the missing plane."

More of my optimism left with the sound of the departing Blackhawks.

"We'll find them," Casey assured me. "We've faced worse." He put his hand on my shoulder. We both knew I hadn't.

I nodded. "Let's check the area. If they were able, they'd leave something for us to go on." That was nothing but pure, white hope.

The three of us began searching.

"Jack," Andy called. "Over here."

Around the side of the barn he'd found a muddy area. "Hear me out on this. I think some POS set that car on fire and rammed it into the barn."

The car had come through the main door, crashed into some bales of hay, trapping whoever was in here. I picked up a broken board. "These were broken before they were burned." The broken edge was blackened. I skirted the mud. "There's a wrench by the pump." I glared out into the dark desert. Not even the moon was out tonight.

A cold wind whipped through the ashes around us sending a thousand glowing cinders swirling into the air. They faded as they fell and vanished. "Maybe they escaped."

"They made it out of the barn." Andy stood shoulder to shoulder with me. "If they're out there it's going to take a while to find them."

I'd been hunting out here. Despite the level appearance the terrain could suddenly fall away. In places it drops hundreds of feet to more desert below. At night you wouldn't see them until it was too late.

It had been nearly eight hours. We checked around the barn and out into the sagebrush searching for tracks.

» § «

"Roger, I'll tell them. Sarge," Casey called as he hurried toward us. "The Blackhawks took a swing on the way back to base. They found something not far from here." He said into the microphone, "Go ahead."

"It's about two klicks due west of you," Sloan's voice came over the radio. "We got the heat signatures of a helicopter, three men, and a campfire."

I took the mic from Casey. "Roger, Sloan. I owe you. Out."

"What if it's campers?" Andy asked.

"No." I scanned the area with my night vision scope.

When we got closer the sound of gun fire ripped open the night. The shots came from the direction Sloan had said they'd spotted the helicopter.

I shifted into automatic. It was the only way I could get through what I feared had happened.

It didn't take long to surround the area. As we got close the helicopter took off. We arrived at the camp sight to find only a severely injured Pierce laying on the ground by the fire.

I glared down at him. "Where is she?"

"Damn it, Trace. Do I look like I know anything?"

I motioned for someone to shine a light on him. "What happened?" I asked as I lifted the compress on his shoulder.

"You tell me. She's your woman. Who the hell did you piss off this time?"

I put a new compress on his wound. "Where are the others?"

"I don't know." His voice grew weak. "Sullivan started shooting at us again and Burt and Hollister took off when the sniper stopped shooting." He moved to face me.

"Stay still."

He relaxed. "She saved my life. I owe her." He pointed. "All I know is she ran in that direction." After a short pause he said, "Sarah Buckingham left a long time ago."

"Get a chopper in here," I said to Casey.

Pierce reached up. "Find her, because Hollister will kill her if *he* does."

I'd come across Hollister a few times. He was one mean sociopath. He hated women. And if that woman was with me, it was a death sentence if he found her.

Casey's radio crackled to life. I heard Sloan say they'd called off the search and they were headed our way at top speed.

"Jack." Andy pulled me aside. "I'm scared as hell. There's nothing. Pierce doesn't know anything, we can't find anything in the dark, and I want my wife back." He glanced around. "I think we should go back to the burned out barn. It makes sense. If they got away, that's where Sarah would go and I'm sure Ensley is with her."

We loaded Pierce in the chopper.

"Sloan, take us back to the barn."

Chapter Thirty

"Who are you?" I asked Mr. X for the third time.

No answer again. He was listening to the helicopter off in the distance.

"I'll just call you Mr. X then." I stood and tried to get a look at the aircraft making the noise.

He stopped me. "Ensley, stay down. Sullivan is still out there. We're going back to the barn so Trace can find you." He turned and started walking.

I took his arm. "Thank you. I'll do my best to keep up."

With the idea of Jack finding me I felt lighter.

I was thinking about being safe in Jack's arms again when Mr. X pulled me to the ground. He put his hand over my mouth and whispered, "Quiet. Don't move."

Above, on the bank of the dry riverbed, someone ran past us. A few minutes later we heard a motorcycle start up and speed off.

Mr. X let go of me. "That was close."

"Was that Sullivan?"

"It was." I heard him chuckle. "If he's lucky the gas I left in his tank will get him to a road." He helped me up. "I'm leaving you in a few minutes. From here, you can make it back to the barn and Trace.

Be careful." He pointed to the incoming helicopter. "Hollister and Burt are still out there." He handed me a gun. "If you see either one, shoot them. Don't hesitate. I'll have your back as long as I can. Now, stay low and move fast as you can. And for God's sake, stay out of trouble." With that he left me.

He didn't make a sound as he moved away. Seconds later, I swear he vanished.

On the bank of the dry riverbed, I was surprised to find I was already on the burned side of the fire. Moving as fast as I could, I hurried toward the still burning barn. I was almost there when I heard Sarah.

"Ensley, over here." She hugged me. "How did you get here?"

"A man came out of the dark and saved me from No-neck. He took out No-neck just as he was about to beat me to death."

Behind us stood Mr. Evil and No-neck. Past them I saw their helicopter.

I'd slipped the gun my rescuer had given me in the pocket of the jacket he'd also let me have. Now, I had to stay out of No-neck's reach.

"Where's the other guy?" he demanded. "The one who knocked me out." He took a menacing step forward. "It gave me a headache. I'm mean when my head hurts."

"How are we supposed to tell the difference?" Before I could wrap my hand around the gun in my pocket, No-neck grabbed me.

I jerked hard against his punishing grip. He raised his fist again.

"Knock it off. You'll kill her if you hit her. They want them alive and in one piece. I'm not blowing a payday because you have a bad temper."

"Hey, where's the other one? She was just here." No-neck was out of patience.

I looked around, Sarah had disappeared.

No-neck slapped me. "Where is she?"

My face burned and my temper flared. I brought my knee up in an effort to impact his groin. My jeans scraped across my battered, stiff knee. I missed.

"Shit." He raised his fist.

I thrashed to pull free. I had to get to the weapon in my pocket.

"Will you knock it off? Let's find the other one and get the hell out of here while they're still at the other spot." Mr. Evil scanned the area. The only light came from the flames. "I don't want to wait around for that sniper to start up again, or for those Blackhawks to come back."

"He's going to find us. Damn it to hell." Mr. Evil got in the front seat. "I do not want to face him again. Let's get out of here."

No-neck got in the passenger seat.

They weren't paying any attention to me so I slipped on the headphones hooked to the seat in the back.

Mr. Evil started the engine. "He was tortured two and a half weeks ago by the best. He's back, maybe not at full strength, but close enough to make me not want to tangle with him. If *they* think she'll draw him out, we're up shit creek. I've faced him when he wasn't mad. This." He jerked his head toward me. "Isn't going to sit well with him."

They? So there was someone else behind our kidnappings.

The craft lifted. I threw off the headphones and lunged for the door. I hit the ground hard. The desert floor wasn't that far away. The combination of the force of the helicopter taking off, plus the wash from the rotors, coupled with the one large clump of unforgiving sagebrush I landed on, equaled more scrapes and bumps. At least it hadn't knocked the wind out of me.

Instead of flying off they set back down.

I squeezed my eyes shut. Great.

No-neck jumped out of the passenger's side and aimed his gun at me. "This is your last chance. Get the hell back in here." He popped off a shot to make his point.

"Damn it. They're going to hear that," Mr. Evil shouted.

"I'm going to start putting bullets in you until your friend shows up."

"I'm here," Sarah said.

"Good. Hands on your heads."

"This is it," I said as we walked toward the man with the gun. "He's mad enough to shoot us."

"If he does—it's been nice knowing you."

Sarah sounded so brave. "It can't be over. I've got too much to do." My heart thumped hard. I was so cold my chest hardly hurt. "I need

..." Oh, what the hell. If I was going to die it didn't matter. "I need to—"

All she said was, "We'll make it."

When we got to the chopper, No-neck said, "Next time, I'm going to shoot you. Both. You've already made us miss our rendezvous. They're not happy and I'm pissed. If this comes back on me and I don't get my money, you're going to be the first casualty." He glared at me.

Mr. Evil shoved us toward the back door of the craft. "Damn it. They're paying extra for all this crap." He scowled at us. "Let's get the hell out of here. We've got to get a head start. There's no way we can outrun those Blackhawks."

"We don't need to. They won't shoot us down with them on board," No-neck said.

My heart sank. We were going to be flown away to who knew where. Away from normal—whatever that was now.

The helicopter took off. The fire below was a shimmering crescent in the desert. The only thing in the scorched area was the campfire Sarah and I made. It glowed bright and strong.

No-neck turned to me. "You jump out this time and I'll use you for target practice." To make his point, he aimed his sidearm at me. "Got it?"

I nodded and turned away. I wasn't going to let him see me cry. No. I *was not* going to give up. "How can you be so—?"

Sarah shook her head. They'd handcuffed her with her hands above her head again. She was right. It wasn't going to do any good to fight with this guy. With their attention on flying the helicopter and scanning the ground below, I took a chance and moved to her. I reached in her pocket for the handcuff key, gave it to her and moved away.

I looked out into the blackness below and hated the two men in the front seats.

The night slipped below the craft like an ocean of ink. Ocean. I'd never get the chance to stand on another beach wrapped in Jack's arms. They'd hold me as long as they were able to force Jack to do what they wanted. When I was no longer useful, they'd kill me.

No. I would not let that happen. I'd never been a victim. I wasn't going to be one now. "This is crap." I scrambled to my feet and grabbed the pilot by the neck. He reacted by jerking on the controls. I put the knife I'd taken from Ponytail to his throat.

Sarah had managed to free herself from the handcuff. She stretched the chain of the handcuffs across No-neck's throat.

I pressed the knife against the pilot's neck. I'd left my headset on so he'd hear me. They weren't the only ones who could threaten. "We can do this the easy way and you can land so we can call for help or I can systematically slit your throat. I'll give you enough time to get to a hospital or I can cut it right now and we'll take our chances. Your choice."

"Bitch."

"Yeah, well, I get cranky when two of pieces of garbage take me away from—Land this thing, now." My demand came with more pressure to his carotid artery. Ponytail liked his knives sharp. The slightest force against Mr. Evil's skin and a rivulet of blood ran down the pilots neck.

By the time we were on the ground, Sarah had no-neck's weapon. I'd taken Mr. Evil's sidearm and held it on the two furious men while Sarah handcuffed them. Done, Sarah called out a mayday on the radio.

The man who answered identified himself as a military pilot. "We're almost there."

»§«

Two large helicopters landed fifty yards away.

A sinister river of night lay between the new helicopters. Three men were silhouetted against the aircraft's lights as they walked toward us. Between the sounds from the three helicopters and the dust the rotors swirled up, visibility and hearing were limited.

"Sarah, what if they're more bad guys out looking for this set?" I called over the diminishing den of the engines.

The shapes marched with determination in our direction. The spotlight of the other side's aircraft cloaked the men in a wash of silhouette. The men stepped into the stream of unforgiving night.

There was something familiar about one of them.

We stood our ground. Our would-be captors were our shields as the newcomers advanced.

The engines grew quiet and the sand settled as I pushed my gun into Mr. Evil's back.

The men were twenty feet from where our light stretched into the night.

The others were ten steps from the light.

Five running paces from us.

"Jack?" It came out as a whisper. I abandoned Mr. Evil and hurried to him.

Sarah went to her husband.

Jack held me. "Are you all—?"

I didn't let him finish. I kissed him.

I heard someone say they'd let the pilots know.

I wasn't letting go of Jack.

"Are you all right?" he whispered as I held on to him.

"How did you find us? They kept switching our locations and the men guarding us—" I kissed him again. "You were so close. Ten minutes."

He held on to me without saying anything. Finally, he whispered, "Is this how you felt when you were looking for me Christmas Eve?"

"As if you were in the center of an endless maze. Every path lead to another dead end, and each dead end felt like a blow to your heart? Then, yes."

"God, I'm sorry," he whispered.

There is nothing in the world that is hotter than a man in uniform. Jack in a uniform is way off the scale. I kissed him again. I knew there were other people around. I didn't care.

"Those two kept telling us they were supposed to keep us alive. I was sure we—"

"Doc, are you okay?"

I realized I hadn't answered him. "My hands hurt, and my knees are sore and I'm hungry and thirsty, and I'm so glad to see you I don't care. Jack, I," I stopped. This wasn't the time. In the middle of the desert, with the stink of burned sagebrush and barn surrounding us, and all the others standing so close, this was not the time. It had to be the right time, the right place. Sarah's words echoed in my head, 'Never put off anything. Still.

He held my arms. "You've been through a lot. Let me see your hands and knees." We went to the big helicopters. In the light, I saw the tiny pebbles still imbedded in my palms. "Your face is bruised and your lip is cut." I knew that frown. "Who the hell hit you?" I knew that tone. It was way past dangerous. Way down. "No-neck." I pointed to the man Casey was securing in the other helicopter.

Jack left me. "Get that son-of-a-bitch out here," he shouted at Casey.

I hurried after him. I knew it wasn't just the bruise on my face that had Jack so angry, it was everything that had happened. Starting with the torture of Christmas Eve and ending with the slap I'd gotten.

"Shit. Jack," Andy left Sarah.

"You piece of shit, first you kidnap these two women, then you haul them out in the middle of the desert." Jack took a deep breath and let it go. "Then you hit a woman a third your size."

Andy hurried forward, "don't, you'll—"

Too late. Jack hit No-neck so hard he bounced off the side of the helicopter.

"Never mind." Andy watched No-neck drop to the ground as Sarah joined him.

Jack held his chest. "Damn it."

"You shouldn't do that," I said. "You're going to aggravate your ribs."

"I'm going to aggravate a whole *hell* of a lot more than that." Jack stood over No-neck. "Get up. Now." His fists were clenched and he'd forgotten the pain of his fractured ribs.

"If I were you, I'd stay put," Andy advised the man on the ground.

Casey pushed the guy with his foot. "If his ribs weren't broken, you'd have gone right through the side of this chopper. Then we'd have to walk home and that, my busted-ass friend, would put me in a real bad mood."

I knew better than to get between Jack and anything making him angry. It was an easy lesson. I'd only seen him mad a couple of times. Tonight made three. I looked down at the man on the ground. He had, at the very least, a broken nose. I knew I should help him. I thought about it for a second. He hit me and he threatened to shoot me. Nope. He was on his own.

Mr. Evil looked down at No-neck and shook his head. "I told you. You're lucky there're witnesses and he's busted up."

Jack turned his attention to Mr. Evil. "I see you haven't come up any in the world, Burt. Still working for the wrong side. This time, I'm not going to be as forgiving." He walked over to him and said something. Whatever it was it left Burt squeezing his eyes shut and shaking his head. Jack motioned to one of the soldiers. "Get this garbage out of here." He walked back to me and took my hands. "Let me take care of your hands. They have to hurt."

"Not anymore." I wrapped my arms around his neck.

"You know we're not alone," he whispered.

I heard Casey laugh. "I don't think I've ever seen anyone quite that excited to get a free helicopter ride."

In the light from the Blackhawk, Jack pulled out a bottle of water and was about to pour it over my hands.

"May I drink that? We haven't had much since they took us."

He gave me the water and reached for another bottle. "They weren't doing a great job if they wanted to keep you alive."

I took a hold of the front of his uniform, and pulled him close. "Do you know how sexy a man in uniform is?" I smiled at him.

He tensed, the good kind, as he whispered back, "You're making me crazy, Ens." He moved back. "Let me see your hands."

I held out my battered palms. "How did you know to search for us out here?"

"We found Pierce's friend. He was so eager to help he drew us a map."

I had a feeling the *eagerness* was more self-preservation than a desire to help.

That had to be Ponytail's smelly friend. "It's a big area and you were so close."

I watched as he popped another stone from my hand. "You're good at this. You have a gentle touch." I whispered in his ear.

He smiled.

242

» § «

I'd never ridden in a Blackhawk. They move right along. When we were in the air I said, "I have to tell you something."

He tightened the blanket around my shoulders and tapped his headset. "Later."

We landed at Gowen Field outside of Boise. When we were inside one of the hangers, I saw how bad I looked. My t-shirt was ripped, both of them. My jeans were torn and my blazer was filthy and destroyed. Again. These adventures were definitely shrinking my blazer collection. "Is there a bathroom here?" I asked. "I'd like to wash off some of the filth."

One of the NCO's showed Sarah and me to the closest one.

"Wow. You'd think I'd been kidnapped and left to die in the desert," I said. Jack had bandaged my hands so I dampened a paper towel and washed my face. "What were the odds they'd find that guy and us?"

"We're lucky women. More than you know. Less connected men would still be searching. They don't loan Blackhawks to just anyone. I hope, no, I know they'll find out who's behind this. I wouldn't want to be them when they do."

"Did you see the fourth man's face?" Sarah asked.

"Not well enough to recognize him again."

There wasn't much to be done about my t-shirts. I took off the most damaged one and turned the other around. It wasn't comfortable, but it covered the scrapes on my stomach.

When we came out, Jack and Andy were leaning against Jack's truck waiting for us. We told them about what had happened from beginning to end. "Jack, those two knew about what happened at Christmas," I said.

"Interesting," Jack opened the door and we entered a room off the hanger. "Sullivan was the sniper. We're tracking him, but the way he operates, he has a couple of backup plans. I'd like to know more about the man who got you away from Burt and Hollister.

Casey was waiting for us. "Ladies, I brought food. It was close, fast and hot." On the table was a couple large pizzas and water.

"Thank you. This is great," I said.

"You've come through again," Sarah said as she selected a slice.

"Tell me again what happened at the safe house." Jack helped himself to a slice as he sat next to me.

I went over the agent going to check things outside and hearing the crash in the garage. "It had to be Ponytail who drugged me. He knew you and Andy. He said you'd put that scar on his throat."

"I did." Jack smiled. "His name is Pierce. He's going to be in the hospital for a while."

"He said you'd had dealings with him before," Sarah said. "He mentioned it didn't end well."

"No. It didn't." Jack opened a bottle of water. "He's going to be in prison for a long time. He won't be a problem for us again."

"He saved me, sort of. He came to my aid more than once. I wouldn't have made it if he hadn't pulled me out before the barn blew up." I glanced over at Sarah.

She shook her head and said, "Pierce's sidekick shouldn't be hard to identify. He'll be the stupid one, with all the money, trying to hire a hooker. He's driving a gray Chevy Nova with a dent in the blue fender." She gave them the license plate number. It was something that hadn't occurred to me. I was lucky to have been kidnapped with her.

Casey smiled. "Oh, we've already had a discussion with the smelly Mr. Bell. That's the reason we were headed in your direction."

"I'd like to know who Ensley's Mr. X is," Sarah said as she took another slice of pizza.

Jack and Andy exchanged looks. Andy got up and moved away from us, his phone in his hand.

"He has to be the one who turned on the emergency beacon," Sarah said.

Casey came back in. "We found this secured under Burt's helicopter." He laid an evidence envelope on the table. In it was a square device. "That's where the distress signal came from."

Jack picked it up and turned it over. "Did you trace it?"

"Sorry, it's been professionally scrubbed. My bet is CIA."

I slumped back in my folding chair. "No." I closed my eyes against the memories from Christmas Eve. "Don can't be behind this." Why wouldn't he let go? He had to know I'd never go back to him. No matter what.

Jack reached over and took my fingertips in his hand. "It doesn't mean it's him."

"Then who?"

"That is an interesting question." Andy sat down beside Sarah. "It appears we have an interested third party out there. One that's not out to kill us, for a change. This one is more of a guardian angel. Which makes me happy."

"Me, too." Sarah kissed her husband.

"Mr. X saved me from Hollister. He was about to beat me to death when Mr. X showed up. He knocked Hollister out and took me back to the barn." I indicated the jacket I was wearing. "He gave me this so I wouldn't freeze and the gun I gave to Sarah."

"Let me see the jacket," Jack said.

I took it off and handed it to him.

Methodically, he searched it. He pulled an envelope out of an inside pocket. It was ordinary, the kind you buy in a box of a hundred. Jack and Andy exchanged looks.

"Open it," Andy urged. "Maybe it will give us some answers."

Jack hesitated then slit it open. Inside was a sheet of paper. He sat in silence.

"Jack?" Andy asked. "You okay?"

He cleared his throat, but remained silent. Finally, he read, "Jack, Take care of her. Dad."

We looked at each other, no one knowing what to say.

Jack carefully folded the letter and slipped it back in the envelope. He laid it on the table as if it would burn him if he held it a second longer.

"Well, then," Andy didn't take his eyes off Jack. "That was unexpected."

"What did he look like?" Jack asked without taking his eyes from the envelope.

"He was dressed all in black and wore a balaclava. I couldn't see any of his face. He was nice." That sounded stupid. I thought back. "He was about your size and despite the fact that he knocked out

Hollister, he was gentle with me. He cared enough to make sure I was warm and he gave me the gun."

"Casey," Jack called. "Bring latex gloves."

When he came to the table Jack said, "Have this checked for fingerprints."

Casey snapped on the gloves, took the note, and left.

Sarah and I ate, Jack sat stone still, and Andy looked concerned.

I had to break the strained quiet. "Jack, what's going to happen to Kevin Clark. I mean because he's FBI." It wasn't much, it wasn't relevant, and it sure didn't matter.

"Agent Clark is resting uncomfortably in a jail cell," was all he said.

"It turns out he was our leak. Brad was," Andy smiled, "not amused."

I could imagine. "Do you have any idea who in Spirit Springs is feeding the Big Bad information?"

"Big Bad?" Jack lifted his gaze from where the envelope had been.

"That's what Sarah and I call the faceless person determined to make our lives miserable." I paused. "It isn't Lacey, is it?"

"I doubt it. Looks like I'm going to be doing some housecleaning at the office."

"What I'd like to know is how Sullivan found us." I said.

The two men looked at each other as Jack said, "He never left. After Christmas he hung around, probably in Mullen, waiting for another chance. When you came home he scrambled to put this haphazard plan in motion. The only thing he did right was make his escape."

Why hadn't I thought to tell them this before? Oh, right, I was focused on seeing Jack again and being saved. "The mystery man drained the tank on Sullivan's motor cycle. He said Sullivan wouldn't have enough gas to make it to a road."

"Andy," was all Jack said.

"On it, Sarge," he said as he moved away from the table.

"Do you think they'll find him?" I felt like I was six as I crossed my fingers under the table.

Jack shook his head. "Draining the gas was a good move, but Sullivan always has a backup to his backup."

"They were going to use us as leverage against you both." I laid a half-eaten third piece of pizza down.

"I know."

"How?" I looked over as Andy joined Sarah. He shook his head.

"Ens, they've been trying for years to find a way to stop us. When we get home you're going to get a security system, and I'm getting you a big dog."

"What if he doesn't like the cats? Or Lois?"

He smiled. "That's what you're concerned about? If the dog will like your cats or my dog?"

"Yes. What else?"

He shook his head. "How about your life?"

"I'll be fine." I tugged him close. "I have you."

Just then Casey returned. "Burt and company aren't talking. They're not amateurs." He sat down beside me. "They will. It's going to take a little more persuasion."

"What did you find in the helicopter?" Jack asked.

"A cargo compartment with *some* information. You ladies were headed out of state for sure. If I had to guess, the next trip wasn't going to be your last stop."

"Is it over?" I asked.

"No," was all Casey said.

» § «

The sun sparkled off the Boise River as we drove across the bridge and out of town. I sighed as I relaxed against the seat, we were heading home. His new old truck was hitched to the back of his big truck. "I don't like the fact that you didn't find out who was behind all this," I said.

"We did and we didn't."

"That's it? You did and didn't."

"Yes."

"Jack, you," I glanced over at him. There wasn't any point in asking. Besides, I figured it was above my paygrade. I understand the need to keep things secret. My dad used to give me a don't-ask look when I had too many questions.

"We're sure the two men who chased us in Seattle were hired by the same group who kidnapped you and Sarah. The pros are questioning them along with Burt and Hollister." He thought about that for a long minute. "Why chase *us* if they were after you? They had to know they weren't going to succeed."

"I'll tell you this. You were right, there *was* more than one faction out there." He turned onto the freeway.

Should I bring up the subject of the lie? I knew it would change the warm wonderful feeling I had sitting near Jack. Still it needed to be settled.

Epilogue

The three-hour drive was wonderful. I was with Jack and no one was trying to kill either of us. All in all, a good morning. Now.

We pulled into my driveway. "Come in. I'll make some coffee and we can just be together."

He smiled and shut off the truck. Inside, no animals hurried to greet us. Lois was with Jane and the cats.

I turned on the coffee maker.

As I waited for the first cup to fill, I saw Jack standing at the desk in the library. The dark wood of the bookshelves and the leather chairs in the room were a compliment to his presence. I took the cup and put another one on. When they were finished I walked down the short hall and handed him the coffee. I leaned against his arm as he held the picture I'd sent my dad before he retired. I took the photo and said, "It's crazy, but in a way, if it weren't for this picture, I wouldn't be here right now." This simple photo had changed my life dramatically. The last few days were a testament to that.

He frowned at me. "You wouldn't?"

"It's true," I said as I sipped my coffee. "Dad wanted a new picture of me." I traced the edge of the silver frame with my finger. "I guess my high school graduation photo had started to yellow with age." I shrugged. "Sophie insisted if I was going to have my picture taken I needed a makeover. I thought it was—let's just say I wasn't excited about it." I smiled at the memory of Sophie standing in the doorway to my office, her hands on her hips, refusing to move until I said yes. "As always, she had a compelling argument. We went to a spa having a next-model promotion. Even the name of the place sounded silly, *Ordinary to Extraordinary*." I laughed. "Silly, but life changing."

I picked up the picture as he put his arm around me.

"I came out looking like someone else. Part of the package was a model-style photo shoot at the end of the day. That's the picture I sent to my dad. Sophie bet me I couldn't keep the look up for a week. I, of course, took the challenge. Two days later one of the other scientists at work asked me out. He wanted to know how long I'd worked at JPL." I shifted uncomfortably. There was no way Jack could understand how that man had made me feel. He'd never been invisible. "I'd worked there for three years. Worse, his office was four doors down from mine. He'd seen me every day for years and never noticed me. From then on, I decided the change was worth it. You know the rest."

He took the picture from me. I can always tell when he's struggling with something because his mouth tightens and a line forms between his eyes.

He led me into the living room and we sat down on the couch. He set his coffee on the table and pulled me next to him.

"If it weren't for this picture, I wouldn't be here either." He paused. "I went to Ralph's office the day it arrived." He held up the framed photo. "I was struggling with everything that had happened in Africa and Dave's death, losing my men, having to kill that girl. The day I got out of the hospital, I went to tell him how sorry I was about the way things had turned out. Did you know he was up for a third star? Instead of playing it safe," He glanced at the picture. "When I walked into his office, he was standing behind his desk smiling, despite losing his command, his star and his career. He said, 'Want to see a picture of my daughter? I can't believe how she's changed. I guess D.C. agrees with her.'" Jack laid the photo on the end table and pulled his wallet from his pocket and rested it on his thigh.

"You looked so happy, so full of life. I wanted desperately to feel that way again. I thought I never would." He opened his wallet and slipped out a picture in a tattered photo sleeve. "Ralph gave me this that day. I don't know why."

I took my picture.

"When I got state side I looked at life through the bottom of a scotch bottle for too long. You heard Andy say, 'It's her. She's real.' That's because," He paused and took a breath as he contemplated what to say. "One night Andy and Stan found me in a—let's say I wasn't in the best place. I was one drink away from oblivion—which is where I spent most of my time then. I had your picture in my hand. They sobered me up. The first question Andy asked me was who the woman was in the picture. I told them it was from an old assignment and that you weren't real. Stan knew, but never said a word."

It all came back to choices. Had I not made the decision to go with Sophie that day, not only would I have been lost in a life of obscurity, Jack might not have pulled out of his depression. I closed my eyes. Everything counts.

Everything.

I felt Jack's arm tense around me. Not the good kind. I opened my eyes and glanced up at him. His face was tortured with anxiety. I twined my fingers through his and held on tight.

He relaxed and turned his attention back to the photo. "A couple of weeks later, Ralph called. He told me he had a job for me. All I had to do was get here and it was mine. I did okay for a while. A couple of months into the job, my grandmother died. I started to slip. That's when Ralph showed up with Lois. Between the two of them and your picture, I made it through." He paused. "The first time I saw you was when you and Cole came to visit Ralph. You were more beautiful than your picture."

I sat there in silence as I remembered my tortured days and nights in D.C. The anguish of not knowing if I'd be able to come back and knowing all the time I had no choice. I swallowed my tears and touched my photo. The edges were frayed, the paper yellowed and soiled, and the plastic sleeve split.

"You deserved more than I was able to give you then," he said. "I was dealing with nightmares, and depression. I couldn't be with anyone. I was having a hard time being with me. I had nothing to offer you. The night Ralph was murdered, I was afraid you'd be nothing more than a beautiful face in a picture, a fantasy I'd conjured up to stay sane. I was wrong. I know that sounds disturbing and I wouldn't blame you if you—"

"I understand." I ran my finger over the worn edge of the picture. It looked as if it had been taken out and viewed a thousand times. "It was your anchor." I reached into his pocket and took out his phone. "This was my lifeline to you on Christmas Eve. I held onto it so tight," I paused remembering the heartbreaking fear of that night. "I was afraid if I let it go, you'd be gone and I'd—" I felt a shudder rip through me. "In D.C., my Kindle took the place of your phone. I needed something to anchor me to reality. That's why I was so upset when Brad kept taking it away from me."

Putting his fingers under my chin he turned me to face him and kissed away the tears on my cheek.

He watched as I got up from the couch, leaving behind the warmth of his touch. I went into the library and returned a minute later. I handed him the only other small picture they'd taken that day three and a half years ago. I sat back down next to him and tugged his arm around me. I took the old photo and handed him the new one. "That one's outlived its usefulness."

For a split second, I didn't think he was going to take the new one.

He did.

He turned the photo over, his eyes grew dark as he blinked back emotion. I'd written on the back: *For Jack, To a new beginning. Love, Ens.*

I hope you enjoyed the further adventures of Ensley and Jack. The next book, Redemption Road is waiting for you.

About the Author

When Peggy isn't thinking up new ways to kill people, or how to blow something up she is growing orchids and blueberries, or taking her new 9mm to the range. She loves watching mysteries with her small but expanding zoo of two cats, two Spinoni. Outside lives a small flock of hungry Mallards complete with offspring, a gaggle of vexed Canadian Geese, the burgeoning covey of quail, and the hundreds of tiny toads who showed up this spring. The toads number has dwindled, but they are ever busy keeping the mosquito population at bay.

The dogs are clowns and the cats have learned to avoid the dog's large webbed feet. All four domestic animals are interested in the feathered crowd outside.

Her garden is an ongoing experiment. Gardeners in Idaho know that to grow anything other than sagebrush you have to make your own soil. That is the fun and the challenge of a thriving garden in the desert.

Also by Peggy Staggs

Ensley Markus Mysteries

House at Road's End

Deception Road

Spirit Road

Redemption Road

Crossed Roads

Justice Road (Coming soon!)

Laura Barlow Adventures

Cold Place in the Sun